A WOULD-BE SAINT

Have friends 17

A WOULD-BE SAINT

A NOVEL

by

ROBIN JENKINS

sense of humour? 13 /5 66

LONDON
VICTOR GOLLANCZ LTD
1978

ISBN 0 575 02506 9

IF 6403

MADE AND PRINTED IN GREAT BRITAIN BY
THE GARDEN CITY PRESS LIMITED
LETCHWORTH, HERTFORDSHIRE
SG6 IJS

PART ONE

Gavin Hamilton —see <u>Holy</u>
<u>Wilhe's Prayer</u>

I

A S A C H I L D of eight that summer of 1918 he took for granted that all people in the world existed for his delight.

Neighbours thought that he was the least demanding and most independent wean they had ever known. His need of them and the joy he got from them went on in his imagination, which was very private.

The people of the world were the inhabitants of Auchengillan, a mining community in Lanarkshire, too small for a town and too scattered for a village: a pleasant countryside of fields with daisies and buttercups and cows and larks' nests, more fields green with potatoes or yellow with corn, burns with minnows, and hedges with wild flowers and butterflies. Seen from all over were the bings of the three pits, smouldering like volcanoes.

During that last summer of war his great secret worry was that he would forget his father, a machine-gunner in France. It would have been easier to remember if his mother had been willing to talk about his father, but she sat for hours in silence, staring into the fire, with a duster or a spoon in her hand. Sometimes when he came home hungry from playing football she would murmur in a dreamy voice that she would make his tea in a minute; but after waiting patiently for an hour or so he would start to make it himself.

He loved his mother too, but he didn't understand her. Whenever he laughed aloud at some story he was reading she would whisper, "Wheesht," as if there was a baby sleeping. His father on the other hand when they had gone walking through the fields had made him laugh till he had a lump in his throat.

In the Co-op. store he once overheard women saying what a pity it was that wee Gavin Hamilton was becoming so secretive. They blamed his mother. He needed his father home again. Sandy Hamilton, they said, was a cheerful young fellow liked by everybody: he'd crack jokes with the flies on his counter.

Before the war his father had been a barman in the Auchengillan Arms.

At school because he was clever and sweet-tempered his teacher

Miss Carmichael liked to sit beside him, giving help that he didn't need and others did. In the playground the twelve-year-olds of the qualifying class, much bigger and heavier than he, knew him as the wee boy from Primary 4 who when playing football tackled so hard that sometimes he had to be told to take it easy.

One sunny afternoon at the end of July when the wild roses were in bloom and in France the Germans were being bloodily defeated he set off alone with girr and cleek for a tour of his world.

His girr bounced on bumps in the road like a happy dog. From behind its hedge Jock, the Nicholsons' old Airedale barked, not because it was angry at having its sleep disturbed but because it wanted to come with him. Once he had let it come but it had kept knocking the girr down or seizing it between its teeth.

Soon he was away from the houses and puffing up the track to the disused quarry. More than ever like a dog his girr wanted to dart off into the thickets of briers and brambles as if to sniff out frogs or hedgehogs. He had to work hard to keep it under control. He had never told anyone, not even his father, but he thought he was the best goer of a girr for his age in Auchengillan.

The quarry was where miners off duty played cards or pitch-and-toss. He rattled his cleek against his girr to let them know he was coming and wasn't a policeman. He didn't know why, but gambling was against the law. The miners always had whippets with them, trained to yelp in warning if policemen came anywhere near.

In a sunny den amongst the bushes men were seated on the ground playing cards. Even if he hadn't known who they were he could have told that they were miners because of a wonderful quietness they had, and a way of lifting back their heads gratefully to let the sun shine on their pale blue-speckled faces.

Old Mr Wishart who lived in the cottage next door had been a miner for 50 years. He had told Gavin that miners learned quiet-ness during the long hours they spent lying on their backs or crouched on their knees in dark spaces so small that there was scarcely room even for one man.

Gavin liked and trusted the miners.

They looked up and smiled at him. They knew who he was, Sandy Hamilton's boy. They ordered their whippets to stop snarling.

One of them spoke to him. This was Mr Simpson, known as "Blackie". Sober, he was the quietest of all; drunk, though, on

Friday or Saturday nights, he could be so violent that it took three policemen, their helmets knocked off, to drag him to jail.

The contrast between the big burly black-moustached man peaceable and him raging fascinated Gavin.

"How's your faither, son?" asked Mr Simpson.

"Fine, thank you, Mr Simpson."

"That's grand. How many Germans has he killed?"

"I don't know, Mr Simpson. He never says onything in his letters aboot killing onybody."

"He would not, sensible man. I'm the stupid yin for asking. Tell him, son, that Blackie Simpson's waiting for the day when he'll draw him his first pint. Nae pint will taste better. Tell him that, son."

"I'll ask my mither to tell him when she's writing."

"You do that, son. Noo that the Germans are on the run at last it'll no' be long till he's hame again."

"I hope so, Mr Simpson."

The other miners smiled and nodded.

One winked. "Is this you aff on a run wi' your girr?" he asked.

"Yes, Mr Syme."

"Tak care."

"Thank you. I always take care."

As he raced off he heard them laughing. Perhaps like lots of other people they thought he was just a bit too well-mannered, made so by his mother. But their laughter did not dishearten him; instead it cheered him up. If these quiet men with the big strong gentle hands thought his father would come home safe surely he would.

From the quarry a narrow path with a fence on either side ran through the sloping fields. Corn still green grew above, below cows grazed. Cows lying in the shade of trees always reassured him. He liked the sounds they made, the warm smell off them, and the way they swished their tails to drive off flies.

Because of long grass and nettles it became harder to keep the girr rolling. His rule was that if he had to carry it more than six steps he must turn back; and he never cheated. So, straining his right arm, he propelled the girr on, with many wobbles and one or two falls. Falls, though, didn't count.

Soon with stung knees he came out on to a wider dusty earth road. It led to the rows of brick houses the miners came from, called Brandy Neuk, under a huge smoking bing.

He knew boys and girls who lived in Brandy Neuk. If he was to go down there, over the bridge with moss like bright green mice on its parapets, among the houses and the whippets and the pigeons and the washings hanging out and the women gossiping and the girls skipping and the boys playing football, he would have a right. Nobody would ask him what he wanted, nobody would shout to him to go away.

He had a right to go anywhere in Auchengillan. It was his world.

He decided not to visit the Neuk this time, but raced along the earth road towards the shops. White butterflies twinkled about him. It was warm. He had his jersey sleeves rolled up.

Below him on his right was the main road that in one direction went to Cadzow and then on to London, so he had been told; in the other direction it went to Glasgow, passing through Lendrick a mile and a half away where his Hamilton grandparents lived though he couldn't remember ever having seen them. They and his mother had fallen out. Since it had happened before he was born he couldn't be to blame. They had fallen out with his father too, but he didn't know if that was because his father took his mother's side or because his father had been part of the quarrel, whatever it was. He had no Forsyth grandparents. They had died long ago when his mother was a girl. He thought he had uncles and aunts and cousins somewhere, but he wasn't sure.

The shops were the centre of Auchengillan. Opposite them, across the main road, was St Andrew's Church, where he went every Sunday morning with his mother, and sometimes in the evening as well. The shops were Quigley's "jenny-a'-things", where you could buy all kinds of interesting things like peeries and Jews'-harps; the Auchengillan Arms where his father had worked; Brisbane's fruitshop that also sold sweeties; and the Co-op., where you didn't use ordinary money but checks made out of stuff like celluloid.

Beside Quigley's there was a wall about five feet high. On its other side was a steep drop into a burn. Usually men sat on it to chat but if they saw a policeman coming they would jump down, joking and dusting their trousers. Gavin didn't know why sitting on the wall wasn't allowed. Big boys sometimes walked along it, to prove how steady their nerves were. He had once seen Jim Flanagan do it with his eyes shut.

Today four men were seated on the wall. Like the card-players they were miners on the night shift. When they came home from the pit at six in the morning they washed and went to bed. They liked to get up about two in the afternoon to enjoy some fresh air. Gavin knew this because he had friends whose fathers were colliers. He had visited their houses.

One of the men called to him. It was Mr Clelland whose son Jackie was in Gavin's class.

"Is your faither still a' right, son?" he asked.

"He's still safe and well, Mr Clelland."

"That's champion. Be sure and tell him we were asking for him."

The three other men nodded.

"I will, Mr Clelland. Thank you."

He felt more confident than ever that his father would be protected from harm by this regard that everybody had for him.

The pub was shut at that time of day, but he knew what it looked like inside, not because like cheeky boys he'd pushed open the door and keeked in, but because once, years ago, his father had taken him in and set him up on the high counter. He had even let him taste beer. He had whispered into his ear not to let his mother know.

A green tramcar rattled past, with showers of sparks, on its way to Lendrick. Two weeks ago he had gone with Charlie McGill and Davie McLuskie to the pictures there. They had seen *The Clutching Hand*. Charlie had hidden under his seat at the part where a panel in the wall opened and the clutching hand appeared.

As he passed Brisbane's he hoped that Nellie's new false teeth weren't hurting her gums any more. Yesterday when he was in buying potatoes she had turned her back and taken them out. Others in the shop had smiled. He hadn't. People in pain weren't funny. Even when Charlie McGill got the strap and made faces and howled for mercy and even wet his trousers he never laughed, though nearly everybody else did, including girls. All those with more than three spelling errors and fewer than six sums right got the strap. The same boys and girls got it every day. Charlie was one. He knew he was going to get it and tried to prepare for it by spitting on his hands. He thought that would lessen the pain but it never did. In the playground he showed his hands all red and swollen to anyone who would look. He would try to smile.

Past the Co-op. was a tenement with closes. At one closemouth some women were gossiping. Among them was Mrs Lindsay whose man Jim had been to the war but was home again with a leg missing.

"Hello, Gavin Hamilton," she cried. "Whit's the news aboot your faither?"

"He's fine, Mrs Lindsay," he replied.

"Thank Christ for that. May it long continue."

As he raced away he felt anxious. She shouldn't have said "Christ". People were always saying it, people he liked too, but it was wicked to say it all the same. His mother had said, "Don't worry. They'll be punished." He hoped no one would be punished, but if Mrs Lindsay was, if she had to be, he prayed that it would not take the form of something terrible happening to his father. Perhaps God thought she had been punished enough already.

Behind the Co-op. building was the open space where he and his friends often played football. Some would be playing there now. They would be keen to ask him if he wanted a game, for they knew he was a good player. If there was somebody else waiting for a game he and this other boy would have to decide who was to be cock and who hen or sometimes pug or engine. Then they would ask one of the captains: "Cock or hen?" Or "Pug or engine?"

He continued along the main road. In a little while he would have to cross it.

Two boys were strolling towards him, smoking douts picked up off the street. They were barefooted and had dirty jerseys. One was Jim Flanagan and the other his pal Harold Murphy. They were Catholics and often fought with Protestant boys. They went to their own Catholic school where, it was rumoured, they were taught by the priest that Protestants were heathens who would never go to heaven.

Gavin wasn't afraid of them. They had never done him any harm. Like everybody else they liked him. Perhaps this was because he himself liked everybody, even Harold Murphy who said dirty things and once took out his pintle to show it to some girls.

Jim Flanagan grabbed at the girr.

"If I tossed this ower the fence, wee Hamilton," he cried, "would you rin hame and tell your mammy?"

The fence of railway sleepers was thick and high. He would find it very difficult to retrieve his girr and he would be very sorry to lose it; but he wouldn't cry and he certainly wouldn't tell his mother.

"He'd want a sook at her diddies," said Harold, with a snigger.

Gavin had seen too many babies being fed at the breast not to know what Harold meant. It puzzled him though that Harold ~humour~ should think that he was still such a baby as to need to do *that*. He was a better football player than Harold.

"I bet she's got nice diddies," said Harold, with another snigger.

Gavin could not see how a woman's breasts which were meant for giving babies milk could be nice or not nice. Maybe those that gave too little or no milk at all weren't nice. He had seen women squeezing and babies turning blue in the face from sucking too hard.

Jim handed him back his girr. "Is your faither still winning the war?" he asked, with a grin that showed some teeth were missing.

Gavin nodded. His father was helping to win it anyway. Jim's own father was a miner. Jim was going to be a miner himself.

"He's a machine-gunner, isn't he?" Jim asked.

"That's fucking dangerous," sneered Harold. "The Germans try to kill machine-gunners first. I read it in the paper."

"Shut up. Gavin's faither's no' going to be killed."

It's in the Lord's hands, his mother often whispered. Well, whoever the Lord was He certainly wasn't Harold Murphy with the big dirty ears and pimply chin.

"Watch when you're crossing the road, Gavin," said Jim, like a big brother.

"I will, Jim. Goodbye."

"Goodbye, Gavin."

Before he had gone twenty yards he heard yells of pain. He looked back. Jim was banging Harold's head against the fence. It was only half in fun. Jim wasn't simply paying Harold back for saying those nasty things about Gavin's mother and father. Boys often turned on their friends for no reason except that they felt like hitting someone. Gavin never understood that. He never wanted to hit anyone. It wasn't because he was a wee jessie either. At football he wasn't afraid to tackle boys twice his weight.

He crossed the road, very carefully, and took a path that led through more fields past Burnbank Terrace, a long brick tenement with a pend in the middle leading through to the backcourt. He knew boys and girls who lived there, among them Willie and Jessie Findlay whose father had been killed in the war. He had once seen Jessie weeping in the playground. Somebody said she had hurt her knee playing peaver, and so she was holding her knee, and so she had been playing peaver; but Gavin had known from the way she was crying that it wasn't because of her skinned knee which would get better, but because her dad had been killed and she would never see him again.

He knew four other boys whose fathers had been killed.

He hurried past the pend. Some girls playing in it caught sight of him. "Was that wee Gavin Hamilton?" Luckily they didn't give chase and make a fuss.

At last he was back in his own avenue of small stone cottages. His legs were weary, his arm ached, and his hand was cramped.

Mrs Ferrier was standing by her gate talking to Mrs Lawrie.

Unlike the women at the closemouth they wore hats. They always did. People who lived in Hawthorn Avenue considered themselves superior. Most of them owned their houses.

"Juist a meenute, young man," said Mrs Ferrier, as he tried to sneak past.

He stopped.

"Whit's the latest word of your faither?"

"He's still safe and well, thank you."

"No news of him coming hame? He's done his bit, unlike mony I could name."

He always found her voice frightening. She never seemed to say good things about anybody. It was said she was blind in one eye and suffered severe headaches. Her bad eye was all yellow.

"He'll have to wait till the war's over," he said, as politely as he could.

"Is that whit your mither says?"

"Yes, Mrs Ferrier."

"Hm. She was in sich a hurry to see him go, so why should she be in an equal hurry to see him come back?"

That was muttered to Mrs Lawrie but he easily heard it. Grown-ups often spoke as if he wasn't there.

This wasn't the first time he had heard neighbours hinting that his mother had urged his father to be the first in Auchengillan to volunteer. He didn't know if it was true because he had been only four at the time and he had never liked to ask his mother.

"It's nearly over now, son," said Mrs Lawrie, who was fatter than Mrs Ferrier and kinder. "He'll soon be hame."

As he trudged on wearily he heard Mrs Ferrier say that there must be something wrong with Marion Forsyth's head. No normal healthy young woman, even if her man was away at the war, would sit and sulk at home.

It was true that when neighbours came knocking at the door his mother would whisper to him to keep quiet and out of sight until they had gone.

She was in the room or parlour gazing at his father's big photograph on the chiffonier. In Gavin's secret opinion the soldier's hat with the badge was a little bit too big. But he liked the brave way his father was smiling. No one smiling like that could ever be killed.

Why then was his mother frowning and pouting? Her large pale brow made the one, and her red mouth the other, very noticeable.

But he could see nothing wrong with her head. There was no place where it was soft, say, like in an apple or potato. Her hair, black and shiny as tar, had been let down and flowed over her shoulders.

He tried not to remember what Harold Murphy had said about her "diddies", but they stood out so proudly in her pale blue blouse that he couldn't help noticing them.

"I'm back," he said, after a while.

"So you are," she murmured. "So you are."

2

ONE AFTERNOON TOWARDS the end of August a game of football was being played in the open space behind the Co-op. building, in rain that had started as a drizzle and had become a steady downpour. Lights were on in houses though it was only four o'clock. Some of the players had long ago begun to grumble that it was daft to go on playing: they'd catch pneumonia or worse still get a hammering when they went home soaked. Others, more dedicated, either paid no heed to these whimperers or else gave them scornful glowers. One of the captains, Tommy Grierson, his fair hair hanging over his eyes like a Highland cow's, was provoked once into shouting at the most persistent moaner: "Shut up, Willie. Look at wee Gavin. He's no' half your size and he doesnae want to stop. Dae you, Gavin?"

Eagerly Gavin shook his head. It was a lot heavier because of his sodden hair but if it had been as heavy as an iron ball he would still have been keen to play on. His side was winning by twenty-three goals to fifteen and he had scored six himself. Besides, he felt exalted at being allowed to play with these older boys.

He'd been knocked down several times and was covered in mud. Once he'd been back-heeled on the shin, where there was now a big black and purple bruise. As well as scoring goals he had prevented some by resolute timely tackles. Angus Clelland, a poor player himself because his knock-knees gave him bad balance, had jeered at him: "At this rate, Hamilton, you'll be playing for Glesca Rangers yin day".

Only one thing could have made him happier: that was if he had known that his father was waiting at home for him. But as he dodged, dribbled, passed, and shot he hadn't time to think of anything but the game.

Therefore he was slow to understand when Davie McLuskie, who was goalie for his side, shouted out of the murk: "Gavin, here's an auld man wants to talk to you".

"If he's come to tell you you've to go home," said Tommy, "juist you go, Gavin. You've done great."

With reluctance Gavin took his eye off the ball and peered through the rain.

Davie hadn't been kidding. There was an old man with a black umbrella standing beside the heap of half-bricks that was one of the goalposts.

Two or three of the shivering disenchanted players, hoping that the coming of the old man might mean the abandonment of the game, showed an interest in him.

It was Grandpa Wishart. Gavin was surprised and not very pleased. He liked Grandpa, but there were times when the old man, just because he was an old man, forgot that Gavin was eight now and not four.

He passed Willie Findlay whose skinny face was spotted with mud and who looked as bitter as a soldier left too long at a dangerous post.

"You're lucky," he muttered. "I wish it was me going hame."

Davie McLuskie was relieved to see Gavin. "I don't think he's weel," he muttered. "He's greeting."

And, terrible to see, Grandpa Wishart, who had once been trapped hundreds of feet under the earth for ten days without food, was in truth weeping. He held up the umbrella with one hand and with the other groped for Gavin's face, as if he was blind as well as old and feeble.

Embarrassed but sympathetic, Gavin tried to reassure him. "It's a' right, Grandpa. It's nothing. I'm juist wet. Look, it's no' even bleeding." He showed his bruised shin.

It was, though, he now realized, very sore.

Behind him the game had been stopped. Tommy had picked up the ball. He ran towards Gavin.

"Whit is it, mister?" he asked. "Has Gavin to go hame? Whit's the maitter?"

Afterwards Mr Wishart was to maintain to everybody, including his wife of 53 years, that he deliberately chose that time and place to tell the lad, when his friends were there, not because they would give him comfort, for weans were never very good at that, no blame to them, but because they gave him company. Gavin was just a little fellow but he had already learned that the only way to get any happiness out of life was by having friends and trusting them.

The truth was, though, he was so overcome at seeing the brave little boy all muddy and bruised from pitting himself against much bigger boys that he just blurted out the awful news.

"Gavin, your mither's juist had a telegram. It says your faither's been killed."

Gavin noticed that Grandpa was wearing house slippers. He must have forgotten to put on his boots. Gavin wanted to think about this and smile at it for it was quite funny. This news about his father was too enormous to be dealt with there and then.

His friends were silent. Three of them had fathers at the front, in danger of being killed. Willie Findlay's father had already been killed. Others had fathers who worked at the coalface where it was dangerous too but not so dangerous as the war.

Tommy Grierson put his arm round Gavin's neck. "Never mind," he muttered.

They all nodded and said, "Never mind, Gavin".

They knew it was a useless silly thing to say but they couldn't think of anything else.

Gavin looked round at them all. He saw something to like in each anxious face.

Willie Findlay began to sniffle. He hid his face in his muddy hands.

"Does it juist say killed?" whispered Angus Clelland. "Does it no' say how?"

"It tells that in a letter that comes efter," said Jack Syme.
"That's whit happened when my Uncle Eddie was killed."

"I think you shouldnae hae telt him here in the rain, mister,"
said Tommy, in a kindly voice to the old man. "You should hae
waited till he was hame wi' his mither."

They all nodded again. At home, where it would be dry and
warm and bright, and everything was familiar, news like this might
not seem quite so desolating.

"It's a fucking shame," muttered Archie McGill.

Others repeated it. "A fucking shame." No other words could
have expressed so well their bafflement and pity.

Grandpa Wishart roused himself. Later he was to claim that he
waited purposely for a few minutes to give Gavin's friends a chance
to lend their support, but the truth was he had slipped into a senile
dwam of helplessness. He was 73 and afraid of death. He had left
his old wife weeping sorely. And he had just given a child he loved
the cruellest of blows.

"We'd better get hame, Gavin," he said.

"Will you be a' right, Gavin?" whispered Tommy.

Gavin nodded. He was shivering but that was because he was
feeling cold. "I hope we win, Tommy," he said.

"That doesnae maitter. We'll a' go hame."

There was some heartfelt agreement from the others.

"Any time we play," said Tommy, "you'll get a game."

"Sure thing," they all said.

"The morrow?"

"Well, maybe no' the morrow, Gavin."

"Then the day after?"

"We'll see."

"All right."

Tactfully ignoring Grandpa's hand held out to take his Gavin
marched off with the old man. After a few steps he turned to see
what his friends were doing. Perhaps they had just been being
polite when they had said they wouldn't go on with the game. But
no, they were still standing all together, like cows at a gate waiting
for the farmer. They waved. He waved back.

He and Grandpa crossed the backcourt of the Co-op. building.
Weeks ago at a wedding there he had shouted with the rest of the
boys and girls, "Hard up. Bowl the money." When the money was
scattered he had managed to snatch up two pennies. Remembering
all that cheered him up a little.

They went into a close and up the stairs. It was chilly and dark in there. Gavin had a feeling that lots of promises which had been given him had suddenly all been broken.

Two women were standing at the closemouth. One was Mrs McLuskie, Davie's mother. The other was Mrs Lindsay whose husband had had his leg blown off.

Mrs Lindsay put her hand on his head. "Did you tumble into the burn, son?" she asked, laughing.

"Terrible day, Mr Wishart," said the other woman.

To Gavin's horror Grandpa said in a very shaky voice, "You've nae idea hoo terrible, Mrs McLuskie. Gavin's father's been killed. The telegram came juist half an hour ago."

"Christ Almighty," muttered Mrs Lindsay.

Then she did something even more shocking. She showed her teeth like a fierce dog and shook her fist at the sky. Gavin was to remember it all his life.

Who was she so angry with? Was it the Germans who had killed his father and blown off her husband's leg? Or the people who had sent the telegram? Or God who had let the war happen?

From the closemouth to Gavin's house took more than fifteen minutes. If Gavin had been on his own he could have done it easily in five. Grandpa was very slow. He had to rest often. Once one of his slippers came off. His umbrella kept bumping against walls, fences, lamp-posts, and trees.

Luckily they saw only one person in Hawthorn Avenue. This was Mrs Nicholson who owned Jock the Airedale. She didn't notice them for she had an umbrella too.

Gavin had been dreading that everybody in the avenue would be at the house, all come to say how sorry they were. He did not trust his mother to be nice to them.

There was nobody. Perhaps they had already been and now were gone back to their own houses. His mother wouldn't have wanted them to stay long.

He did not expect her to run and hug him. He was too wet and dirty. In any case, whatever she was going to do to show that he and she must suffer this terrible loss together she would not do it at once, she would wait, she seemed always to be waiting.

She was sitting in the room on one of the best chairs, with her hands clasped on her lap. She was wearing a black dress and looked beautiful. She was not weeping.

"He's wet and cold, Mrs Hamilton," mumbled Grandpa, from

19

the door. "He kens. I've telt him. Maybe I shouldnae, maybe I should hae left that to you, his mither."

"Thank you, Mr Wishart. Gavin, thank Mr Wishart for bringing you home."

"Thanks," whispered Gavin.

Grandpa fled.

The telegram was on the chiffonier beside his father's photograph. He stared at it fearfully.

"Can I get reading it?" he asked, after a few minutes.

"It's for you as much as it is for me."

He picked it up, trying not to dirty it. It just said killed, it didn't say how.

Uneasy, not knowing what he was supposed to say or do or even feel, he pretended that it took him much longer to understand the telegram than it really did.

Never had he felt less at home with his mother.

He wished she hadn't dressed herself in black. He wished she would stop smiling as if she was leaving whatever crying had to be done to him.

He didn't want her to cover her face with sackcloth and ashes as it said in the Bible, but this holding of her head higher even than usual, and this proud smiling, did not give him courage as she seemed to think it should.

He wished that he could go away and sit by himself for a while in some lonely place, and try to get used to the certainty that he would never see his father again. He thought of cows munching contentedly.

He didn't want to think of his father lying in mud with his face shattered by bullets.

Mr McFarquhar the minister when reading out the names of men in his congregation who had been killed in action always did it with more pride than pity.

Miserably he thought he saw what Mrs Ferrier might have meant by saying his mother was wrong in the head. Women were expected to break their hearts if their husbands were killed. He had seen Mrs Findlay outside the Co-op. once, unable to stop weeping. Women trying to comfort her had wept too. She had been very grateful to them.

He had never seen his mother being grateful to anyone.

3

MOTHERS WITH CHILDREN in the penny-buff usually
waited outside the school to take them home.

One day, three weeks after his father's death, as Gavin came out
of the gate with some of his friends, one of these women, as he
thought, stepped forward and gripped him by the shoulder. He
thought she was going to tell him how sorry she was about his
father.

She was much older than the other women at the gate, and
wore a black hat from which hung down a black veil obscuring her
face. He thought she looked more angry than sympathetic. Like
him she had an armband. He was sure he had never seen her
before.

He noticed some younger women glancing at them curiously.

Perhaps she was mistaking him for another boy.

"I'm Gavin Hamilton," he said.

"I ken wha you are." She had a stern voice. She was tall for a
woman.

He was too polite to ask her what her name was.

"Let's walk a bit," she said. "What I've got to say is for your
ears alane." She addressed his friends. "Off you go, boys. I want
to talk to Gavin."

They were accustomed to seeing him being stopped by people
wanting to speak to him about his father. It used to be interesting
but not any more. So they raced away, clouting one another with
their schoolbags.

"I'm no' supposed to talk to strangers," Gavin said, politely.

"That I'm a stranger," she said bitterly, "is a disgrace that lies
at somebody else's door, no' at mine."

He didn't understand. "I've to hurry hame. I've to go messages."

"Whit I've got to say is mair important. Do you ken wha I am?"

He shook his head. He had no idea.

"I'm your grandmither. My name's Hamilton too. You're no'
the only one that's mourning. You lost a father, I lost a son."

Under the veil tears ran down her cheeks. They did nothing to
make her face look softer and more lenient, but they removed his
fear of her.

"I had to learn frae strangers that my son was deid," she said.

He hoped she wasn't blaming him for not sending her a telegram. He had never sent anyone a telegram in his life.

He knew his mother would have wanted him to run, but he felt obscurely that this tall hard-faced rough-voiced woman, if she really was his grandmother, had rights too. So he kept stoically by her side, praying that she wouldn't try to take his hand. Whoever was to blame for the quarrel he must show that he was on his mother's side.

"Your grandfaither would like to see you," she said.

He looked ahead to see if his grandfather was waiting.

"He's at work. He's a smelter. He makes guid money. How wad you like to be a smelter yin day?"

He didn't tell her that his mother wanted him to be a minister.

"When the time comes your grandfaither could get you in. He's weel thocht of. It's a well-paid trade. We live in Lendrick. 60 Somerville Place. A tiled close. Inside bathroom. Four rooms and kitchen."

She stopped. In another minute they would be at the shops.

"You don't say much."

Perhaps there was no special reason why she and his mother had fallen out. Perhaps they just hated each other.

"She's got you weel trained."

She put out her gloved hand and touched his head before he could draw back.

"There's nae need to tell onybody aboot this meeting," she said. "It's oor business, yours and mine, naebody else's."

She didn't want him to tell his mother.

"I hope you understand?"

He nodded to show he understood but he hoped she didn't take it to mean that he was promising not to tell his mother.

"That's a promise," she said, "and it's no' honourable to break a promise. 60 Somerville Place. A red-stone building. Two up, middle door. Bring a friend if you like."

Then she walked away before he could protest that he hadn't really promised anything.

He was amazed that so unsmiling a woman could be his father's mother. It must have been from his grandfather that his father had got his cheerfulness. Everybody thought that it was from his mother that *he* got his seriousness.

By the time he reached home he had made up his mind that he would have to let his mother know. He just couldn't see how he could keep it hidden and yet be loyal to her.

Since his father's death she had become more lively, and even laughed and sang. Neighbours, he suspected, were strengthened in their belief that she wasn't right in the head. The Wisharts kept asking him kind but sly questions about her.

That afternoon she was ironing clothes. Before his father's death she had always been a bit untidy, leaving buttons unfastened and laces loose. Now she had become pernicketty and was never satisfied with her appearance though he kept assuring her there was nothing wrong with it.

He sometimes wondered if her taking excessive care with her dress and her so suddenly becoming light-hearted were her ways of breaking her heart.

"You're looking very solemn," she said. "Did somebody steal your scone?"

"I met somebody."

"Did you indeed? And who was this mysterious somebody?"

"I didn't really meet somebody. Somebody met me."

She laughed. "Is there a difference?"

He considered and decided there was a big difference.

He sighed. "It was my grandmither."

His cautious words were like a hammer striking her head. She turned pale. The iron stopped. There was a smell of burning. The white petticoat was being scorched.

"Something's burning," he muttered, miserably.

She still held on to the iron but did not move it. She stared down at it with her red mouth twisted with hate.

"She was waiting for me ootside the school gate. I didnae know her."

The petticoat would be ruined.

"She telt me where she lives. She asked me to go and visit her and take a friend. I didnae say I would."

"I'm glad you didn't, for if you had I would never have spoken to you again all my life."

Again he considered. Was that the same kind of exaggeration that he and his friends often used, without meaning it? "I'll bet you a million pounds." "If you dae that again I'll kill you." He decided it wasn't: she really meant it.

"Well, I didnae," he said, feebly.

"And you never will, while I'm alive. Do you understand?"

"Yes." This time it *was* a promise.

"Good." She lifted the iron. Not only the petticoat was scorched,

23

so was the sheet beneath. Yet she laughed, and her face was bright again. "I've made scones. You can have one with your glass of milk."

"Thanks." But he was thinking that though he liked new-baked scones and milk they were hardly substitutes for an explanation as to why his mother hated his grandmother so much.

He had a terrifying vision of her placing the hot iron against his grandmother's cheek, under the veil.

4

WHEN THEY HAD passed their qualifying examination pupils of Auchengillan Primary School went on to Lendrick Advanced Division, where the boys concentrated on woodwork and metalwork and the girls on sewing and cookery. Tickets were issued free to travel to and from Lendrick on the buses that had recently replaced the tramcars. Tales were told of the excitement and fun of those journeys. Like his classmates Gavin was looking forward to them.

Unknown to him his mother kept an appointment with Mr Richardson, the primary headmaster, on a Wednesday afternoon in April, almost four years after the death of her husband.

She went dressed elegantly in a blue coat trimmed with black fur.

A white-whiskered man of 64, Mr Richardson had not expected so handsome and fragrant a young woman. This was a bonus. He could not stop himself snorting in appreciation. He felt tempted to hold her small blue-gloved hand.

"Your boy, Mrs Hamilton," he said," is one of the most able I have encountered in 40 years of teaching."

She took the praise very calmly. "I've always had good reports."

"I would like to suggest that he be put forward for the bursary examination at Cadzow Academy next month."

This time she couldn't quite hide her surprise. "Cadzow Academy? Well, why not?"

It was the top school in the county. Even for fee-payers the scholastic standards were very high. The bursary-winners were the cleverest and most ambitious pupils from all the best primary schools. No Auchengillan pupil had ever so much as competed for a bursary. That wasn't to say it never had any pupils capable of winning one. There had to be a rare combination of exceptionally bright eager pupil and far-sighted sacrificing family.

"Mind you, he would be up against the cream of the county," the headmaster warned her.

"But you think yourself he might do well enough?"

"I think he has the ability to go on to the university itself. He does not say much, your Gavin, but I once got out of him that he would like to be a doctor."

"He has never said any such thing to me. He knows I would like him to be a minister."

"A minister?" The headmaster could not help looking glum. "Well, I'm bound to say he'd grace the position better than most. He's not just very intelligent, he's got a gift rarer even than that: he never makes children not so clever as himself feel small."

"Is it an honour then to show respect for dunces?"

Disconcerted, the old man still answered stoutly: "Yes, it is. There's not a child in this school would grudge him success."

"Whether they would grudge it or not would make no difference."

"It would to Gavin."

The headmaster was thinking that if the boy had taken his good looks from his mother it must have been from his dead father that he took his magnanimity.

"There are trusts set up to help war orphans with their education," he said.

"We want no charity."

"It wouldn't be charity. Your husband earned it."

"So he did. Well, Mr Richardson, I'd be obliged if you would put Gavin's name forward."

"With pleasure. The examination's next month. On a Saturday."

"Thank you. I know it's your duty to make sure that the cleverest children get their proper chance, but I'm grateful just the same. Good day."

From his window he watched her walking smartly across the playground. He was thinking of Andrew Gordon, who had been as clever as Gavin Hamilton but who had been taken by his family from school at fourteen and put down the pit. No doubt as a collier with a black face and weary back he was as happy and useful a member of society as he would have been as doctor or lawyer or teacher, but it had seemed then and still seemed now, a painful waste.

Probably though Andrew would have been cowed and miserable among the budding snobs of Cadzow. Gavin Hamilton had the grace and courage to hold his own in any company. Also, he was a good-looking boy with his jet-black hair and compassionate eyes. Poor Andrew's face, like his hands, had been large and coarse.

Mrs Hamilton's discussion with Gavin was brief.

"Just don't tell me you want to be like your friends, I'll listen to anything but that."

He sighed but said nothing.

"But if you do sit this examination make sure you pass and pass well. You may not mind jealous fools laughing at you, but I do."

He did not think that if he failed anyone would laugh at him. He had a higher opinion of people's goodwill than she. It often had her shaking her head at him, as if she foresaw disasters in store because of his reckless trust.

He did not think though that he would fail.

5

ON A WARM May morning he went to Cadzow on one of the new buses. It was called "Sweet Lavender" and was painted the colour of lavender. He wore his dark-blue Sunday suit and had a fountain pen clipped into his breast pocket. His mother had made up sandwiches in a neat brown-paper package. She had also given him an extra shilling for emergencies.

He had never before been in so large a town but it was easy to find his way to the academy. All he had to do was follow other boys and girls hurrying there. Like him they were well-dressed and could have passed for fee-payers. Except one, a boy with a big mouth and untidy hair who wore a jersey darned at the elbows with wool a lighter green than the rest. He did not slink along trying not to be noticed. He grinned in a friendly way at everyone who happened to glance at him.

Gavin smiled back. At once, showing that he was really feeling lonely, McIntyre, as his name was, ran over and walked beside him.

"Douglas McIntyre. Doug for short."

"Gavin Hamilton."

"Frae Bonnyhill."

"From Auchengillan."

"Is there onybody else frae Auchengillan sitting this exam?"

"No."

"Same here. My heidie said I had nae chance. He said it was cheek me trying. I bet you're supposed to hae a guid chance, Hamilton."

Gavin smiled.

"My faither wants me to try. D'you think it's a' right me haeing on a jersey? They'll no' turn me away at the door, will they?"

"I wouldn't think so."

"My mither says if I win a bursary she'll try to get me a jaiket. At a jumble sale, maist likely."

Academy pupils were supposed to wear the proper red blazers with the motto in gold letters on the breast. They were expensive. Gavin didn't mention it.

"We're poor, you see. I've got twa brithers and three sisters. Hoo many hae you?"

"None."

"Nane at a'? Oh, I wouldnae like that. You don't mind me walking wi' you?"

"No."

"Would you mind if I sat beside you?"

"No."

"No' to cheat or onything like that. I'll juist feel a bit less nervous. I must say, Hamilton, you don't look nervous."

So during the examination in the great hall with the stained glass windows and the black-gowned invigilators McIntyre sat at the desk on Gavin's right. Once he winked ruefully but that was all the communication he attempted. He had no fountain pen and had to use one of the pens provided. It had a scratchy noisy nib.

The first paper consisted of an essay, a passage for interpretation, and some general knowledge questions.

Gavin was finished in good time. McIntyre, he noticed, was still writing and scoring out desperately when the call came to put pens down.

"Arithmetic in the efternin," said McIntyre, as they went out into the playground. "I'm better at arithmetic. Some hopes!"

He kept close to Gavin. After they had eaten their sandwiches they joined in a game of football with some other of the more carefree candidates. Most of the rest stood about anxiously discussing the morning's paper and worrying about the afternoon's.

As usual when playing with boys of his own age Gavin was outstanding.

"My goodness, Hamilton," panted McIntyre, "you're a great player."

"Did you ken," he asked later, "that Cadzow's famous for fitba'? They've won the Secondary School Shield mair times than ony ither school. I bet you'll be playing for the first team yin day. Me? I'm a ham."

When they came out of the examination hall again later in the afternoon and compared their answers with those of others Gavin found that he appeared to have all the twenty sums right, but McIntyre that he had at least eight wrong.

They walked together to the bus stop. The same bus would do for them. Bonnyhill was about halfway between Cadzow and Auchengillan.

"I hope I get a bursary," said McIntyre. "It's to please my dad, you see. He's in the sanatorium at Hairmyres. He's got consumption. He'd like me to be a doctor. Some hopes! Whit does your faither dae, Hamilton?"

"He was killed in the war."

"Too bad."

Yes, it was too bad, but perhaps it wasn't as bad as having your father dying of consumption in a sanitorium. Gavin's mother was often scornful of the small pension she was paid, but she also kept telling him to hold up his head, there wasn't a person in the country who would dare not to honour him for his father's sake. Who would honour McIntyre for having a father in the sanatorium? Who would make allowances for his darned jersey and his common way of speaking?

As he rose to get off the bus McIntyre patted Gavin on the shoulder. "Goodbye, Hamilton," he said. "I don't think you'll be seeing me in September."

"I hope I will."

"Do you really? You're no' juist saying it?"

"I mean it."

"Thanks. Thanks a lot."

On the pavement McIntyre stood waving eagerly.

"Good luck," murmured Gavin, "good luck."

*   *   *

His mother wanted to know how he had got on, how grand a building the academy was, and, especially, what kind of boys and girls he had met.

"They were all right."

"Oh, I know they were a lot more than just all right. Mr Richardson said they were the cream of the country. If you become an academy pupil there will be no more Charlie McGill or Davie McLuskie coming to the door to ask you out to play. Mind that. If you want to rise in the world you've got to associate with the right people, those that dress well and speak nicely and have good manners. These Auchengillan friends of yours couldn't be more common. You know that."

He did not know it and he hoped that he would not have to give up his old friends, but he did not want to argue with her in this typically exalted, slightly hysterical mood. She could plunge straight from it into stony depression.

He did not tell her of McIntyre. She would never have understood if he had said that what had impressed him most of all that day was the courage of McIntyre, not only in wearing a jersey among all those smart suits and not being ashamed, but also in having a father with consumption and showing, without a trace of bravado, how much he loved him.

He hoped that he and McIntyre became friends.

6

ON HIS FIRST morning as a Cadzow Academy pupil his pals Charlie McGill, David McLuskie, and Jockie Aitchison were waiting for him at the bus stop opposite the church, at eight o'clock. They had promised they would be there to see him off, wish him luck, and admire his red blazer.

They had thought it would be a jolly occasion but when he appeared they became subdued and shy. They hadn't realised he would look so like the young toffs who lived in the part of Lendrick known as "up the hill" and who would never in a million years speak to them. They hung their heads and grinned stupidly at his shoes; even these were new and highly polished. Their own were worn and dirty: Charlie in fact had on sandshoes with his big toes showing through. A minute or two before Gavin arrived Charlie had been boasting that he was going to ask Gavin to let him try on the blazer; but he did not ask and his friends didn't hold him to his boast. His jersey had stains of tar on it. It would have sullied the splendid blazer. They would all have looked daft, him wearing it and them looking at him wearing it.

"We were frightened you mither wad be wi' you," muttered Davie, as if to excuse their diffidence.

"Better no' say 'mither', Davie," said Charlie. "They'll say 'mother' at Cadzow."

Though they all laughed, including Gavin himself, they were aware of the great difference between "mither" and "mother". In "mither" was faithfulness to old friends and old customs; in "mother" could be pretension, conceit, and even betrayal.

The bus came. They mumbled goodbyes. They could not help showing in their voices and in their faces that though he was only going to Cadzow eight miles away they knew that he was really setting out on a journey that would take him further from them than if he was going to Canada.

As he sat in the bus he tried to persuade himself that they were wrong and he would still be their friend; but more clearly than they he saw the difficulties. When he came home every night he would have hours of homework to do, not to mention of violin practice. On Saturdays it was possible he would be playing football for one of the academy teams. On Sunday he went to church twice: he would meet none of them there. In two years they would leave school and go to work. With luck he would continue at the academy and afterwards perhaps go on to university. And of course all the time he would be making new and different friends among the boys at Cadzow.

But even if he had given up this chance to "rise in the world", as his mother put it, and had gone with them to Lendrick Advanced Division he would still have grown apart from them. He liked reading books, they didn't. He was learning to play the violin, they thought it was a cissie instrument. He went to church, they were heathens and proud of it. He saw nothing wrong with trying to speak correctly and politely; they thought, curiously, that they would be lowering themselves. He never swore, they did often. They said dirty things about girls, he was shocked. His mother wanted him to be a minister, their mothers would be pleased if they got any kind of work at all.

It was a few minutes before he came out of his introspections and noticed that there were several academy pupils in the bus. They were chatting as if they had known one another for some time. Probably they were fee-payers from "up the hill" in Lendrick. They said "don't" instead of "didnae" and "I" instead of "Ah" without having to think about it first.

Only one of them showed any interest in him. This was a girl of about fifteen, with such dark skin that he wondered if she was an Indian. Seated directly in front of him, on the window side, she must have got a good look at his friends saying goodbye. She wasn't likely herself to have friends with tarry jerseys and torn sandshoes.

At Bonnyhill there was no McIntyre.

This was a disappointment he had prepared himself for, but his heart still sank. He hardly knew McIntyre, yet he had often thought of him. In his prayers at night he had never forgotten to ask that McIntyre's father be made better.

At Cadzow as he was setting off to walk to the school he was startled to hear a girl's voice behind him. "Just a minute, Sadeyes," it said.

It was the girl with the dark skin. Her own brown eyes were far from merry. Though she had spoken quite sharply her accent struck him as too refined to be Scottish.

They walked side by side.

"My name's Hallad," she said. "Rachel Hallad. What's yours?"

"Gavin Hamilton."

"Is this your first day?"

"Yes."

She must be a fee-payer. Her blazer was no better than his—his mother had insisted on buying the most expensive—but she wore it with careless assurance, as if she had more at home. And she soon showed an impertinence that Charlie McGill would have blushed at.

"Those three boys that saw you on the bus," she said. "Are they your friends?"

Tell her, he heard his mother saying, as genteelly as you can, to mind her own business. That way she will respect you more. Don't think she's interested in scruffy characters like Charlie McGill or Davie McLuskie. She just wants to find if you're fit to be an academy pupil.

"Yes," he replied. "Yes, they're my friends."

To his surprise she looked pleased. "I suppose you won a bursary?"

"Yes."

"I hope you're not going to become a teacher."

He wondered what she had against teachers. "I don't think so," he said. Not the kind anyway that used a strap.

"Good. Why do all clever poor boys in Scotland become teachers? It's a great pity."

"Why?"

"Teachers remain childish, intellectually and morally."

"Is your father a teacher?" he asked.

She appreciated his irony. She laughed. "Am I talking like someone whose father's a teacher? I suppose I am. Sorry. No, he's a writer."

Gavin was impressed. "A writer? Of books?"

"Tomes, actually. Utterly unreadable. About politics and economics. What's your father?"

"He was killed in the war."

"Oh." She sounded more angry than sorry. "How beastly. I didn't approve of the war."

The idea that the war could be approved of or not was strange to him. Lots of people in Auchengillan hadn't liked it much, but they had all accepted it as necessary. Besides, Rachel could have been only seven or eight when it began. It seemed very impertinent of her not to approve of what the king, the prime minister, and the government, not to mention the Rev. Mr McFarquhar, had said were the four bravest, noblest, and most Christian years in the country's history.

"It was supposed to make Britain a land fit for heroes," she said. "Well, look at all the unemployed. Look at the miserable pensions. Look at the way we're treating the Germans. What we're doing of course is making sure there will be another war one day. Just in time for you to fight in it, if you were foolish enough."

She left him at the girls' gate.

No person had ever disturbed him more. She had given him glimpses of difficult decisions ahead. It wasn't going to be enough to believe what he was told, do what he was told, study hard, win prizes, and play football for one of the school teams.

In the playground among the hundreds of red-blazered boys he saw one, all by himself, leaning against a wall, and wearing a blazer that was maroon not red. It was McIntyre. With a feeling of relief and joy he made for him through the crowds.

7

HAVING DONE VERY well in the busary examination Gavin was placed in the top form 1A. McIntyre who had just scraped through found himself at the bottom in 1E. Therefore they saw each other only at intervals, lunch-breaks, and on the bus.

Gavin's classmates, the "swots" of 1A, claimed his attention with their enthusiastic discussions of all kinds of subjects, including Latin and Shakespeare. McIntyre, not in the least thin-skinned, sometimes gate-crashed these intellectual groups, making jokes that only Gavin appreciated. They called Gavin an idiot for having such a friend and told McIntyre that his place was with the childish dimwits of 1E, exchanging comics and cigarette cards. They made clever sarcastic remarks about the wrong colour of his blazer.

There was another group with which Gavin was popular and from which McIntyre was excluded. This was the footballing fraternity, those good enough to play for a school team. After a few games with the junior eleven Gavin had been promoted to the intermediates. He had quickly become one of their stars. Every second week they played away, against teams in Lanarkshire, Renfrewshire, and Glasgow. At the home games in Cadzow McIntyre sometimes turned up and cheered loudest of all.

Gavin was often worried because he was not doing more to help and protect McIntyre, especially as McIntyre never uttered a word of reproach or complaint or resentment or envy. He had never known anyone so devoid of self-pity. It amazed him that among these hundreds of boys he was the only one aware of McIntyre's goodness. It seemed to him to shine out of McIntyre's face.

On the day after the results of the first-term examination were given out Gavin and McIntyre were seated at lunch eating their sandwiches and comparing marks. Gavin was drinking tea. Often McIntyre couldn't afford to buy a cup. He couldn't today.

He was pleased with his marks.

"What did you get for English?" he asked, eagerly.

"88."

"88? Great. You must be first."

"First equal. A girl got 88 too."

"I got 60. Not bad. My best mark, as a matter of fact. Fifth in the class." He consulted a slip of paper. "English 60. Maths 39.

French 32. That's my worst. Science 44. History 51. Geography 55. Not too bad, eh? I mean they cannae throw me oot if I get 60 for English. Can they?"

"Of course not."

"My average is 45.1. Whit's yours?"

"86."

"Crikey! You must be first in the haill year."

"Pretty near it anyway."

"You'll be dux of the year."

"There are two more term exams."

"You'll dae juist as weel in them."

"I hope so. Is your father home yet?"

McIntyre sighed. "No. Maybe he'll make it for the New Year."

"Isn't he keeping better?"

"No' very much. He wants me to stick it here. But it'll get harder."

"Do you do all your homework, McIntyre? I mean——" What he meant was did McIntyre have peace and quiet at home to study. There were those two brothers and three sisters.

"Sure. There's a wash-hoose naebody uses at night. I sit in there wi' a caun'le. It's quiet onyway."

"But isn't it cold?"

"I wrap an auld coat of my mither's roon' me."

He didn't talk much about his mother.

Gavin had never spoken to his about McIntyre. He couldn't have borne hearing her disparage his friend.

A few days before the Christmas holidays McIntyre was absent. There had been nothing wrong with him the day before.

Discreetly Gavin asked some boys in 1E if they knew what was the matter. They hadn't even noticed McIntyre was off.

He was off the next day too.

Rachel Hallad noticed. She sat beside Gavin in the bus.

"Where's your indomitable friend?" she asked.

He savoured the word: indomitable. How true it was.

"He's absent. He was absent yesterday too."

"What's the matter with him?"

"I don't know."

"Haven't you asked?"

"Nobody seems to know."

"Do you think something's happened to his father?"

He was surprised. He had thought McIntyre's father was a secret that only he knew.

"Douglas told me," she said, gently.

"Do you mean his father may have come home from the sanatorium?"

"Yes. I hope alive."

"Yes. Oh yes."

Her saying Douglas reminded him that he and McIntyre seldom used each other's Christian name. He wondered why. Addressing other boys he called them Bill or Peter or Charlie and yet he did not feel as close to them as he did to McIntyre.

They passed through Bonnyhill.

"How would you like to pay me a visit during the holidays?" asked Rachel. "I could meet you at Lendrick Cross."

"I'd like that. Thank you." It would be interesting to see her house and to meet her father who wrote books.

"Do you think Douglas would like to come too?"

"I don't know. Would you like me to ask him?"

"If I see him I'll ask him myself. We'll fix a date later. My father's keen to meet you both. I often tell him about you. You're a fascinating pair. Did you know that?"

He had told his mother about her. His mother had been pleased. She had made enquiries. The Hallads were well-to-do. They lived in a big villa "up the hill". They had once lived in France. Mrs Hallad was dead: it was thought she had been a Frenchwoman. They were said to be Jews but only ignorant people would hold that against them. They were the kind of friends he ought to cultivate.

McIntyre came back the day the school broke up. He was waiting for Gavin outside the room where they ate their sandwiches. He looked a little downcast.

"Hello, Hamilton," he said. "I've come to say goodbye."

"Goodbye?"

"I'm leaving. I just came to hand in my books and say goodbye to you. My mither said I'd to thank you for her."

"But why are you leaving?"

"Dad dee'd. A week ago. I kent a' the time it was going to happen but I kept kidding myself he'd get better." His voice was faltering.

"I'm very sorry, McIntyre."

"Weel, onyway, I saw him. At the end. You didnae, Hamilton. I was luckier than you. It's expensive at the academy and we're poor. Onyway I'd never hae got much further. I was kidding myself."

"What are you going to do?"

"Join the scruff at Bonnyhill Advanced Division. Till I'm fourteen. Then wi' luck I'll land a job. We could dae wi' the money. Well, goodbye, Hamilton, and thanks a lot."

"Goodbye, McIntyre. And good luck."

If they had been men they would have shaken hands, if they had been girls or women they would have embraced or kissed cheeks. Being boys, and Scottish boys at that, they nodded, smiled, and turned away, McIntyre to hurry along the corridor and Gavin to walk slowly into the room crowded with exuberant boys.

No one asked him about McIntyre, no one knew that McIntyre was gone for good. If they had been told they would not have cared.

As he sipped the hot sweet milky tea he prayed, asking simply that McIntyre be given a fair chance.

8

ON THE DAY of his visit to Rachel Hallad three days after Christmas, while he was waiting for the bus to take him to Lendrick he was assailed by shouts of abuse from a close in the Co-op. building. "Fucking academy toff! Creeping Jesus Hamilton! A penny one please to Lendrick!" This last in an exaggeratedly posh voice.

He could not see who the shouters were but one sounded like Charlie McGill. He would have liked to go and try to persuade them that he was still the same Gavin Hamilton who had played with them just a few months ago; but they would have run away still shouting insults. If they had stayed to listen they would have jeered. They would have been justified, too. He wasn't the same. His mother would have said that he was much better: he spoke properly, he knew Latin, he had friends whose fathers were bank managers or doctors or teachers. He did not think himself that he was better. He didn't blame Charlie and the others for yelling at him, but he would have liked to be able to explain that he didn't really deserve their contempt, that in his heart he was still their friend, it was only external circumstance that obliged him to have nothing to do with them.

He would have liked too to tell them about McIntyre, not in order to show himself up in a good light as having befriended someone as poor as themselves, but to put a sweetness into their minds.

As he stepped on the bus, with the abusive shouts redoubled, he heard in his mind his mother's scornful voice: "Don't tell me you're worrying about what Charlie McGill, a halfwit, thinks of you".

He wondered if McIntyre's friends in Bonnyhill had looked on him as a traitor. If so, were they now rejoicing that he had been forced to go back to them? Or, unconsciously influenced by McIntyre's goodness had they always wished him well and were now unhappy on his account?

One change in himself that Gavin had to admit to was that he was no longer able to take for granted that people existed for his delight.

His mother said that he was growing up and learning sense.

Rachel was waiting for him at Lendrick Cross. She wore a long light-grey fur coat, with hat and gloves to match, and long red boots. She had put on lipstick. The breath that could be seen coming out of her mouth in the damp cold air seemed scented, as if she had been drinking wine. She looked more French than Scottish.

She addressed him in French. "Bonjour, jeune garçon aux yeux conscientieux."

"Bonjour, mademoiselle," he murmured.

"Ou est votre ami?"

"Son père est mort."

It should have seemed callous talking about McIntyre's loss in French, here at Lendrick Cross where the people passing were so dourly Scottish; but somehow it wasn't. "Son père est mort," even spoken with a Scottish accent sounded more tragic than "His father is dead" or "His faither's deid".

Rachel though now preferred English. She looked grim rather than sad. "How do you know?"

"He came back to school to hand in his books and say goodbye."

"He didn't say goodbye to me."

"I don't think he had time."

They set off "up the hill".

"Your prayers did no good then?"

He hadn't ever told her of his prayers for Mr McIntyre, but it would have been easy for her to guess. He had once admitted to her that he did pray every night. "Don't you feel silly?" she had asked. "Or sneaky?"

They passed Somerville Place. He saw the nameplate on the wall. The tenement was of red sandstone. He had never been to 68. He had kept a promise and been unkind.

"I'm sorry I said that about your prayers," said Rachel. "It was abominable."

They were already among the big villas.

"No human being can help another," said Rachel. "That's my belief. So you might as well pray. Have you ever tried to keep alive a fledgling that's fallen out of its nest? You put it out on the lawn hoping its mother will see it. Though how she could pick it up and carry it away, goodness knows. You take a pipette and try to drip milk down its throat. Though why a bird should like milk, again goodness knows. You make pellets of bread. You look for a worm and cut it in pieces. You line a box with grass. All useless. It just dies. It's the same with people. I don't mean they die physically like the bird but they do, little by little, in their minds; *you* would say in their souls."

These seemed strange things for a girl dressed so richly to be saying. Was it because she was Jewish?

"I don't suppose you understand a word of what I'm saying, but I mean it, I've thought about it a lot. It's the reason why I have no faith in the future of the human race. Of course Gavin Hamilton with the conscientious eyes thinks I'm talking nonsense. He thinks everybody's good at heart. He thinks the war was fought for civilization as it says on the medals. He believes everything his teachers tell him. He believes in God."

Gavin listened seriously. It was perhaps silly to compare people in trouble with small birds fallen out of nests, but it was true just the same that he had not been able to help McIntyre except by praying for him.

As for believing in God, he had thought that just as everybody was bound to approve of the war so everybody must believe in God. Charlie McGill and Davie McLuskie once, impaling earwigs on pins, had glanced about guiltily as if they felt that God or some spirit of goodness was watching and might, for they granted to Him omnipotence, impale them. The earwigs themselves as they wriggled were proof of God's existence. Everything that had life was proof. To say that you didn't believe in God was like saying nothing was alive, the whole world was dead.

Rachel stopped at her gate. This was wide enough to let a horse and carriage through. She watched her guest closely as he looked at the large grey stone house with its two ornamental turrets that gave it the appearance of a small castle. She knew how inconvenient it was as a place to live in with its enormous high-ceilinged rooms so difficult to heat adequately, and its primitive kitchen; but to someone friendly with ragamuffins and living in a house similar to those in which ragamuffins lived (for so she guessed) "Ivanhoe", for such was its ridiculous name, must look very impressive. It had been built by her grandfather, a prosperous silversmith in Glasgow. It had a small wood in its garden.

Her guest, she saw, was looking delighted, and not in the least resentful or covetous.

"Do you know Silverbanks Street?" she asked.

"I've passed it."

"You must know then that the houses there are slums. Many are single rooms. The rest room-and-kitchens. There are no bathrooms. The lavatories are outside on the landing. Each one is shared by four families."

He nodded. Many of the houses in Auchengillan had outside lavatories which were sometimes shared.

"It's not uncommon for a family of eight or more to live in a room-and-kitchen."

He counted. In Davie McLuskie's family there were seven, and they lived in a room-and-kitchen.

They were walking up the long wide driveway. He had never seen a garden with such huge trees in it. One was a monkey-puzzle.

"There are twelve rooms in this house," she said," and only my father and I live in it. (Not counting the two servants.) Do you think that's fair?"

"I suppose it isn't."

"What would you do about it then? Would you take the family of eight from Silverbanks Street and put them in here, and put my father and me in their room-and-kitchen?"

"Would you agree to the exchange?" he asked. "I expect *they* would."

39

Once again she appreciated his irony. "I jolly well wouldn't: though I call myself a Socialist."

He was interested in the name in gold Gothic letters on the glass above the big front door. He had read *Ivanhoe* the book.

"I'm a hypocrite, of course," she said, as she opened the door and went in.

"I thought you said it was impossible for one human being to help another," he said, smiling, as he helped her off with her heavy coat.

She was now seen to be wearing a black dress with a large white collar. He was reminded of Rebecca the beautiful Jewess.

On the wall was the head of a stag. Red carpet covered the floor all the way up the wide staircase with the massive banister.

A middle-aged woman with grey hair appeared. Rachel introduced her as Mrs Sempill, the housekeeper.

"Is Dad busy?" asked Rachel.

"Well, he's in his study but he said you had to take the young gentlemen to see him there. He seemed to think there would be two."

"One couldn't come."

Gavin was looking forward to seeing Mr Hallad the author and also the study where the books were written.

His mother had made enquiries about Mr Hallad too. "Used to be a professor, they say. A dabbity of a man, with a beard not unlike the king's. Always wears a big black hat, like Guy Fawkes. Must be very clever if he's been a professor and if he's written books, but Miss Peden (Miss Peden was her colleague in the ladies' outfitters) says that he's simple in some ways. He came into the shop once looking for a suitable present for a young lady—his daughter I suppose. Miss Peden suggested a box of hankies. She said he looked at her as if she had just said something terribly clever. Maybe he thinks everybody's very stupid. He bought the dearest box in the shop. Trust Socialists to look after themselves well."

Rachel paused with her hand ready to knock on a handsome mahogany door.

"Anything my father says," she said, "no matter what it is, he means, he's not joking."

Then she knocked and went in.

In front of the fire, on the other side of the biggest desk Gavin had ever seen—it was twice the size of the one in the rector's room in Cadzow Academy—was standing a man hardly any taller than himself, smoking a cigar and wearing a long red velvety gown, with tassels. He had a black beard, sallow sunken cheeks, and brown eyes, much craftier than Rachel's. He gave the impression that he thought his opinion on no matter what subject better than anyone else's.

If I get the chance, thought Gavin, I would like to ask him if he knows the rules of moshie. What is the meaning of "up for smout".

He noticed the title of one of the books on the desk. It was *Politics and Ethics* by Benjamin Hallad.

"Ah, so you are Rachel's friend with the conscience," said Mr Hallad, coming forward to shake hands.

Surely, thought Gavin, everyone has a conscience. If Rachel hadn't warned him he would have said her father was joking. Certainly he was smiling broadly, but then Gavin had had a teacher once, Mr Fulton, who had always smiled like that when giving someone the belt.

"Rachel tells me that you worry about your responsibilities to other people."

But did not everybody? Gavin could think of no one who was not concerned to some extent about such responsibilities. He had seen Harold Murphy upset because his young sister was ill.

"But where is your friend, the insuppressible Douglas, who lets nothing him dismay?"

"His father died. He's left school because he couldn't afford to stay on."

"He has gone out of our orbit," said Rachel, bitterly.

"What a pity. Poor lad."

"We can't help him so we should forget him," she said. "He ought not to have been at the academy in any case. He hadn't the talent."

Her father smiled at Gavin. "Have you noticed how our dear Rachel is so quick to adopt extreme or untenable positions."

"I've just been telling him that in my opinion no human being can help another."

Again he smiled at Gavin, looking more than ever like Mr Fulton with the tawse in his hand. "Well, here is one untenable position that we can dislodge her from."

"He loved his father," she said. "How can we help him there?"

"Can we not offer consolation?"

"By saying we're awfully sorry? What good is that? He'll just have to hide in some corner and get over it himself."

Or in a wash-house, thought Gavin.

"Is not literature, my dear, full of consolatory masterpieces? 'Fear no more the heat of the sun.' And there are the comforts of religion."

"The only way we could have helped was by giving him his father back, this time in good health."

"Alas, we lack the Orphean music to draw tears down the iron cheeks of Pluto! But, like all other human things, grief is not permanent. Other considerations inevitably take over."

"Like leaving school and going down the pit to work? He wanted to be a doctor."

"Speaking as an economist, I must say he will be fulfilling a more useful rôle than as a doctor. But could he not have continued his studies if some benefactor had provided the funds? Supposing of course he has the intellectual capacities. I think you hinted he does not."

"What benefactor?"

"I agree he is not likely but that is not to say he is impossible."

"It's because he's possible that makes his unlikeliness so shameful."

"You put forward a philosophical position, my dear, to the effect that no human being can help another because of the impenetrable isolation in which we all live. Now I find that you are simply condemning human selfishness. What a thoroughly dead horse to flog. Wouldn't you say so, Gavin?"

Gavin wished that they hadn't used McIntyre's misfortunes as their battleground.

He remembered how, when he heard anyone showing off his knowledge, McIntyre had winked and whispered, "I bet he doesnae ken the rules of moshie. He doesnae ken whit's 'up for smout.'"

Mr Hallad and Rachel certainly didn't know. Nor would they find it in the hundreds of books all round them. It was a secret of a tribe too remote.

They had begun to talk about the novels of Sir Walter Scott when Mrs Sempill came in and said that tea was laid out in the drawing-room.

ONE DULL MORNING in June 1926, Gavin with the rest of
4A was busy writing out a translation of a passage from Homer's
Iliad when into the hushed room came, tiptoeing almost, Miss
Fordyce, his form teacher. People who interrupted a lesson of Mr
Soutar always did it with this furtiveness, even the rector himself,
for the Classics master, irascible and very deaf, distrusted all move-
ments likely to produce noise.

Miss Fordyce scribbled on the pad on his desk. Only those in the
front seats heard her sighing, but everybody in the room heard Mr
Soutar's loud ambiguous snort.

"Gavin," said Miss Fordyce, astonishing the whole class, Gavin
included, "would you please put your books away and come with
me. Yes, bring your case."

They could see that her nervousness wasn't just the usual kind
intruders showed in Mr Soutar's room. She looked a lot older,
some of the girls thought. Usually brisk and pink, her face was
now dull and pale.

They deduced that something must have happened at Gavin
Hamilton's home. There were looks of enquiry and sympathy, but
no murmurs. Those would have meant moving the lips. In Mr
Soutar's room that was risky.

Some girls gave Gavin encouraging smiles as he walked to the
door. One of them, a sentimentalist, thought of Hector "of the
glancing helm," slain by Achilles.

In the empty corridor Miss Fordyce stopped and tried, clutching her black gown, to hide behind magisterial sternness. Instead
she looked maternal and on the point of tears.

"Gavin, I'm sorry, but the rector's just had a telephone message
from the Lendrick police," she said. "I'm afraid your mother's
dead. A stroke, it seems."

She had meant to say it ever so compassionately, but she had
blurted it out like a callous fool.

She had confided to her mother once that Gavin Hamilton was
the kind of son she would have been proud of if she had ever got
married. Without being in the least a prig, he had never been known
to do or say a mean or unkind thing. "Anybody's to be pitied,"
her 81-year-old mother had replied perversely, "that hasn't learned
to harden his heart by the time he's twelve."

As his form teacher Miss Fordyce knew of his intention to

become a minister. She had never heard him talking about religion and had supposed that his interest in it was sensible and level-headed, like her own indeed. Therefore she was quite shocked to find him doing, or at any rate trying to do, what all Christians ought to do, she knew, but thank God seldom did, that was, when confronted by the death of someone loved, reject human grief and find too immediate consolation in thoughts of eternal glory. Surely he was too young, too sensitive, and too honest for that. Yet how else to interpret this would-be beatific smile and these dry eyes?

She told herself she was being hysterically unfair. His father had been killed in the war. It could be that all his grief had been exhausted then. It was asking too much of any child to expect him so soon after that blow to react in any normal way to this still more dreadful one.

"Would you like me to go home with you, Gavin?" she asked.

"Thank you, Miss Fordyce. It's not necessary."

"Do you have relatives close by?"

It was curious how he shook his head and yet murmured, "My grandparents live in Lendrick".

"They'll look after you, I'm sure. Come back to us as soon as you can."

As she watched him disappear through the swing door looking lonely and yet composed she realized that though he was well-liked and popular because of his exploits on the football field, he never appeared to have any really intimate friends. This could be because no other pupil came from Auchengillan: his closest friends might be there. He had been friendly with that uncouth boy from Bonnyhill who had worn the wrong colour blazer, and also with that strange girl Rachel Hallad who had gone to live in London a year or so ago.

10

IN THE BUS he tried not to wonder about his mother's spirit. Heaven was a mystery, to be solved only by the dead. That was his belief.

There were moments when he did not think of his mother at all, but of a woman whom he had never seen and who, he hoped,

44

was alive and well. This was McIntyre's mother. Like a guardian ghost she had visited his imagination for many months.

What good was consolation, Rachel had asked, and he had understood then what she had meant; now he understood more deeply. Yet he wanted everyone in the world to console him. If people no longer existed to give him delight surely they did to give him comfort?

Once, closing his eyes, he felt so desolate that it was as if not only his father and mother were dead but everyone in the world, except him.

When he got home Mr and Mrs Wishart would not be there with their white-haired and shaky-handed sympathy: both were dead. Mrs Ferrier and Mrs Lawrie would be, and other neighbours. They had not liked his mother much and they did not approve of his still being at school at an age when their own sons were at work, but they would do their best to be helpful.

What if his grandmother was there? The police, looking for relatives, would have sought her out. She might not try to hide how pleased she was.

At Auchengillan when he got off the bus he saw some men seated on the wall. They were miners on strike. They looked as quiet and peaceful as ever but if a policeman came they would not budge. It would be a small defiance but behind it would be a great pressure of hate and resentment. During the General Strike some weeks ago, when he had not been able to get to school, he had seen miners, among them Mr Simpson, face up to Sergeant Duff and other policemen with pick handles.

They had stretched a wire rope across the road to prevent black-leg buses from passing. They had overturned one.

Every day of the General Strike his mother had walked to Lendrick and back. No dirty-faced colliers were going to keep her from her lawful work, she had said. What right had they to think that they knew better than a gentleman like Mr Baldwin, the prime minister? Soldiers ought to be sent with bayonets to force them back to the pits where they belonged.

His own sympathies were with the miners. He had been sorry though that they had tried to use force. It seemed to him that in any dispute in which both sides thought they were in the right, honour lay with the one that yielded, not out of fear or weakness but out of a desire to avoid hatred and the violence it produced. That side must, he was sure, prevail in the end.

The men on the wall must have heard about his mother. He could tell from the way two of them waved. He waved back, feeling very grateful.

It was his grandmother who opened the door. She wasn't dressed in black and there was no sign of tears on her face. Instead she looked, as he had feared, pleased.

With her were Mrs Ferrier and Mrs Lawrie. They looked at him sadly but he saw that though their grief and pity were sincere —Mrs Lawrie was weeping—they were also, secretly they thought, pleased like his grandmother. What they had called his mother's pride and his own upstart ambition had been humbled, as they had known all along would happen. Having been proved right they could not help feeling satisfied.

"It it true?" he asked.

In Mrs Ferrier the satisfaction of her secret self became then less important to her than her wish to comfort him. She pushed forward and, not sure what form of physical contact was in order— after all she wasn't a relative and in any case had never been in the habit of embracing or kissing her own sons—took the cap from his hand.

"Aye, Gavin," she said, "it's true, I'm sorry to say."

"Where is my mother?"

His grandmother stepped between. She snatched the cap from Mrs Ferrier's hand and hung it on a peg, but not before she'd glanced at the maker's name inside.

"In her room," she said. "The ambulance brought her. She's no' coffined. I don't think you should go in juist yet."

"I would like to see her."

He spoke to her as if she was a stranger.

"Naebody's going to stop you frae seeing her," she said, harshly. "Later would be best, that's a'."

"Sometimes, Gavin," whispered Mrs Ferrier, "it taks a wee while for peace to come into a deid face. That's whit your grandmither means."

"I would like to see her now."

"Naebody will haud you back if you're thrawn," said his grandmother. "Naebody will get the chance to say you were prevented."

She went before him to the door of his mother's room. She flung it open, deliberately without respect.

"A minute should be long enough," she said, and left him.

46

He was greatly relieved that she had not come into the darkened room with him, to supervise his grieving.

The blinds were drawn. His mother's costume jacket, pink in colour, was draped over a chair. Her shoes to match were in front of the wardrobe; one lay on its side. There was the scent of her perfume in the room.

He held her shoe in his hand for a few seconds before placing it, with care, beside the other. He could hear her footsteps in the room.

She was lying on the bed under a white sheet. As he pulled this aside, very gently, he was reminded of the lady in the ballad "The Gay Goshawk", who had "schemed" death in order to be brought to Scotland where her sweetheart was waiting for her. When he had pulled aside the sheet as Gavin was doing now she had looked up and laughed "with lily-white cheeks and leamin' een" and asked him for "a chive of bread and a bottle of wine".

That was, his English teacher had said, one of the happiest moments in literature.

In contrast his mother was very silent, and the expression on her pale face was one of dismay and disappointment: as if, the moment before death struck, she had called for help and no one had come to give it.

He could not remember her in life asking for help, even from God.

With his hand on her cold brow he thought of McIntyre.

His grandmother opened the door and came in.

"That's long enough," she said, taking him by the sleeve. "It's no' healthy to be by yourself at a time like this."

For a few moments he was minded to shout no, and shake off her kindly but also revengeful grip. She did not want anyone to know it, perhaps she did not want to know it herself, but she was at long last getting her revenge and in the depths of her soul was having to enjoy it.

"Your grandfaither's still at his work," she said. "He'll be in at the back of six. Jobs are hard to haud on to these days. There's tea made. You're big enough for tea."

His father had once told him that *he* hadn't been allowed to drink tea until he had left school and started work.

Could this be her way of hinting that he was too old to be still at school?

"I'd like to go for a walk," he said.

"Didn't I tell you it's no' guid for you to be by yourself? Come and hae tea."

As he watched Mrs Lawrie sip her tea genteelly and heard Mrs Ferrier slurp hers noisily and saw his grandmother nod and nod and nod, a desire grew in him and beat against the bars of his soul: the desire to escape from these women and go to some place where he would be alone. As he looked at the face of each of them it was as if a door slammed in his mind. If more people had been present more doors would have slammed.

Alone, with no faces to see, the effect would surely be opposite, doors would open and his spirit would be free.

This was wrong, he knew. It was going against everything he believed in. For all the pain they caused, and the frustrations, the company of people was as necessary as food.

II

ON THE SUNDAY following the funeral he was in his room putting into his case the books he would need for Monday's lessons when his grandmother came in. She never left him alone for long. Even when he was in the bathroom she came knocking on the door.

"Whit's this you're daeing?" she asked.

He had been struck by the sharp suspiciousness with which she spoke to everyone: even to Mr McFarquhar, the minister. She seemed to think that the whole world had been in the plot to poison her only son's mind against her. Her own husband was not absolved. She seldom spoke to him except in an accusing or scolding voice. A big worn-out man with a flushed flabby face, he pretended it amused him but it was easy to see that he was mortified. He would have been much friendlier to Gavin if he hadn't been afraid of her.

Gavin explained.

"That's something we've got to talk aboot," she said.

She folded her arms. With her it wasn't, as with children in school, a gesture of submission. Just as her black dress was hardly proof of mourning.

"Things hae changed," she said.

His mother was dead: there could be no greater change. His grandparents had moved into his house without asking him and

were preparing to stay. It had a garden and a low door, unlike
68 Somerville Place, two-up, middle door; and there would be
no rent to pay. It was really theirs by right in any case, she had
told him. Dying in his dotage at the age of 79, his great-grandfather
had left the house to Gavin's father and not to Gavin's grandfather as he should. His father had been willing to ignore the will
and let justice be done but his mother had refused. That refusal,
Gavin had gathered, had been one of the causes of the estrange-
ment. Other causes were easy to guess.

"You're oor responsibility noo," said his grandmother. "It'll be
made legal, though it doesnae need to be: we're the same flesh and
bluid."

The house and all its contents were his, but apart from a few
shillings a week of war orphan's pension he had no money. At the
funeral he had met one or two distant relatives of his mother but
they had not been much interested in him.

"So there will be nae mair school," she said.

He was stunned. He had taken for granted that he would be
returning to the academy. He had resolved to work harder than
ever, for his mother's sake.

"We're plain folk," she said. "We've always been plain folk. We
hae nae ideas abune oor station. We ken oor place."

Remembering McIntyre's courage, he himself could not whine.
Perhaps in his case it was more unfair, for he had done very well
in all the examinations; and, though this didn't really count, he
was one of the best players in the school's first eleven.

Somebody else would have to tell her how unfair it was. He
could not. He could think of no one who could.

"If it's money I could pay you back later," he said.

"Oh, it's always money. But it's something else. It's a maitter o'
principle."

He wondered if it was a matter of spite.

"I've been doing well."

"Why shouldn't you? Your faither was clever at school. So
was I."

It would be no good appealing to Mr McFarquhar. He would be
sure to say something about adversity being good for the soul.
Besides, he had said that he didn't think Gavin was cut out to be
a minister.

Gavin was not known at school as a softie. He had it in him to oppose this spiteful act—if it was spiteful—with unrelenting determination. Whatever any lawyer might say he could refuse to accept his grandparents as his guardians, and he could insist that they leave his house.

If he were to say to her, "If you make me leave school and ruin my career I will never speak to you in my life," he would stick to it, whatever the consequences. He had understood his mother's stubbornness so well because it was in his own nature too.

"If you're thinking we're going to put you intae the steelwork whaur you'd hae to dirty your hands you neednae worry. I've been talking to Mr Ballantyne, the lawyer in Lendrick. As weel as a lawyer he's a factor too. There could be a job clerking in his office if you could bring yourself to ask wi' proper humbleness. You're faur too proud."

He was amazed that she knew. Everybody else thought he was too meek, and so he was; but he was aware often of a fierce pride locked in him. If he let it break loose he would defy not only this hard-faced, spiteful, stupid, old woman, but the whole world even if it meant destroying himself.

12

ON TUESDAY MORNING he stopped a bus in Auchengillan and handed a parcel of his books to a boy he knew, asking him to give them to Miss Fordyce. With them was a letter to her saying that owing to a change of circumstances he was obliged to withdraw from the school.

There was time only for McDiarmid to cry, in astonishment, "Why? What's up?" and for him to answer, "I'm not coming back".

As the bus drove away he saw the incredulous faces of other academy pupils staring out at him. There would be a lot of talk at the school about his leaving. There had been none about McIntyre's.

That afternoon when he was out for a walk he met Charlie McGill. Charlie worked for the Co-op. delivering messages on a heavy bicycle.

Charlie stopped. He was wearing a striped apron like a butcher's. Behind his ear was stuck a cigarette. A few Sundays back Gavin had come upon him with a girl in the grass at the old quarry. Charlie's trousers had been at his feet.

"Hello," he said.

"Hello."

"I'm sorry aboot your mither."

"Thanks."

"And aboot you having to leave school."

It must be known all over Auchengillan by this time.

"Can't be helped."

"It's no' right. You worked hard. She's an auld bitch."

Gavin smiled.

"I was speaking to Davie last night. Ken whit he said? He said you're no' lucky. But for yin thing. It's true, Gavin. Whit are you going to dae noo?"

Gavin wondered what the one thing was. "I've to go and see about a job in an office on Saturday."

"Where? In Glesca?"

"No. Lendrick."

"Whit aboot your fitba'?"

So *that* was the thing. "What do you mean?"

"Somebody said he saw in a Cadzow paper that the Hearts and Queen's Park were interested in you. Is that true?"

"Well, they wanted to know what I intended to do once I'd left school."

"Noo you've left sooner than you thought you'll be signing up for the yin that maks the best offer. You see, they like to sign a player when he's young and nurse him along. You could dae a lot better for yourself playing fitba' for a big team than staying on at school and becoming a teacher. You're the heidy kind o' player they're a' looking for. Weel, so long. I'd better hurry."

"So long, Charlie."

It wasn't quite a reconciliation, but at least it was a truce. Something was gained. It was not all loss.

Three days later Miss Fordyce appeared on the doorstep, looking resolute. His grandmother confronted her.

"My name is Fordyce. I'm from Cadzow Academy. Gavin's form teacher. I've come on behalf of the rector. May I come in?"

His grandmother was reluctant. "He's left school. Didn't he tell you that in his letter?"

"Are you his grandmother?"

51

"I am. And his guardian too till he's of age."

"The rector thought that if I was to explain the position to you in person, Mrs Hamilton—it is Mrs Hamilton?—"

"Hamilton's the name."

"——you might reconsider. We are assuming that it was your decision and not Gavin's."

"Assume whit you like. A' right, you can come in and say whit you've got to say."

She showed the visitor into the "room". "There's nae need for you to be present," she said to Gavin.

"I would much rather he was present," said Miss Fordyce. "I would like to know what he thinks."

He had never seen Miss Fordyce so agitated. It was as if she needed her black gown to give her her usual air of imperturbable authority. He noticed her glancing furtively at his father's photograph. The only photograph of his mother on display in the house was in his room.

"The rector thinks, Mrs Hamilton, and I think too, all Gavin's teachers think, that it would be a terrible waste if he weren't to be allowed to finish his education. I'm sure you don't quite understand the position. Gavin's a very modest boy. Perhaps he hasn't made it clear to you how brilliant he is. It would be the easiest thing in the world for him to win substantial bursaries that would put him through university. He would bring honour to your family, Mrs Hamilton."

"Every word you've juist said proves to me hoo right I was. It was pride and ambition that were the ruination of his mither. It's up to me to see that they don't ruin him."

Miss Fordyce was taken aback. Suddenly she realized there were family enmities involved. She had no right to interfere. But she felt bound to question that absurd accusation of pride.

"I don't understand, Mrs Hamilton. Gavin is considered to be a very unassuming boy. I'm sure no one's ever heard him boasting."

"That's no' the way his pride works. He's my ain flesh and bluid. I ken him better than strangers."

Miss Fordyce would have liked to appeal to Gavin, but as a woman in authority herself she could not encourage him to criticize his grandmother, especially in the woman's home.

"If it is a matter of money, Mrs Hamilton," she said, blushing, "I would be very pleased to help. It would be only a loan, of course.

52

Gavin could pay me back later. I assure you he could have an excellent well-paid career ahead of him."

"We can afford whit we think needs to be afforded."

"You mean this is final, he's really not going to be allowed to finish his education?"

"Dae you think it's only at school a body's educated?"

"Of course not. Would it do any good if the rector himself appealed to you personally?"

"The prime minister himself wad get the same answer that I've gi'en you. This is a Hamilton affair. The Hamiltons will settle it themselves."

Miss Fordyce rose. "It's not as simple as that, Mrs Hamilton. You must remember Gavin has been with us for four years. We're bound to feel some responsibility for him."

"Feel whitever you like."

At last Miss Fordyce turned to him. Her face was pale. "I'm dreadfully sorry, Gavin. In fact I'm appalled." She had to bite her lip to restrain a sob. "It's disgraceful. But don't feel too bitter. Don't let it defeat you."

Then she remembered what she ought not to have forgotten for a moment: that hardly a week ago his mother had died, and for that reason alone he must be feeling crushed. On top of that heavy blow had come this other, all the more difficult to bear because it could so easily have been prevented.

She could not keep tears out of her eyes.

At the door she could hardly bring herself to be polite to his grandmother.

Gavin was in his own room when his grandmother looked in. He had a glassie in his hand, ready to be plunked. Up for smout.

"Why didnae you tell her whit you think?" she asked. "That I'm daeing it oot o' spite."

"Are you?"

"Whit satisfaction would I get, spiting a woman that's deid?"

The question seemed to be put more to herself than to him. It was she who answered it, not with words but with a smile the most evilly satisfied of all the smiles she had shown since his mother's death.

It had far more menace in it than the angry shouts and brandished pick handles of the miners.

PART TWO

Holy Fair —

LIKE WISE-LIKE folk in small towns everywhere, the inhabitants of Lendrick were in doubt that some people were better-off than others, or better-looking, or even better-living, but they were never so sure about better itself. As far as goodness went everybody, apart from known rogues, was pretty much alike.

Once, over 100 years ago, a religious revival had taken place in the town, to its own astonishment. For a whole week there had been conventicles on the green sloping fields subsequently known as Preachers' Braes. Sermons had been ranted, psalms ecstatically bellowed, and love of one's fellow-man not only proclaimed but even felt. This last though had not lasted, luckily it was thought: it would have made ordinary social intercourse in the town unexciting. Still, when the glory was gone and everybody was sunk back into the old comfortable limitations, some flickers of regret must have remained.

When the Lendrick Rangers Junior Football Club was formed in 1881 and a suitable arena sought for its activities the fields of Preachers' Braes were chosen. They were within easy walking distance from the town Cross, and the slopes on which in the past the converts had knelt made good vantage points for spectators hoping to see, not the Spirit of the Lord, but something quite as earnestly desired, goals scored by the Rangers.

Bigots who protested that it would be sacrilegious to play football where once souls had been given to Jesus seemed to have been vindicated when for many years the team enjoyed little success. Once it reached the semi-final of the Cup, and six times it finished in the top six of the League. Such feats were worthy enough but not glorious, and it was in search of nothing less than glory that the men of Lendrick and district flocked faithfully to Preachers' Braes every second Saturday from October to May.

At last, in the season of 1931–1932, that glory was almost in sight. Never had it been more needed. Many men were out of work. Faces were grey with worry, breath was bad with the eating of too much bread and margarine, clothes were threadbare, and tempers were on edge because of the peevishness of wives. Goals did not put meat on the table, as those bitter wives too often pointed out, but they did give moments of ecstacy that lifted the soul as no choice gigot could.

It was unanimously agreed that the team's run of successes in Cup and League was largely because of Gavin Hamilton, aged 21, the best right-half ever seen at Preachers' Braes. Some were inclined to wonder if his skill as a footballer could be connected with his clean living as a man. He had never been known to utter a bad word on or off the field, he drank nothing more intoxicating than Iron Brew, he did not smoke, he had never groped a girl far less fucked one, and he was the Superintendent of St Andrew's Parish Church, Auchengillan. But then on the other hand Grunter Houliston, aged 34, the team's bow-legged surly centre-half, who deserved as much credit for its success as Hamilton, cursed and blasphemed, drank heavily, smoked 40 fags a day, and fornicated with loose women.

It had to be accepted therefore that there was no necessary connection between a man's private morals and his public performance, whether as a footballer, a clergyman, or a politician.

One showery afternoon in April the Rangers were playing Spittal Rovers in the sixth round of the Junior Cup. The biggest crowd in anyone's memory was there to watch.

Present among the dignitaries in the private enclosure in front of the pavilion was the Rev. Andrew McFarquhar, 63-year-old minister of St Andrew's Church, Auchengillan, wearing a scarf over his clerical collar. A man among men, he did not want to be a damper on robust expressions of joy at good play and rage at bad.

Christianity to Mr McFarquhar was not a religion for milksops, peacemongers and sentimentalists. It was for stout-hearted men who when struck a blow repaid with one twice as hard. In this way, he believed, were bullies and Huns properly chastised; sometimes even they were redeemed. He had two great regrets in his life: that he had never played rugby for Scotland, and he had been too old to be a combatant in the Great War.

He was much prouder of Gavin Hamilton, the speedy footballer, than of Gavin Hamilton, the pious Sunday school superintendent.

Gavin had long been a worry to him. He had watched with impatience as the lad had let himself be victimised by his ogress of a grandmother. He had not approved either when about a year ago the said ogress, having been smitten by the Lord with paralysis, so that she could no longer talk but only gibber, young Gavin, instead of feeling pleased that his prayers were at last answered (what was the good of prayer if it couldn't be used to encompass the downfall of foes?) had devoted himself to looking after her, his grandfather, whose job it ought to have been, having by this time been reduced to snivelling senility, though he was only five or six years older than Mr McFarquhar himself.

In his pulpit he had had to praise so exemplary a grandson, but seated by his fireside with a dram in his hand he had grumbled that returning good for evil was all very well, but if indulged in nationally it would mean the ruin of the empire.

There was a case in point right in front of his eyes that very minute. Spittal Rovers had a huge brute of a left-half who had evidently been instructed to maim Hamilton as early in the game as possible. This was a tactic often adopted, and in a manly sport permissible enough. Several times already he had sent Gavin sprawling. Virile stuff, deservedly applauded by Spittal supporters. What ought to have been done then, and what the Lendrick supporters, among them Mr McFarquhar himself, demanded as their right, was that Gavin, a well-built young man, should have knee'd the big ape in the groin or poked a finger in his eye, when the referee's back was turned. Instead he went on playing sportingly. Once indeed, after being roughly upturned, he had held out his hand in friendship. Small wonder Ryan was provoked to even wilder brutalities. Demonstrations of superior virtue won no admiration and softened no hearts. That had always been Mr McFarquhar's experience.

A few yards from the minister a young woman of twenty-two was standing, expensively dressed in a red coat trimmed with black fur. She had a pale thin-lipped face that often looked cruel. At such times she was really trying to look contemptuous. Born in Lendrick, she did not admire the people she lived among. She thought most of them were coarse and ignorant. In love with Gavin Hamilton, she despised him for believing that in Lendrick, worse still in Auchengillan, a lifetime of service and fulfilment could be spent. She did not want to marry a "good" man, she wanted to marry one that was well-off and lived in a select district like Newton Mearns in a house with at least five bedrooms and two bathrooms, in an acre of garden. Why shouldn't she, since she had lived in such a house all her life, except that unfortunately it was in Lendrick.

She was Julia Bannatyne, daughter of the lawyer in whose office Gavin had been a clerk since leaving school. For her sake her father had given him chances of advancement: he had not taken them. He wanted to remain poor and humble; yet he struck her as being dangerously ambitious in a spiritual sense. He acted as if the good-will of everyone was important to him; yet he could be so self-sufficient that she herself often felt excluded. He did good deeds; but she sometimes wondered if he did them out of pure compassion and not out of a wish to show up the selfishness of others, including herself. His grandmother had done him the greatest wrong, therefore he showed her the greatest forgiveness. As a way of getting revenge it was very effective. What the causes of the old woman's mental agonies were was not easy to tell, but Julia was sure being beholden to him was one of them.

It would be easy for him to get out of Lendrick. All he had to do was sign on for Queen's Park, the famous amateur club in the First Division. They were keen to have him. With his ability he would win a place in their first eleven. They would not pay him any money but influential well-wishers of the club would find for him a lucrative job with social status. Her father knew a director of a whisky firm who was ready to provide such a job. Instead he went on playing for this petty junior team, out of loyalty to people who, if the word had been in their vocabulary, would have called him a prig.

Another spectator in the private enclosure was Gavin's grandfather. He was present in defiance of his wife. She couldn't speak or write but she could still give commands with her eyes. She had ordered him to stay at home and look after her. He had fetched Mrs Ferrier to keep her company. It wasn't his fault that she detested Mrs Ferrier.

His eyes watered whenever the crowd roared its applause of some particularly clever piece of play by Gavin. He told strangers that he was Gavin's grandfather. It was childish, but he had all his life not much to brag about, except perhaps the size of his pay packets during the war, and it had been Nellie who had bragged about them.

He had never forgiven himself for not having stood up to her when she had made Gavin leave school.

Among the Lendrick supporters on the terraces were Charlie McGill and Davie McLuskie from Auchengillan, wearing bonnets and mufflers. As a married man with a child Charlie had less money to spend than Davie, who had very little. Both were unemployed. Davie had bought a packet of Woodbines. They stood with their hands in their pockets, smoking and shouting. They had been Lendrick supporters since they were ten. Like other boys of that age they had got in by begging men to lift them over the turnstiles. Now that they were become men they felt that they deserved a richer, prestigious team to support, such as Glasgow Rangers. If they could have afforded it they would have been at Ibrox Park that afternoon.

There was no longer enough glory for them in watching Lendrick Rangers, even if one of the stars was their old school friend Gavin Hamilton. They had once called him a traitor, and they had been unfair. He was not a snob either for he visited smelly old women and took them presents. He had introduced his swanky girl friend Miss Bannatyne to Charlie and his wife in Lendrick main street. He had once given Charlie a loan of a pound, or rather had made him a gift of it. Charlie had told no one, not even Davie. He had said that he needed the money to buy special foods for the baby which wasn't thriving. Most of it had been spent for that purpose, only a shilling or two being retained for some pints and fags. If, giving you money, Gavin had thumped you on the back and called you a cadging bastard, the taking of it would have been less humiliating.

Charlie and Davie were sure they knew what Gavin was up to. He would play for Queen's Park, build up a reputation, and then get a transfer to a big professional club. Being an amateur he would keep the fee himself: it could amount to thousands of pounds. Also he would marry the Bannatyne dame. As an only child she would come into her old man's money. Gavin would be knee-deep in clover. Keeping in with God had its advantages.

2

AT THE END of the game, with the Rangers victorious by four goals to two, Gavin himself having scored one, he was especially keen to shake hands with Ryan who had treated him so roughly.

Ryan not only turned away but muttered, "Go and fuck yourself". Gavin smiled as if he had been generously congratulated.

It would have been an exaggeration to say that when confronted by insulting viciousness like this he was never disappointed or indeed angry. He simply believed that to return meanness with meanness, hate with hate, spite with spite, and violence with violence, increased the amount of meanness, hate, spite, and violence in the world.

In the dressing-room his teammates went about naked, drinking beer in uproarious celebration. Grunter Houliston told a joke of extreme obscenity and shook his big penis in illustration. Gavin laughed with the others but not so heartily. He deplored their crudeness and their frequent blasphemous use of Christ's name, but he gave them credit for their comradeliness and unselfishness on the field. Some had it in them to be true Christians. But if he had tried to convert them they would have been embarrassed or affronted: they would have said they saw nothing wrong with the way they lived, they were as good as their neighbours and that was good enough for them.

In Lendrick and Auchengillan there were no opportunities to be rich or famous, but there were many to achieve what was more meritorious; a reputation for unselfishness. Foolish people might not want it for themselves but they could not help being impressed by it in others. They might call a man who had it a mug, but in their hearts they would honour him. Christ was at work in them whether they acknowledged Him or not.

His teammates teased him about Julia, decorously enough. No doubt behind his back they made cruder jokes. They couldn't understand why he wasn't already married to her or at least engaged. They thought her the best catch in town. If he had told them that what he could not accept in her was her callousness they would have retorted that he was a bloody fool. She was quite right, they would have said, to show a hard face to enviers and moochers. The world's wealth not to mention Lendrick's was unfairly divided, that was true, and it would always be true. Jesus Christ hadn't done anything about it, and neither would Ramsay McDonald. Anyone lucky enough to have more than his or her share was wise to stick to it.

She was waiting for him, in her small red car. Before the game he had explained that he had promised to visit Tommy Grierson that

62

evening and tell him about the game. His suggestion that she should come with him had made her angrier still. She had better things to do on a Saturday night than sit shivering in a damp miserable house, with sticky-fingered brats pawing her stockings. She would have to put on a show of amiability. This she refused to do. She had her own standards of honesty to maintain.

She was afraid that one day he would committ some act of utterly irresponsible and ruinous goodness.

She kept her temper. "You can go and see Grierson any evening," she said. "He's not going to run away."

In an accident in the pit three years ago Grierson's back had been broken. He hadn't walked since.

She was not rebuked for her callous remark. Gavin left people to rebuke themselves. Often the effect was to make them more vindictive.

"You think they enjoy your visits," she said. "Are you sure you don't make them feel uncomfortable?"

"Tommy was very kind to me once."

"Yes, so you've told me. But I can't see what you've got in common now."

Certainly not love of God. Crippled for life at the age of 24 Grierson had no reason to love God. He was married too to as ugly a woman as Julia had ever seen. Yes, Elspeth Grierson coped heriocally with a bedridden husband, two young children, ill health, and extreme poverty. Scotland was full of heroines like her. Julia preferred to salute them from as far away as possible.

"Well, we can't stand here all night," she said. "I'll drop you at the Cross. You can get a bus there."

She noticed how stiff he was as he got into the car. After every game his legs were bruised and sore.

If he had gone home with her as she had hoped she could have kissed those bruises and rubbed soothing ointment into them. With a little luck, quiet music, dim lights, and a soft voice, she might have enticed him into making love.

They drove along the main street. It was crowded with men returning from the match and women shopping. Her car was recognized. If she had been alone in it people would just have stared; a few might have made faces of dislike. With Gavin beside her she shared the waves and smiles he got. She could not help thinking that as an unrepentant snob she was really closer to them than he was. Everybody was snobbish. Even the worthy Mrs Grierson,

63

bringing up her children on the parish, must know people she looked down on.

She stopped at the Cross. "What about coming to *my* church tomorrow morning?" she asked.

"All right."

"Call for me at the house. If it's dry we'll walk down together. While the bells are ringing. Afterwards we'll have lunch together. Please don't say no."

"I wasn't going to say no. I'd like that."

"Thank you, darling." She leaned over and kissed him.

She felt him trembling, if not with desire then surely with the effort to restrain desire. The day when he would throw away his scruples and pull down her knickers might not be so far off after all. Thereafter marriage would be certain and soon. All his concern, compassion, and love would be for her, and for their children. He would be less altruistic; to compensate she would be more.

As she turned the car "up the hill" she saw him for a moment in her rear window. He looked happy. Surely it wasn't because those drunks were making a fuss of him. Surely too it wasn't because he was looking forward to an evening in a dreary house with an embittered cripple. It must be because he was thinking of her.

3

ALWAYS AT Lendrick Cross he remembered Rachel Hallad in the grey fur coat. Some time after his mother's death he had got a letter from her in London. Some girl at the academy had written and told her about him. She had said that she was very sorry to hear about his mother, but not about his having to leave school. If he had stayed on and gone to university he would have ended up as a teacher or worse still a minister, with an inevitable stunting of his conscience.

He thought of McIntyre too. He had met him once. About a year ago, after a game against Bonnyhill Violet in Bonnyhill, he had been told that there was someone at the pavilion door asking for him. He had been dismayed to find McIntyre dressed in the uniform of the Argyll and Sutherland Highlanders.

"Couldn't get a job," McIntyre had explained cheerfully. "So

I joined up. Regular money to send hame. A mooth less to feed there."

"You're the last person I would have expected to become a soldier."

"Why d'you say that?"

"You always avoided fights. If anybody insulted you you laughed and walked away."

"I still laugh and walk away."

"But you could be ordered to kill."

"Only enemies."

"Not *your* enemies, McIntyre. You'd never kill them."

"Whit aboot yourself, Hamilton? I couldnae believe it when I heard you'd to leave school. I'm sorry aboot your mither. I ken how you felt. I was going to write. By the way, I hear lots o' Senior clubs are efter you. I'm no' surprised. I've never really got ower it, Hamilton, you being sae guid at Latin and geometry and French, and yet sich a great fitba' player. You could play for Scotland at Hampden yin day. My faither used to say that maist fitba' players had their brains in their feet. If they tried to think wi' their heids they made a mess o' things. It's true. Your brains are in your feet and your heid. You should hae heard the Bonnyhill supporters talking aboot you. But I'll hae to hurry. There's somebody waiting for me. Sure, a lassie. So long, Hamilton, and stick in."

"So long, McIntyre, and good luck."

He had been unable then and was still unable now, to imagine McIntyre thrusting a bayonet into a human belly, with the necessary hatred.

If it was to save itself from being used for evil purposes goodness needed its own kind of cunning and stubbornness.

His grandfather was home before him, and was feeding his grandmother scrambled egg from a spoon. She had a bib round her neck. As Gavin looked in she gazed at him with an appeal for help mixed with malevolence. He had once seen a cat with its insides squashed by a lorry dying with that kind of look in its eyes.

"If you've time, Gavin," murmured his grandfather, "I think she'd like you to play her a few tunes on your fiddle. I think they ease the pains in her head."

"Yes, of course." He smiled at his grandmother and nodded.

"You were the best man on the park, Gavin, as usual. If we keep that up we'll win baith the Cup and the League."

"Someone threw a bottle at the referee."

"So I heard. I didnae see it myself. I'm no' surprised, mind you: some o' his decisions were awfu'. The Rangers should hae had twa penalties at least."

The stricken women pushed egg out of her mouth with her tongue. It was her way of letting them know they were neglecting her.

Gavin then said for the first time something he had been thinking about for months.

"I may have to give up the game."

His grandfather was so startled he left his wife's face half-wiped.

"Football seems to provoke so much violence," said Gavin.

"Men shout terrible things, but they don't mean them. I shout myself."

"Not viciously."

"Weel, I'm no' sae sure. Maybe we get rid of a lot of badness in us at fitba' matches. So maybe it does us guid."

"There was fighting among the crowd."

"Och, juist a couple of drunk fools taking a swipe at each ither. That's nothing."

Gavin saw tears of exasperation appear in his grandmother's eyes. She gibbered painfully.

"She doesnae like us to talk aboot fitba'," said his grandfather. "She never did. God help me, I think it was because she kent it gie'd me pleasure. Think o' that side o' it, Gavin, when you talk aboot gieing it up. You'll no' like me saying this, but you gie a lot mair pleasure playing fitba' than you dae preaching religion."

That was the trouble, thought Gavin. Football had taken the place of religion in Scotland. Christ the Redeemer was of less consequence than the scorer of the winning goal.

4

IN THE POCKET of his jacket was his copy of the New Testament. He did not intend to read out of it at the Griersons' but he liked to feel that it was always there if he needed it, like a wild-west sheriff his gun. People thought that he had no humour. They did not know that he often made fun of himself.

Passing the brightly lit Auchengillan Arms which as usual on Saturday night would be packed with men who ought to have been

66

spending what little money they had on food for their families he smiled as he recalled his own jest to the Bible Class, that perhaps it would have been a more fruitful miracle for future temperance-workers if Our Lord had turned wine into water and not the other way round. It had been reported to Mr McFarquhar who, thinking that his own fireside drams were being obliquely criticized, had found an early opportunity to tell him that the worst form of pride a Christian could be guilty of was to think that he could improve on Holy Writ.

Just past the pub he met Charlie McGill and Jackie Clelland on their way to it. They did not stop. "Hello, Gavin," they muttered. "You played a blinder today. When are you signing for the big Rangers, eh?"

It never occurred to them to ask him to come with them into the pub where after all he could have drunk lemonade. They seemed to be under the misapprehension that the companionship would be objectionable to him, as well as the whisky.

It was raining by the time he reached Burnbank Terrace where the Griersons lived. They had had to leave their colliery house in Brandy Neuk after the accident. He held on to his hat as he entered the pend. Many times as a boy he had played headers and moshie in it when it was too wet outside. A gas lamp just outside lit up one half of it and made the other half all the darker. Girls had liked to frighten themselves by seeing bogey men.

Someone was standing there, in the darkest part, against the wall. It was a young woman. She seemed to be ill, from the sounds she was making; then he realized that she was crying. At her feet was a small suitcase. At first he thought it was a dog.

"Whit d'you think you're staring at, you cunt," she muttered. "Mind you ain fucking business."

She sounded though more miserable than vicious. There was a smell off her, of cheap scent or alcohol, and of unwashed underclothes.

He touched his hat. "I'm sorry. Is there anything the matter?"

"Hae you got a fag?"

"I'm sorry. I don't smoke." Suddenly he knew who she was. "You're Jessie Findlay."

Who long ago in the playground had crouched, as a child of eight, weeping because her father had been killed in the war.

Later on she had become foul-mouthed, unchaste, dishonest, and even violent. She had been in the hands of the police for thieving and assault. Some people said that losing her father must have had a lot to do with her going so terribly bad; others added that her mother marrying again hadn't helped; but most were of the opinion that the seeds of badness must have been in her from the beginning, God knew why or how. Other girls who had lost their fathers hadn't let it twist their minds. And Jim Ogilvie, who her mother had married and by whom her mother had two other girls, was a decent enough man if a bit lazy.

She had finally gone off to Glasgow where, it was rumoured, she had become a prostitute.

So now she had come home. It looked as if she had been turned away by her mother and stepfather. Her brother Willie had emigrated to Canada years ago.

It would have been enough, as an ordinary Christian, to murmur that he was sorry, express a hope that things would turn out all right, and then hurry away, not so fast as to give the impression he was fleeing, but not so slow as to give her a chance to pursue him with profanities.

So he might have done, if that memory of her weeping in the playground had not, he felt, involved him in some profound kinship and responsibility.

"Aye, I'm the terrible Jessie Findlay," she said. "And I ken you. You're Gavin Hamilton."

"Yes."

"You came to the hoose wi' Willie. I thought you were the best-looking boy I'd ever seen. Your faither was killed in the war, like mine."

"Yes. I believe you went to Glasgow to work."

"Work? That's a good yin. Weel, you could ca' it work."

"And you decided to come home?"

"I came back to Auchengillan. I've got nae hame. I'm going to hae a wean."

More than ever the sensible morality of not interfering appealed. She was her mother's responsibility, not his; or her brother's; or her former friends', if she had any; or the man's whose child she was going to have; or the paid authorities' whose duty it was to take care of women in her plight.

"Christ, I wish I had a fag," she said, wearily. "I'm dead beat."

Suppose, he thought, this was Germany and she was a Jewess. In that case the consequences of helping her might be a beating up and imprisonment. Here in Auchengillan he would simply be

68

laughed at as a simpleton, trying to show that he was better than everyone else.

"They slammed the door in my face, the cunts. If I had ony money I wouldnae need them. I wouldnae need onybody. It's going to cost ten quid, maybe twenty, to get rid of this." She tapped her stomach. "You havenae got twenty quid to spare?"

"You mustn't think of that, Jessie. Life is sacred."

"Sacred? Christ, that's a laugh. They didnae think it was sacred during the war."

They heard footsteps. A man and woman came into the pend. The man muttered something, making the woman giggle. Evidently they took Gavin and Jessie for lovers.

"Whit are you daeing here onyway?" she asked, when they were gone.

"I'm visiting Tommy and Elspeth Grierson."

"Elspeth Grierson that used to be Elspeth McDonald? A big ugly-faced bitch she always was. She never had a good word to say aboot me, that one."

"I tell you what, Jessie. I'll go and make my apologies and then I'll come straight back."

"Whit hae I to wait for? Whit's going to happen?"

"I'd like to help you."

"How can you?"

"I could take you home with me."

"You live in Hawthorn Avenue. Among the snobs, I used to think. A'right. I'll wait."

"Wouldn't it be better to stand out of the pend? It's very draughty in here."

"It's very wet oot there."

They could hear the rain pelting down.

"I won't be long. I promise. Don't worry. We'll think of something."

As he went off she laughed. It was not a pleasant sound; but surely it was despair causing it, not cynicism.

5

IT WAS ELSPETH who opened the door, with dummy-teated Robert in her arms.

"We were beginning to think you had forgotten," she said.

"I'm sorry, Elspeth. I'm afraid I can't stay. Something's happened. I'll just come in and say 'hello' to Tommy."

"Is it your grandmither?"

"No. Nothing like that."

In the bare clean living-room that was also the kitchen and bedroom Tommy was lying in the set-in bed, reading by very poor gaslight that night's sporting edition of the *Evening Times*.

Three-year-old Elsie was playing on a rug in front of the fire.

"Hello, Gavin," said Tommy. "Tak the man's hat and coat, woman. He deserves to be pampered. Listen to this: 'Hamilton played his usual cool and effective game. He must be about the best prospect in the Junior League. We hear that Queen's are still favourites.' Whit d'you think o' that?"

"Gavin's no' staying, Tom."

"In the pend," explained Gavin, "I met somebody I used to know. She was crying. I promised I would help her."

"Who is she?" asked Elspeth, suspiciously.

"Jessie Findlay."

"I thought sae. That trollop. I heard she's back. So her mither threw her oot. Quite right. Before she contaminated the ither girls. Excuse me for saying this, Gavin, but you're juist the kind she's been dying to get her claws intae. Isn't that so, Tom?"

Presented with a subject more interesting, Tommy lowered the newspaper. He grinned. "Weel, she was a bit of a terror."

"It's nae joke. Warn him to hae naething to dae wi' her. He's your freen', so warn him."

"He's a grown man. He's got the use o' his twa legs. He can rin awa' if he wants to."

"You've said yourself that Gavin's like a wean when it comes to trusting people. She's rotten to the core. She'd ruin him and laugh while she was doing it."

"Don't get sae worked up, pet. A' Gavin said was that he wanted to help her. He didnae say he was going to mairry her."

"Don't say sich a thing even as a joke."

Gavin winked back when Tommy winked at him, though he didn't quite understand what Tommy meant by it. It was a pity, he thought, that the cares of bringing up her family on a pittance, and of looking after her broken husband, had turned Elspeth so unforgiving.

"Nobody's rotten to the core, Elspeth," he said.

"She is. Do you ken whit she did when Mr Rankin, heidmaister of Lendrick Advanced Division, was going to gie her the strap for insolence?"

"Watch you don't shock Gavin," said her husband, with another wink.

"She took off her knickers: juist stood there in front of him and took them off and shook them in his face."

Little Elsie looked up: "Whit for did she take off her knickers, Mammy?" she asked.

"Never you mind. You get on wi' your playing. That, Gavin, was Jessie Findlay at fourteen. Since then she's gone from bad to worse."

It seemed to Gavin more heinous for a man to strap a girl than for that girl to remove underclothing. The meek, or at any rate the powerless, were often goaded into desperate measures.

"And in Glesca," whispered Elspeth, "she's been a whure for years."

"That's whit they say," said Tommy.

"Her ain mither's one of them that say it."

Gavin suddenly grew anxious. If Jessie was gone the best opportunity he had ever had to test his fitness to call himself a Christian would be lost.

"Your ain mither, if she was alive," said Elspeth, "and your grandmither, if she had her power of speech, would be telling you whit I'm telling you. In some ways, Gavin, you're too simple. Gie that slut half a chance and she'll drag you doon."

"She's only 22, Elspeth. Perhaps I might raise her up."

Elspeth for a moment looked as if she would snatch the dummy from Robert's mouth and stick it into Gavin's.

"Good-night, Tommy," said Gavin. "I'll call in again soon and tell you about the game."

"You might hae something mair interesting to tell me," said Tommy, with his most unintelligible wink of all.

6

A S W E L L A S a fag she needed a drink, and something to eat, and a place to sit down in out of this fucking cold. Spasms of nausea, weariness, and anger shook her. What she wanted above all was for somebody to be made pay for her misery. It ought to have been Breen. She should have stuck a knife into his pimply back. But he was well out of reach now, and anyway he had pals far handier with knives than she.

Next on the list for kniving was Ogilvie, her stepfather.

To be fair, though, it hadn't been him who had ordered her out of the house. It had been her own mother.

Even if she had been stinking with pox her mother shouldn't have thrown her out. Mothers were supposed to love and protect their kids no matter what. Anyway, these scabs on her face weren't syphilitic. That was to say if that creepy doctor Breen had brought wasn't a liar.

Wearily, she thought of Gavin Hamilton. The other boys, including Willie, had called him Creeping Jesus. He had said that he would help her. All it would amount to would be sympathy and maybe ten bob. The more Christian people were the less likely they would want to have anything to do with her. She always thought of Christians as respectable, not as good. She accepted their right to despise her but she hated them for it. In their place she would have despised a scabby whore stupid enough to get herself pregnant.

Hamilton had sounded shocked when she had spoken about getting rid of the wean before it got a chance to be a wean. Life was sacred, he had said. Fifty to one he was still a virgin. Likely he thought that between a man and a woman belly to belly there was always a feeling of love and tenderness. She could tell him of hundreds of times when it had been very different.

But he wouldn't come back. That big bitter-faced bitch Grierson would have talked sense into him. Best forget him. Yet what else was there? She had no money. No one in Auchengillan would take her in. Most of the boys she had gone to the quarry with were now married men; any that weren't married wouldn't waste the price of a pint on her. As for the girls she had known once, like Netta McLuskie, they too were married, with weans. They might whisper into her ear the name of some old hag in a back street in

Lendrick who did abortions with a soup spoon, but that would be the limit of their help.

"Fuck them all," she muttered.

But she could not really blame them. In their place she would have done the same. They had troubles of their own.

She had sunk down on to the ground when she heard running footsteps. It was Hamilton.

"Sorry for keeping you waiting," he said, helping her to her feet.

"I've got plenty of time."

"Your hands are frozen." He picked up her case.

She was in a daze. "Where are we going?"

"To my house. You'll be all right there."

"Hawthorn Avenue, isn't it? I've walked alang it hundreds of times. It smells nice when the hawthorns are in flourish. Bad man's flourish we used to ca' it, Christ kens why."

"Christ's crown of thorns was thought to be made of hawthorn."

He had always spoken seriously like this, whether about moshie or football or Jesus Christ.

She decided not to ask him what would happen when they got to his house. Scare a rabbit and it bolted under a hedge, never to be seen again.

It was raining heavily. Her hair and feet were sodden. She could hardly walk for weariness. Last night she had slept on a stair landing. She thought of lying in a warm bath, with a fag in her hand and a gin-and-orange within reach.

But if she was cosy and warm and safe so would be the little bastard inside her. It would thrive. What she ought to do was jump off a high wall. With her luck she'd probably break both her legs and still be pregnant.

They passed three men making for the pub. Two of them recognized her. So they should have: she had kissed their pricks in the old quarry.

"Christ, did you see who that was? Jessie Findlay, Willie's sister."

"Anybody that wanted his hole got it frae Jessie."

"That wasnae Gavin Hamilton wi' her?"

"It was, Jesus, whit a combination!"

"Don't mind them," murmured Hamilton.

She hated him more than she did those bastards laughing at her. She would rather have gone into the pub with them. At least they might have stood her a drink and given her fags. Afterwards they would have taken their payment up against a wall.

In Hamilton's presence she felt filthier than she had done after she had received the discharge of six men at a stretch.

He was the one she ought to make pay.

He could not have ushered her into his house or helped her off with her wet coat more considerately if she had been his pregnant wife.

The kinder he was the more he would have to pay.

From inside a room an old man's voice cried: "It that you back already, Gavin?"

"Yes, Grand-dad."

"That's no' Julia wi' you?"

"No. It's someone else."

She wondered who this Julia was. There had never been a Julia in Auchengillan that she could remember. It was too posh a name. She must come from Lendrick.

She remembered that when his mother had died his grandparents had pushed themselves into his house. In her own experience too old people were the most selfish and demanding.

He showed her into a bedroom. It was clean and tidy, but cold. In a corner stood a fiddle case. On the dressing-table were photographs in twin frames: one was of his mother and the other of his father.

She had a photograph of her own father in her handbag.

He lit the gas fire. "You'll want a bath," he murmured.

It was his gentlemanly way of saying she stank. She had noticed him looking at her scabs.

"To tell you the fucking truth whit I need maist is a fag," she said. "I'm juist aboot screaming for the want o' one."

"I don't smoke myself," he said," but I think there are some cigarettes in the house. A friend left them. I hope they're not mouldy."

"If they were made of horse shite it wouldn't maitter."

"I'll fetch them. Sit by the fire."

He turned at the door. "I once saw you crying because your father had been killed."

"I cried a lot then. I was young and kent nae better. Where was this?"

"In the school playground. You pretended it was because you'd scraped your knee playing peaver."

74

She didn't remember the incident.

He went over to the wardrobe and took out a leather case. He laid it on the bed. "There are some clothes in here. You might find them useful."

This time he went out.

She lifted the lid. There was a pleasant perfume from the clothes. They were mostly lingerie, a bit old-fashioned but expensive. They must have been his mother's. She took out a pair of lace-fringed cami-knickers and held them against her.

He came in with the cigarettes.

"Were these your mother's?" she asked. "Weren't you keeping them for your bride? For Julia?" She grinned.

"You can have them if you want them."

"After my bath wouldn't I look real high class in this?" she held up a pale pink silken négligé.

The cigarettes were filter-tipped and slightly scented. She didn't care much for them but they would have to do. She lit one at the gas fire. "Were they Julia's?" she asked.

"After you've had a bath I'm sure you'd like something to eat."

"Something to drink too, if you've got onything."

"There's no alcoholic drink in the house. There's milk."

"Where's the bathroom?"

"I'll show you."

She couldn't think of him as a "teenie", not even when he handed her fresh towels like an efficient housewife.

As she lay in the bath it occurred to her that this was a bit of luck that did not have to end too soon. Hamilton was making use of her to practise his Christianity on, so why shouldn't she use him to give herself an easy life for a change? All she would have to do would be to show him that there was still some good left in her. She could weep in innocence as she had apparently done in the playground. It would be easy to make a sucker like him believe that she was ashamed of her past life and wanted help to enable her to begin a new and better one.

The wean, fuck it, was the problem. If she waited too long she'd have to have it. She couldn't do that. She'd bash its brains out the minute she saw it. She'd have to get rid of it. Well, she still had a month or two to spare.

Why shouldn't she, using the tricks of the trade, have Hamilton eating from her hand? She'd noticed him looking at her breasts. What if he saw her pussy? What if he had it rubbed against his

75

face? What if she took hold of his cock? She had once had as a customer a white-haired geezer who Breen had told her afterwards was a minister. He had been shaking with shame, but he had been as desperate to get it in as any plukey boy of sixteen. He would have gone on fucking her, or trying to for he had come in a minute, if his whole congregation had been watching.

Christian though he was, Hamilton would give her anything she asked, if she gave him what bitches gave dogs, as Breen used to say. She'd have to use a little patience and cunning, that was all. Show him first how grateful and penitent and humble she was, let the scabs clear up. Then one night go to him in his bed, with nothing on under her négligé, weeping, breaking her heart, talking about her father, slipping into bed with him, taking hold of him tenderly at first, as if it was part of her distress and her consoling, and then urgently. Jesus Christ Himself wouldn't be able to hold back then.

7

NEXT MORNING, while his guest was still asleep, Gavin hurried to the nearest telephone box.

He rang Julia's number. He had to wait, though he knew she had a telephone by her bedside.

"For God's sake," he heard her muttering. Then "Hello" she said, crossly. "Julia Bannatyne speaking. Who is this?"

"Gavin."

"What's wrong? Has anything happened to your grandmother?" She was always hoping to hear that the gruesome old woman was dead.

"No. It's just that I can't be with you this morning."

"Why not? This is ridiculous, Gavin. It's unfair. It's treating me like dirt. I'm not having it."

"I'm sorry."

"Sorry! Is that all you can say?" she yelled. "Aren't you going to tell me why?"

He did not want to lie, but if he told her the truth she would never understand. "I forgot I promised Mr McFarquhar I would help at the service this morning."

It was only half a lie. Mr McFarquhar expected him to help at every service.

"Well, why shouldn't I join you there, among the boors?"

"You can come if you want, of course."

"Thank you for that eager invitation. Do you know what I'm going to tell you, Gavin Hamilton? I'm going to tell you to go to hell. Go to hell!"

She banged down her telephone.

As he went back to house, more slowly than he had come, he felt worried. Julia herself for different reasons was in as much need of his help as Jessie. Left to herself, she could so easily develop into a typical middle-aged middle-class self-centred woman with a heart as hard as the diamonds in her rings.

He should have told her the truth. It would have been absurd if she had been jealous of poor Jessie. Perhaps she would have joined in what after all was an act of Christian redemption.

At breakfast Mr Bannatyne saw that his daughter was in one of her bad-tempered, self-pitying moods. He knew that her call had been from Gavin Hamilton cancelling some arrangement. He would have been happy himself if the whole relationship was cancelled. It seemed to him very contrary of Julia, who thought she deserved the dearest fur coat, the latest shoes, and her own car, as well as a thousand other things, to imagine that she was in love with a man who, God help him, really believed that material possessions retarded spiritual growth.

8

GAVIN HAMILTON's taking of Jessie Findlay into his house was known throughout Auchengillan by bed-time that Sunday. It was the most discussed topic since the splitting of Sergeant Duff's head with a pick handle during the General Strike.

In the manse by the fireside with drams in their hands Mr Mc-Farquhar and his wife Sarah spoke about it. On these libatory occasions by mutual consent they were at their most dignified, in manner and speech.

Mrs McFarquhar was a severe-looking woman with skimpy white hair. This she had in curlers. Usually tight-lipped, she was made loquacious by whisky, even though she took only the tiniest of tots.

"If he believes he is being a Good Samaritan," she said, "he ought to know that such things will not do today. In any case, the Good Samaritan had the sense to succour an honest merchant who when his wounds were healed went on his way again. This woman Findlay is far from honest. She will stick like a burr. I do not understand why you are smiling, Andrew. It is a disgrace to your parish. He is your Sunday school superintendent. I do not say that he will speak to the children about this woman, but I am sure the children will be saying all kinds of wicked things among themselves. You know I have had doubts about Gavin for some time. He has always struck me as being too virtuous by half. I congratulated him once on having a father who gave his life for his country, and he was quite rude. Yes, in that polite way of his, he was definitely rude. But why are you smiling?"

"You and I, my dear, have sometimes wondered what Gavin's attitude to women really is."

"I have wondered no such thing, I assure you."

"He is a big, strongly built healthy young fellow, a trained athlete, with a body through which the usual many impulses must surge."

"This is strange language, Andrew."

"How does he vent these impulses? That is the question."

"I do not think, my dear, that you should take any more. The agreement was: one normally, two on occasions of particular stress, but never three. That is your third."

"No matter. What I am suggesting, my dear, is that he may well have a sly ulterior motive. Get credit for an act of Christian charity, and at the same time enjoy certain other advantages of the situation."

"I am at a loss, Andrew. Please make yourself clearer."

"I am afraid that would involve me in the use of some demotic language not fit for your ears."

"Or for your tongue, my dear. Do you think she is really pregnant?"

"They say so."

"It is very hard to accept the Lord's will that a woman of that sort who does not want a child and is not fit to have one should conceive, while another woman who has been a Christian all her life and who wished dearly to have a child could not."

"Very hard, my dear."

Like a fire going out, the subject went cold on them. Mr Mc-Farquhar had long ago got over the disappointment of never having a son, but his wife had not. Especially during the war had her regret been great. She would have been the proudest woman in Scotland if she had had a son an officer in the king's army. Indeed, during those magnificent years she had often imagined that she did have a son, called Colin, winning medals for gallantry against the fiendish Huns.

In an alcove in the Gilbertfield Arms some of Gavin's former schoolmates used the demotic language referred to by Mr McFarquhar. The only restriction imposed on them was that Chris the head barman required that all obscenities necessary for the proper telling of stories and jokes should be spoken in lowered voices, lest by some strange chance there should happen to be a customer present who might be offended.

"She's juist whit Gavin needed. An answer to his prayers."

"Now he'll find oot whit his cock's for."

"Trust Creeping Jesus to land lucky. Here we're stuck wi' wives affronted if you hint that there are mair positions than yin."

"And that it neednae always have to be done in the dark."

"And wearing a nightdress doon to her ankles."

"And a chemise as weel."

"No' to mention the stockings for her varicose veins."

"Think of Gavin. There's Jessie, bare as a frog, wi' her legs roon' his neck."

"Kittling his balls."

"Whit aboot her scabs, though?"

"Scabs?"

"Sure. They say her face is scabby."

"Mair than her face maybe."

"Pox, is it?"

"Whit else?"

"Christ."

"Och, it'll juist make it a' the mair exciting for Gavin."

"Still, it's a peety for her."

"And she's got a bun in the oven."

"Some oven."

"It's juist as weel Willie's in Canada. Mind how he was always grousing?"

"Maybe Gavin thinks he's taking Willie's place."

"I expect he thinks that because baith their faithers were killed in the war he's got a duty to her."

"He fancies himself as a Christian."

"Weel, he's got a problem on his haun's I wouldnae like. You and me, we'd juist open the door and say, "Right, hen. You've been here long enough. Fuck off.""

"True enough, that's no' his style."

"And there's the wean. I believe she asked her mither for money for an abortion."

"Gavin would never gie her money for that."

"He'd better watch oot. If you want the wean, Jessie will say, right, it's yours; and she'll bugger off and leave him wi' it."

"Maybe she'll no' bugger off. Maybe he'll hae her as weel as the wean."

"You mean he might offer to mairry her?"

"And gie up Julia? Christ, he'd have to be mad."

"Weel, isn't he?"

"Now, that Julia. I wouldnae mind haeing *her* in bed. . . ."

Standing in the sawdust with which the floor of the Co-op. was freshly strewn every morning, a group of women discussed Jessie and Gavin. One of them came from Burnbank Terrace and was friendly with Jessie's mother.

"She'll no' talk aboot it. I cannae blame her."

"Still, Jessie's her daughter. She cannae shut her eyes to it."

"That's juist whit she wants to do."

"She tried once."

"When it was faur too late."

"Wha's to ken when a wean's starting to go bad?"

"She's talking aboot going to Gavin and telling him he's got to put Jessie oot."

"She's got nae right."

"She thinks it's a shame on her him taking Jessie in when she wouldnae herself."

"It's be a bigger shame on her if she talked him into putting the lassie in the street."

"I understaun' her feelings, mind you."

"He'd never dae it juist because she asked him. He's a determined one."

"Always was. Never said much. But very determined. Especially if he thought whit he was doing was right."

"Will he be sae determined though if Miss Bannatyne has her say?"

"Miss Bannatyne should tak care. They say she's a lot fonder of him than he is of her. That's a difficult position for ony woman to be in."

"But she's got the money."

"It's the wean that worries me."

"Whit wean? There will be nae wean. Jessie will see to that."

"We should a' see to it."

"Whit does that mean? I'm no' in favour o' abortions."

"That's your privilege, Bridget. But whit future would this wean hae? Even if it got adopted into a guid family it would find oot yin day that its mither was a whure and its faither yin o' her customers. It'd wish it was never born."

"Especially if it was a lassie."

9

JULIA HAD MADE up her mind that this time she would not be the one to forgive and give in. She was supposed to be selfish, so selfish she would be. She had plenty of other things to do besides wait for telephone calls or letters. She played golf, visited friends in the afternoon for coffee and in the evening for drinks, went to the theatre in Glasgow with other friends, including a medical student who fancied her, motored to Edinburgh with a girl friend for a day's shopping, did a little work in the garden, listened to the gramophone and the wireless, read a book, and took a basketful of groceries to an old woman in Silverbanks Street who had once been a charwoman in Rosemount, Julia's home. Five times she passed the office in the main street, once walking and four times driving. She didn't even look in its direction.

There were moments when she was struck by fear that this time she had lost him for good. It was then that she realized how much she loved him. Perhaps she did not love him enough, for it was not in her nature to love anyone beyond the point where self-interest was obliterated, but she did love him to the edge of her limits. She had no doubt at all that, leaving priggishness aside, he was a better person than she. If they ever had children he would love them more fruitfully than she ever could, and they would love him more trustfully than they would her. As he got older he would grow richer and wiser in his nature. She would remain pretty much the same all her life, no better and no worse, and never very interesting. She liked possessions too much. She got more pleasure out of stroking her new fur coat than she did out of doing a kindness. That was why she would never grow in humanity as he would. She knew it, she was sometimes ashamed of it, and because of it she was often afraid. It was a great relief that she would have his faith to draw on if she was ever confronted by one of life's tribulations, such as the death of her father or of one of her children.

On Friday afternoon she was in the drawing-room playing over and over again on the piano one of her favourite pieces of music, the Largo from Dvorak's *New World* symphony, when Mrs Sempill came in to say that there was a woman at the door asking for her.

She went on playing the sad but sustaining music. "Is she begging?"

"No, I don't think she's begging."

"Is she looking for work?"

"She's too old for that. She says she's from Auchengillan."

"Oh." Julia stopped playing. She could think of no woman in Auchengillan whom he would have sent as a messenger.

"What shall I tell her?" asked Mrs Sempill.

"Was that all she said, she's from Auchengillan?"

"And that she would like to speak to you. I would say she's put on her Sunday coat and hat for the visit. She's walked up from the Cross. She looks tired."

"I suppose you'd better ask her to come in."

"Will you see her here?"

"Yes."

She went on playing the piano until Mrs Sempill came and announced, "Mrs Ferrier to see you, Miss Julia".

As soon as she saw her Julia remembered having seen her in Gavin's house visiting his grandmother. A nosey old creature with one eye gone bad.

"How do you do, Mrs Ferrier? Would you like to sit down?"

"Thanks. I'm no' staying long, but I'll be glad of a seat. This is a very braw room. Was that you I heard playing the piano?"

"Yes."

"So you and Gavin are baith musical."

"What do you want to see me about, Mrs Ferrier?"

82

"Maybe you'll think I'm interfering, and you'll be offended. I'd be sorry if you were. But I think I owe it to Gavin's mither, and to Gavin himself, for I've kent him a' his life. I've wiped the slavers frae his mooth as he lay in his pram."

"I promise not to be offended, Mrs Ferrier. Has it got to do with Gavin?"

"It has that. Pardon me." She took a handkerchief from her handbag and wiped her own mouth. "I'm still puffed oot wi' climbing that brae."

"Does Gavin know you're here?"

"No, no. Naebody kens. No' even Ferrier. I've took it on myself." Again she paused.

Julia felt sorry for her. "Would you like some tea, Mrs Ferrier?"

"No, no. Certainly not. I'll state my business and then I'll leave."

Julia waited. Mrs Ferrier was going to make an incoherent job of whatever it was she had come to say, but if she was hurried she would get even more muddled. There was a spot of yellow matter in her bad eye.

"You'll no' hae heard o' Jessie Findlay?"

"Never."

"She's frae Auchengillan. Aboot the same age as yourself. In Gavin's class at school, or maybe in the class below him, for I doot if she was ever much of a scholar. Her faither was killed in the war. Like Gavin's. Her mither, a fushionless soul, mairried again, fairly soon efter."

"I wonder, Mrs Ferrier," said Julia, gently enough, "if you could come to the point?" If there was a point. She was beginning to think the old woman was, as they said down the hill in Lendrick, "donnert".

"I'm coming to it. Jessie was an ordinary wee lass, fair-haired, bonny enough in a peely-wally kind of way. But I think she always had a meanness in her een. Onyway, when she was thirteen or so, she became a real holy terror. I'm no' going to shock you, Miss Bannatyne, in your ain fine hoose, by telling you the awfu' things that lassie did and said. Swearing. Stealing. Scarting. And worse. A lot worse. By the time she was sixteen she'd gi'en awa' to dozens whit a decent woman keeps for yin. If you see whit I mean, Miss Bannatyne."

Julia felt like shocking her by saying: "You mean she let all the boys of the neighbourhood fuck her?" The fifth formers in

Julia's private school in Glasgow had not been so prudish in their language as this yellow-eyed green-hatted old woman.

"Weel, to naebody's surprise, Jessie went aff to Glasca, whaur it seems she fell amang evil folk. She sold herself for money."

"You mean, became a prostitute?"

"That's whit I mean. I'm sorry you had to say the word. These are hard times but that didnae excuse her. Weel, to cut a long story short, she came back to Auchengillan last Saturday, in a terrible state, skinny, scabby, and pregnant."

"Poor creature." Julia would have said "Poor bitch" if she had been talking to one of her friends.

"It does you credit to peety her, but wait till I've finished. She wanted money for an abortion. She wanted taken in and looked efter. Whit impudence! Weel, her mither, Mrs Ogilvie as she is noo, showed her the door. She's got twa ither lassies by Ogilvie, aged twelve and fourteen. She didnae want them polluted by Jessie. Ogilvie, a big saft lump, sat by and said naething. Noo I'm coming to the bit that concerns you, Miss Bannatyne."

Julia couldn't help smiling. How in heaven's name could this miserable story take a twist that could concern her?

"There she was, destitute, no' feeling very weel as you can imagine, hameless, minded I should think to go and mak a hole in the Clyde. Then wha should come upon her but Gavin Hamilton."

Suddenly Julia *was* concerned.

"It seems he was visiting the Griersons. He met Jessie greeting in the pend. So whit did he dae?"

"Run away as fast as he could, I hope."

"So he should hae done. But no, whit's guid enough for ither folk's never guid enough for him. He took her hame wi' him."

"Why?"

"Why? Why? To gie her shelter. To feed her. That was his reason and his only reason, in my opinion, though there are some saying itherwise."

"What are these others saying?"

"You get bad-minded folk everywhere. Dae you ken, Miss Bannatyne, maybe I should hae taken that offer o' tea. I'm parched talking."

"Of course." Julia rang, Mrs Sempill appeared, the order was given.

Mrs Ferrier watched and listened with much satisfaction. Having a servant to do the work struck her as an admirable arrangement.

"It must have been last Saturday night that he took her to his house?" said Julia.

"That's right. It was pouring rain."

"Was she still there on Sunday morning?"

"She's still there yet. Settled in. That's why I'm here. He needs help to get rid of her. I tried myself. Yesterday I went to the hoose, pretending it was to keep his grandmither company for an hour or sae. I got quite a shock."

Just then the tea arrived. Julia noticed that Mrs Sempill had used the third best china and the silver teapot. This visitor from down the hill must be impressed but not too much honoured.

Mrs Ferrier was a messy cake-eater and a noisy tea-drinker.

"This is guid tea," she said. "I try to afford the best myself. As I was saying I got a shock when I saw Jessie. There she was, hair washed, face shining (the scabs nearly a' healed), wearing a clean peeny. A' smiles. She'd been reading frae the *People's Friend* to Mrs Hamilton. Auld Hamilton, Gavin's grandfaither was there, looking pleased. Wee Jessie, he said to me, if you can credit it, was a great help, she was cheery herself and made ither folk cheery. Noo he's a man that's had his fibre sapped for reasons I'll no' go into, but he was certainly gratefu' to Jessie. God help us. Whit game was she up to? That's whit I asked myself. That's why I'm here. As I said, she's pregnant. Every lassie that's pregnant is on the hunt for a man to mairry her. Aye, Miss Bannatyne, that's whit I'm saying: the impudent besom could be efter Gavin."

Was this, thought Julia, the act of irresponsible and ruinous goodness that she had always feared?

"What can I do?" she asked.

"If you'll let me advise you I'd say you should go when Gavin's at work and order her oot o' his hoose. You might hae to offer her money."

"Yes. How much?"

"Ten pounds at the very least. She's determined to get rid of the wean, you see."

"I wouldn't like to give her money to help her get an abortion. I think that's murder."

Julia stood up. She wanted to go up to her bedroom to think it all over.

"I hope you're no' offended," said Mrs Ferrier.

"No. I'm glad you came. I'm grateful. Thank you. Mrs Sempill will see you out."

As she hurried out of the drawing-room she wondered if she should have offered this rather sinister old woman money too. Everybody expected to be paid.

10

L Y I N G   O N   H E R bed, she found herself shivering as if at the onset of illness. Without wanting to think about it, she knew that she was at last going to give him up. She had never really convinced herself that she would marry him, and most of her friends had been sure she wouldn't; yet now that she had decided to break with him for good she felt no relief, but only a regret that, she realized, she would still feel when she was an old woman, even if in the meantime she had been married happily enough to some other man and had several children. Wherever she was, in whatever luxurious circumstances she found herself, she would remember him and envy him his sweeter and more durable happiness. She would envy too the unknown woman who, taking the risks, had become his wife.

Even now she felt envious of that disgusting designing creature in his house. When he came home from work that evening *she* would meet him at the door. It would be on *her* that he would smile, so beautifully. It would be *she* who would feel honoured.

She kept the letter as short as she could. She simply said it would be in both their interests if they parted. She wished him well. She did not mention either Mrs Ferrier or Findlay.

It had to be posted immediately, lest she should change her mind.

Telling Mrs Sempill that she would be only a few minutes, she set off, as she thought, to the pillar-box less than 100 yards away, outside "Ivanhoe" where the Hallads used to live.

She dropped the letter in without hesitation, but then, instead of turning and walking back as she had intended, hurried on down the hill to the main street. There she went into the Bank of Scotland. She had a strange feeling that she was not the Julia Bannatyne she knew so well, but some other woman whose purposes she did not quite understand. She felt some surprise therefore when the clerk wished her good afternoon, called her Miss Bannatyne, and with only the quickest of curious glances at her face, counted out in £5 notes the £100 she had asked for. She had to put the money in her pocket as she hadn't brought her handbag.

As she waited for the bus at the Cross some loungers there stared at her in insolent surprise. She was very seldom seen wating for buses.

When she came off at Auchengillan there were more idlers, seated on a wall. Two were elderly men. They looked at her, she thought, as if they had sympathetic advice to give her. She looked at them as if she would have been pleased to listen to it. Of course she could not ask them for it nor could they offer it. She and they were kept apart by that quality which Gavin condemned in others but which he had more of than anyone else she knew. Pride. Hers, though, and that of these unemployed, unshaven, worn-out men were natural and comprehensible and took account of the ways of the world. Gavin's did not.

It was his grandfather who opened the door. He was an example of what happened when a person was drained of natural pride. Everybody admired his devotion to his stricken wife, but everybody thought he was weak and foolish in letting her still tyrannize him.

He looked suspicious as well as surprised. "Gavin's at work," he said.

"I know that." She always spoke sharply to him; otherwise he never listened. "It's not him I want to see."

"It's Jessie," he muttered, accusingly.

She stepped past him. "Is she still here?"

"Aye, she's here. She's reading the *People's Friend* to Nellie."

That, thought Julia, would be a sight worth seeing: the depraved calculating young woman reading a story of unbelievable wholesomeness to the bitter old one.

Julia went into the sitting-room. "Please tell her I would like to speak to her."

"Whit are you going to say to her? Wha telt you? Does Gavin ken you're here? I'm no' sure I should let you speak to her, Miss Julia."

"Please tell her."

He went off grumbling.

She sat down, hands clasped on her lap, and studied the pattern on the carpet. She did not want to have any form of words ready.

Findlay took her time. Perhaps she was in front of a mirror powdering over the scabs and practising a smile of deceit.

When she came in, with a soft knock on the door, she was wearing a handsome blue dress made for a bigger and more stylish woman. It hid her pregnancy: if, that was, there was any to hide. She was fair-haired and quite pretty in a coarse plebeian way. Julia wondered if she would have found the creature's smiles so nauseating if she hadn't known that she was a prostitute.

She tried to see in her what Gavin pitied and thought worth saving. She could not. The rough-knuckled hands especially revolted her. God knew what abominations they had clutched.

"So you're Julia?" she said, in a voice all the more insolent because it was trying to be friendly. "Quite the lady."

If provoked would she shriek obscenities? Probably. Nevertheless Julia was determined not to appease her.

"I'm here on Gavin's behalf," she said. "He is too kind to ask you to leave. You are too brazen to think of leaving. So I am telling you to go. At once."

"That's a fucking lie."

Disconcerted, Julia told another: "He is my fiancé".

"I see nae ring. Do you ken whit I think, Julia? I think Gavin kens fuck-all about this little visit of yours. I'll tell you something else. He's the nicest person I've ever kent in my life, but if there's something no' very nice to be done that he thinks should be done he's capable of doing it without onybody's help. I should ken. I had ideas, but he soon put an end to them."

In God's name what had those ideas been? Julia began to weaken. Perhaps she shouldn't have come. Sending the letter had taken away her right to interfere.

Findlay laughed and stroked her belly. "He doesnae want me to get rid of the wean. Life's sacred, he says. Whit about the millions killed in the war, I asked him, his ain faither and mine among them. Some sacred. But he really believes it. Whit's your opinion, Julia? Do you think I should get rid of it, or do you think life's sacred too?"

Considering the circumstances in which the child must have been conceived, and considering the burden of shame it would have to carry all its life, yes, thought Julia, I think you should get rid of it.

"It's got nothing to do with me," she said.

"Right. Neither it has. That's where you're so different from him. He believes everybody in the world has to do with him. A leper in Africa. A starving wean in India. But I'm sure you've heard of them."

Julia had, too often. She put her hand into her pocket.

"If I were to give you money would you go and leave him in peace?"

Findlay seemed taken aback. Evidently she had not been expecting bribery. "It would depend on how much it was, wouldn't it?"

"A hundred pounds."

As well as astonished, Findlay was curiously dismayed. She had been prepared for a derisory sum. She had been ready to tell Julia where to stick her money.

"You're kidding," she muttered.

Julia took the money out of her pocket.

"A hundred pounds! Good Christ. You must think a lot mair of him than I've been gieing you credit for. Money means a lot to you, doesn't it?"

"And to you."

"I'm no' denying it."

"You would have to go at once."

"Look, the quicker I'm oot o' Auchengillan the happier I'll be. This is nae some kind of joke, it it?"

There were, horrible to see, tears in her eyes. She saw the offer of so much money not as a contemptuous bribe but as an act of great kindness. Therefore she could not quickly enough assume a tough defensive attitude. If she had been offered a paltry sum such an attitude would have been easy.

Was she showing herself as she really was, and as Gavin had seen her to be: unhappy, lonely, and afraid?

Julia felt some regret that she had not offered the money with a little compassion. She herself was not as good a person as she ought to be, or indeed as she could be.

"Whose money is it onyway?" asked Findlay. "Is it your faither's?"

"It's mine. I have a right to give it away if I want to."

"I hear you've never done a day's work in your life. How would you like washing hundreds of dishes every fucking day, including Sundays?"

Julia was about to say washing dishes wasn't the worst thing Findlay was reputed to have done. But she kept quiet.

"If you really mean it," muttered Findlay, "if it's no' your idea of a joke, I'll take it and go."

"And you won't come back? To this house, I mean."

"Nor to Auchengillan."

The money changed hands.

"Thanks," said Findlay, her voice shaking. "I'll go and get packed."

As soon as she was gone old Mr Hamilton hurried in.

"Whit's going on? Whit hae you been saying to Jessie? You've got her greeting."

"She's leaving."

"Leaving? Whit for? When? Does Gavin ken?"

"She wants to go."

"She didnae, half an hour ago. Whit will I tell Gavin?"

"Anything you like."

"Naebody ever tells me onything."

Findlay appeared in the doorway, carrying a green leather case.

In spite of his concern for her the old man said, peevishly: "That's Gavin's case. It used to be his mither's."

"He said I could have it. Thanks for everything, Mr Hamilton. Tell Gavin I'll never forget his kindness."

"But where are you going, Jessie? Gavin will want to ken."

"Better if he doesn't. Say goodbye to Mrs Hamilton for me, will you?"

"I don't understaun'. Naebody tells me onything."

"Well, are you coming?" said Findlay, to Julia. "I expect you'll want to make sure I get on the bus. I'll walk in front, if you're ashamed to be seen wi' me."

They walked together down the avenue.

"The hawthorns will soon be in flourish," said Findlay.

"Do you have some place to go to?"

"I've got a pal in Toonheid. She'll tak care of me. For £100 she will."

They waited at the bus stop. Across the road the men on the wall gazed at them.

"The polis used to chase them aff," said Jessie.

A bus came. They got on, Findlay first. Julia decided not to sit beside her, but in a seat further along.

She was glad that she had sent the letter. Why, though, having broken with him, had she interfered? It would appear to him as gratuitous and callous. He was hardly likely to see it as an act of love.

When the bus stopped at Lendrick Cross she got up. She was

about to pass Findlay without a word or smile when the other woman caught her sleeve.

"Thanks," whispered Findlay. "And tell Gavin from me thanks. And tell him for Christ's sake never to change."

As she stood watching the bus go along the main street, past the office where Gavin was working, Julia felt confused and jealous. What hope had he inspired in that foul-mouthed woman, that she should beseech him never to change? Trust a thief and prostitute, disowned by her family, to give him such advice. It suited the Jessie Findlays of the world that earnest dupes like him should exist.

As her father had said, not altogether in jest, better an alcoholic for a husband than a would-be saint.

All the same, as she walked slowly up the hill she felt sorrier for herself than for Gavin. However absurd and unattainable his ambitions, they gave him confidence and happiness; whereas she, who like everyone else wished for status and enviable possessions, was often doubtful and discontented.

Jessie & Julia n♂ in Pf

PART THREE

In Auchengillan, as in most small communities, the huge events of the outside world were not often discussed or worried about. In 1931, seated on their now liberated wall, the unemployed or night-shift men chatted about football, particularly after the winning of the Junior Cup by Lendrick Rangers that summer, racing pigeons, whippets, and people they knew, and hardly ever mentioned the collapse of the world's currencies. In 1933, in the Co-op. store, women were more likely to be talking anxiously about a neighbour with six children charged with defrauding the parish of £8 than about Hitler becoming Chancellor of Germany. In 1938, munching their stoury pieces and drinking their cold tea hundreds of feet under the ground, miners found it more companionable to exchange stories about a former workmate recently dead of lung disease than to express useless opinions about Mr Chamberlain's visit to the German Führer.

This apparent indifference to the events and the men shaping the history of the twentieth century was not the result of small-mindedness or ignorance. It was simply felt that people known personally were more interesting and sustaining topics of conversation. If they had been asked what they were doing to help the Jews being bullied in Germany or the anti-Communists being tortured in Russia or the Republicans being defeated in Spain, most Auchengillans would have replied that they were sorry for the Jews, the anti-Communists, and the Spanish Republicans, but there were unfortunate folk in their own midst, such as Mrs McKay jailed for a miserable little fraud and old Tam Menstrie on his death bed coughing up black dust, whom they couldn't help either.

One local subject often debated during those years was the moral growth of Gavin Hamilton.

There was that mysterious affair of wee Jessie Findlay, followed by the breaking off of his engagement, if it ever was that, to Miss Bannatyne.

There were times in every man's life, it was generally agreed, when it was permissible and even salutary for heathen patience or Christian resignation to give way, briefly, to natural rage. One such time was when your pigeon during a race arrived home sooner than anyone else's but sat up on the slates ignoring all blandishments, instead of flying straight into its dovecot to have its ring removed. Another was when you lost a good-looking sweetheart with a well-off father. Gavin, it was thought, ought to have looked red eyed and desperate for a week at least, if only for appearance's sake. (A few months later when somebody noticed in the *Glasgow Herald* the announcement of Miss Bannatyne's engagement to a bloke with a posh-sounding name from Newton Mearns nobody bothered to mention it to Gavin. He would only have given her his blessing.)

True, the part he played in the Rangers' victory in the Junior Cup final at Hampden Park would have compensated for the loss of the Queen of Sheba, far less a lawyer's daughter, especially as agents of top clubs like Glasgow Rangers and Heart of Midlothian were crowding round him, with open cheque books in their hands. At the celebration dinner in the Masonic Hall in Lendrick, when in a short speech he declared that he would always prefer to play for his home team than for strangers however famous, everybody applauded, for local patriotism at the time was fizzing in their blood too, but nobody took him seriously. It was the same when he went on to say, for the first time in public, that though football gave a lot of pleasure it was nevertheless just a game and must never be allowed to take the place of more important things. In Grunter Houlisten it would have been whisky talking, in Gavin it was religion: the same thing, more or less. Nobody held it against him, nobody thought he would still be saying it a week later.

He was still saying it, though, years later. He became too fond of reminding Lendrick players and supporters that Preachers' Braes had been given that name because of religious services that had been held there 100 years ago. He never went so far as to say outright they should love all opposition teams and their supporters, not to mention all referees, but he did seem to expect that if a bottle or a turnip was tossed at you by some gorilla from outlandish parts you should not only refrain from hurling it back, you should simply waggle your finger in friendly rebuke; and if a referee awarded a penalty to the enemy, when it was clear to everybody that the player supposed to have been fouled had taken a dive that would have done credit to a Japanese pearl fisher, you ought to curb your temper, sigh, remember that all men were fallible, and be consoled with the reflection that defeat in a game of football was when all was said and done a triviality.

He was made an elder of St Andrew's, the youngest man ever to be given that honour. Where other elders twice or three times his age were content to stay for ten minutes when making their calls he would stay for two hours or longer, until his hosts (who were also his sheep), impatient to have their tea or listen to the wireless or slip down to the pub for a dram, were hoarse with coughing hints.

It was noticed how, though Gavin was very friendly and never failed to stop you in the street and ask with undeniable sincerity how you and your family were, you always felt awkward talking to him, whereas when you were talking to people who wouldn't give a damn if you dropped dead at their feet or if your wife had run off with the insurance man, you didn't feel awkward at all. Some said it was because Gavin, without ever saying a word that could be called preaching, made you feel that there were lots of good deeds you should have done and lots of bad deeds you shouldn't. He was, alas, the genuine article. He was the last person to talk to if you wanted to feel satisfied with yourself.

It was so different with old Mr McFarquhar, the minister. When talking to him or even when just seeing him in the distance you felt that your immortal soul, while not as unspotted as it should have been, was no more spotted than his. Recently he had taken to accepting drams at weddings and funerals.

During the Spanish Civil War old Mrs Hamilton died. From some demented remarks made by old Alec, her husband, he was either accusing himself of having hastened her on into eternity, by putting a pillow over her mouth, or else he was claiming credit for it. It was decided better not believe him. In any case he was dead himself within a month. Gavin came home from work one evening and there was his grandfather dead in a chair.

Though realists pointed out that the two quick deaths had removed encumbrances and allowed him at last the full enjoyment of his home most people in Auchengillan were sorry for Gavin left alone in the world.

Their sympathy instantly changed to congratulation when it was learned, to everyone's astonishment, that his grandparents had left him more than £2,000; by Auchengillan standards a fortune.

With so much money he could buy one of the villas "up the

hill" in Lendrick, a motor car, and clothes suitable for such a jump up in society.

On the other hand, he could provide a free dram per day for a year for all *bona-fide* regular customers of the Auchengillan Arms, his father's old pub.

Or he could buy a pair of shoes and a poke of sweeties for every child at Auchengillan Primary School.

Or he could give £20 to every widow and old age pensioner in Auchengillan.

Or he could wait till New Year and present a bottle of whisky to every household, with a Bible thrown in to balance his conscience.

One evening Mr McFarquhar paid Gavin a surprise visit. He was red in the face and spoke with great solemnity, in a slow thick voice. Hand on Gavin's shoulder, he advised him that whatever he did with the bulk of the money he should at all costs donate some to an African mission. He was convinced, he said, that when the final accounting was done to be able to claim that you had saved the souls and clothed the nakedness of so many blacks would weigh heavily in your favour.

Elspeth Grierson gave the advice that most Auchengillans, joking apart, would have approved.

"You're still a young man, Gavin. You've got your whole life aheid of you. You'll get mairried and hae a family. Keep the money for them. They hae a better right to it than onybody else."

She did not say it, for she did not think she could find suitable words, but the idea of his giving away his inheritance struck her as morally abhorrent. She felt this with Biblical passion.

It was therefore impossible for her to accept so much as a penny. Tommy was not so adamant. He could see nothing wrong with taking, say, ten or even twenty pounds: it would all be spent on necessities, and anyway, since when had it become a sin to take help from a friend?

She listened to him, shaking her head all the time.

"If you were to take a penny, Tom Grierson, I would walk out that door."

"Don't be daft."

"I'm no' being daft. I was never mair serious."

"Keep your shirt on, woman. We'll ask for nothing, and we'll take nothing."

Mr Bannatyne advised Gavin to invest the money. It would be always there if he needed it, and it would keep on growing.

O N E   S A T U R D A Y afternoon in March 1938, when Hitler's troops were marching into Austria, Lendrick Rangers were playing a cup-tie against Cowcaddens Thistle, a team from Glasgow then at the top of the League. The game turned out to be the dirtiest ever seen at Preachers' Braes. On the terraces Cowcaddens supporters swung at Lendrick supporters with lavatory chains. Lendrick supporters aimed tackety boots at Cowcaddens supporters. On the field vicious fouls happened every two minutes. One Lendrick player, kicked in the privates, had to be carried off, writhing, on a stretcher. Thereafter it was the duty and ambition of all the other Lendrick players, except one, to do likewise or the equivalent to one of their opponents.

Gavin Hamilton was the exception. Because he was a peacemaker, his own colleagues were annoyed at him, and his adversaries, noting that he never retaliated, kicked, elbowed, and butted him more than they did any other Lendrick player. At one point his nose streamed blood.

Towards the end of the game, with the score one-all, the referee, either braver than he knew or bewildered by all the shouts of hatred flung at him, denied the Rangers a penalty kick. Intolerably incensed, about a dozen Lendrick men rushed on to the field, not to assault him, as they maintained later, but simply to persuade him that he had made an error of judgement. Nevertheless they gripped him by the throat and other parts. It was Gavin Hamilton who saved him, by pushing the assailants away, more roughly indeed than was necessary, as they were later to complain in half a dozen pubs. He then helped two policemen and some terrified committee men to escort the referee to the pavilion. In the confusion no one was quite sure who ordered the game to be abandoned. Some thought it was Hamilton himself.

Two days later he handed a letter of resignation to the committee. In it he said that he would never play football again.

In the Auchengillan Arms during one of the many arguments about his decision it was pointed out that to give up football because of a break-in by spectators was like a minister giving up religion because there were rogues in his congregation. If every minister was to do that every pulpit in the land would be empty.

Who the hell did Gavin Hamilton think he was? Jesus Christ? Better men than he would ever be had tossed bottles at referees.

Did he think, because his father had been killed in the Great War, that he had some special right to be shocked by a bit of violence? They had a good mind there and then to go to his house in Hawthorn Avenue and ask him to explain himself. Not just in connection with this insulting abandonment of football either. There were too many other ways in which he had made it pretty obvious during the past few years that he considered himself more moral, more sensitive, and more intelligent than anyone else in Auchengillan.

These hotheads were restrained by older men who pointed out that Gavin had only done what he thought right, and his father had once served in that very pub, as cheery and decent a man as ever drew a full-sized pint. Anyway, it was a free country and if a man wanted to give up football or pigeon racing or pissing in the jawbox he had a right to do it without asking anyone's permission.

They began then, in noisy good humour and with much inventive obscenity, to suggest other activities that a free man could give up if he was fool enough to want to.

Among those activities no one thought of including fighting in a war. Yet it was Hamilton's refusal to do just that which was to puzzle and embarrass many Auchengillans.

For at last, on 3 September at eleven o'clock in the morning, there began the biggest break-in in history. Not even Auchengillan could ignore it.

3

ONLY ONE MAN in Auchengillan welcomed the war. This was Mr McFarquhar, the minister, now 75. At his evening service on the day war was declared he had his pulpit draped with the same Union Jack that he had used in August 1914. Waving his arm as if he was holding a sword, he thanked God that at long last the nation was going to be given a chance once more to chastise the villainous Huns and demonstrate to the world that it loved honour more than life.

Only one person in his congregation thought that Christ's message to mankind was being flagrantly contradicted, but quite a number felt that this bellicose ranting might have been all right in 1914, but hardly in 1939. Their own view was that war could probably have been avoided but now that it was a fact it would have to be fought, even if it meant the destruction of half the cities in

Britain and the deaths of many thousands of civilians. Their mood accordingly was one of reluctant acquiescence and unhappy foreboding. Therefore Mr McFarquhar's furious impersonation of Moses leading the Children of Israel out of bondage was regretted.

It was suspected, though spoken aloud by no one, that he must have had too many drams beforehand. It was known that he took one or two before a service nowadays, for there was the evidence of his breath and flushed face; but it had been hoped that his wife would make sure he never took too many. Mrs Farquhar was the best they knew at nipping pleasure in the bud.

Some, seated near Gavin Hamilton, wondered if he too was ardent for war and the punishment of the wicked. In a way the Poles and Jews were like the referee on whose behalf he had intervened a year or so back, except that it was the Germans who were being turbulent now, not Lendrick men. Trust Gavin, these people thought. With his athletic build, his upper-class appearance, his educated way of speaking, his money in the bank, and his lack of dependents, with all these advantages he wasn't likely to remain a private long, he'd soon be enjoying the privileges and comforts, not to mention the pay, of an officer.

As he sat in kirk, with his eyes closed, listening to the minister's bellows of hate, Gavin considered the many reasons why as a Christian he ought to be proud and eager to go and fight.

He liked to feel that he was part of the community, and though most of its members would have been surprised to know it he needed their approval. Always too, as in childhood, he felt deeply beholden.

He believed what he read in newspapers and heard on the wireless about the brutalities of the Nazis. All his life he had hated brutality, especially when it was used against the weak and powerless. As a child he had felt faint with horror and pity when watching classmates being cruelly strapped.

As an imaginative boy he had taken part in many battles of the past; on the side of the brave and the righteous.

Every time he read the letters his father had sent home during the Great War he was moved by the comradeship of the soldiers in the trenches, conveyed so poignantly in the permitted stereotyped phrases. Also the letters that McIntyre sent every six months or so from India were always cheerful and uncomplaining.

It would be an honour to have as comrades men like his father and McIntyre.

But if he became a soldier he would be denying Christ. Because

Christ had been denied so many times this war, and many wars in the past, had come about. It was so much easier to kill one's enemy than to love him.

Several weeks later he told Mr McFarquar that he had registered as a conscientious objector. They were in the church hall, watching some Bible-class students playing badminton. The old minister reeked of camphorated oil. His wife had rubbed his chest with it. She had told him he ought not to be out on such a cold night, but he had felt it his duty to come and see the youth of Scotland preparing themselves to smite the Huns. Since the declaration of war he had been saying eccentric things like this. He had been seen clapping a mongrel dog and telling it that it was British.

After a pause, during which he seemed to be stroking imaginary medals on his breast, he said: "You would learn the true meaning of humility if you were detailed to clean out latrines".

He went forward, picked up the shuttlecock from the floor, stuffed it into his coat pocket, and then marched out of the hall, as if to pipes playing.

The players looked at Gavin in consternation.

"He's away with the shuttlecock, Mr Hamilton."

Gavin took another one out of the box.

Two days later he got a letter from the minister. It commanded him to resign forthwith from his church positions.

He consulted members of the session. They did not approve of his having applied for exemption from military service, but they were plain and honest men, willing to concede that a case of sorts might well be derived from the Sermon on the Mount. They advised him to do nothing about Mr McFarquhar's letter in the meantime.

A week later came a second letter. In it Mr McFarquhar stated that under no circumstances would he provide testimony as to Gavin's sincerity as a Christian. He quoted from Exodus: "And the waters returned, and covered all the chariots, and the horsemen, and all the host of Pharoah that came into the sea after them; there remained not so much as one of them".

The evening before Gavin was to go before the tribunal in Glasgow, Mr McFarquhar appeared on his doorstep.

It was in May. The British army was in difficulties in France. Mr McFarquhar's sermon the Sunday before had been despondent.

"May I come in?" he asked. He kept glancing nervously down the road, like a thief on the lookout for a policeman.

"Of course."

In the sitting-room Mr McFarquhar sat upright, with his black hat on one knee and his gas mask in its cardbox box on the other. One of his fly buttons was undone.

A part of Gavin, a proud, determined, potentially reckless part, wanted to tell his visitor that if he had come with insults then he had better leave at once. Another part, which spoke for him most of the time and by which he was known, the altruistic, co-operative, reasonable part, sympathized with the old man, who wasn't well and had waited in vain for over 40 years for a call to a more distinguished charge.

In the same way that proud part rebelled against having to set forth for the scrutiny of a tribunal of contemptuous men the reasons why his soul was so much more sensitive than other men's souls that it must be excused the duty of killing.

The amenable part on the other hand was eager to have his conscientious objections if not approved or even understood at any rate respected.

Mr McFarquhar dragged his handkerchief out of his trouser pocket, bringing with it some spent bus tickets.

"What I want to ask you, Gavin," he said, in a surprisingly humble voice, "is: How can the meek ever inherit the earth unless the brutes and bullies are crushed?"

But if they use the methods of the brutes and bullies, how can they remain the meek? Gavin did not say it. He would have to be very sure that it was purged of cant and arrogance before he ever said it.

"All my life," said the old man, still meekly, "I have worshipped Christ the Crusader, Christ the Scourge of the Wicked, Christ the Avenger of Widows, Christ the Exterminator of Evil."

Gavin could think of nothing to say in reply. "Would you like some tea?" he asked.

"I have had my visions too," murmured the minister. "When I was a young man I would have gone to Africa to be a missionary, if I had not been prevented."

He was falling asleep. There was a white stain like dried toothpaste on the front of his trousers.

There was a loud knocking on the outside door.

Gavin wasn't surprised to find Mrs McFarquhar standing there. "Is my husband here?" she asked.

"Yes."

She pushed in without waiting for an invitation. "Surely you could see that he's ill?"

In the sitting room her husband was asleep.

"Wake up, my dear," she cried, shaking him.

He awoke and at once clasped his hands guiltily, letting hat and gas mask fall. He was like a child caught sleeping during a service, and hoping to make amends by an access of piety. It was not the Lord though that he was placating. In childhood perhaps it had been his father. Now it was his wife.

She pulled him to his feet. She rejected Gavin's offer to help.

At the door she turned. "You look well fed," she said. "In your position I would feel obliged not to eat a crumb of food brought in by seamen at the risk of their lives."

Gavin did not reply. He did not think many seamen would grudge him his share of food. In any case he had not yet thought out to what extent his countrymen might feel that his being beholden to them was irreconcilable with his refusing to fight by their sides.

4

THE TRIBUNAL SAT in a Glasgow courtroom. It consisted of three members, a sheriff-principal who was chairman, a trade-union official, and a minister of the Church of Scotland. Their task was paradoxical and difficult. Establishment appointees, they could not help making it clear that in their view conscientious objection to taking part in a war so uniquely just as the present one against Hitler's barbarians was a kind of heresy and those who embraced it were wrong headed, perverse, wilful, and self-deluded. They were being asked, as a patriotic duty, to assess the sincerity of heretics.

If an applicant could convince them that he was absolutely sincere in what to them was a delusion he could be granted complete exemption from military service. If he betrayed some vagueness or uncertainty he could be exempted on condition that he did work of national importance such as agriculture or forestry. If he struck them as being actuated more by emotion than by conscience they could make him liable for non-combatant duties only. Lastly, if he did not convince them that he was a genuine heretic but simply had misunderstood his own orthodoxy or was too pig-headed to acknowledge it, he could be transferred to the military register, which meant that he must either obey his call-up summons or go to jail.

The chairman, Sheriff-Principal Sir James Heriot, spoke in a patient urbane voice. Not once during the whole morning did he ask a question the purpose of which was to make the applicant appear stupid or ignorant or devious or cowardly. He was addressed as 'my lord'.

The trade-union official, a burly heavy-faced middle-aged man called Cochrane, did not bother to hide his impatience with those whose objections were political. The Church representative, Mr Borthwick, was just as openly disdainful of those who based their case on Christian grounds but whose knowledge of the Bible was easily shown to be shallow and deficient. For some reason he was not wearing a clerical collar.

Gavin sat on one of the pew-like benches and listened to some cases being heard before his own. There was a hush like a church in the courtroom. There weren't many spectators, but most of them seemed well-disposed to the objectors. There was one soldier in uniform. He had come to lend support to his brother.

It was hard to believe that what was being considered was a fundamental matter: the conflict between the rights of the individual and those of the State. Everything seemed low-key and even casual. Gavin had once attended a small debt court in Lendrick where the issues were minor, such as the non-payment of rent. He had felt more moved than he did here. Women had wept in misery because of debts of a few pounds.

One applicant who said he was a joiner and an International Socialist declared to the tribunal that he had more in common with German joiners than with British army officers.

"Maybe so," muttered Mr Cochrane, "but don't think that would stop those German joiners from gutting you with their bayonets."

"That's because like British workers they've been misled."

"You, I take it," said Mr Borthwick, "would lead them along the proper path."

"I would, if I could."

"That path no doubt would end in revolution?"

"Right."

"Bloody revolution?"

"If it was necessary."

The chairman intervened. "You seem to be saying, Mr Rodger,

that you would have no objection to taking part in a war the purpose of which was the extermination of what you have called the ruling class. Am I right? Is that really what you are saying?"

"It is."

"Then I am afraid I am at a loss to understand why you are here claiming to be a conscientious objector to war."

"I object to killing my fellow workers. I don't have the same objections to killing those who have exploited them and led them into wars."

"I see. I'm afraid the Act does not provide for such distinctions. Any further questions, gentlemen?"

"I'd just like to say, my lord," said Mr Cochrane, "that I know a wheen of workers who would not be very pleased at the likes of Mr Rodger there claiming to be their champion."

"Are you aware, Mr Rodger," asked Mr Borthwick," that you are advocating civil war, the most dreadful kind there is?"

"I'm glad to hear you admit that war is dreadful."

"Of course I admit it. It is the measure of the arrogance of some of you conscientious objectors that you think you are the only people who look on war as evil and terrible. Surely the men who take part in it and suffer its consequences are in a better position to know just how evil and terrible it is? The difference in their case is that they believe the alternative, submission to a brutal enemy, is even more evil and terrible."

Two young men in front of Gavin whispered to each other.

"Big Jim's done for himself, wouldn't you say?"

"He knew it. He's just said what he came to say."

"It's Barlinnie for him."

"Right. Funny thing is he wouldnae kick his lordship's dog, far less his lordship himself."

Rodger came and sat beside them.

"How'd I do?" he asked.

"Depends on what you were after, Jim. You certainly didn't get yourself off."

"I ken that. That Cochrane, calls himself a Socialist. Would you credit it?"

Next was a history teacher, a clever-looking, plump-faced, bespectacled man of about Gavin's age. He was called McMillan.

Sir James enjoyed a little argument with him.

"You say, Mr McMillan, that no good has ever come out of

war. Would you not say that the abolition of slavery was good?"

"I would."

"So good indeed that men might honourably give their lives to achieve it?"

"Give their lives honourably, maybe. But not take other men's lives. That of course is the whole point. But if your lordship is referring to the American Civil War I would like to remind you, with respect, that the real issue there was not slavery but the right of individual States to secede from the Union. Lincoln was willing enough to let the South keep their slaves, but he went to war to prevent their seceding."

"His lordship doesn't need a history lesson from you," sneered Mr Cochrane.

"If this is the view of history that you teach your pupils," said Mr Borthwick, "I am surprised that you have been allowed to continue in your employment."

The three in front of Gavin had formed themselves into a subsidiary tribunal.

"Well, what d'you think? Will he make it?"

"Sure thing. They'll not want him putting wrong ideas into the sodgers' heids. He'll do less harm talking to trees or tatties."

"He'll no' get complete," muttered Rodger. "He's never mentioned Jesus Christ once. It's planting trees for him."

Next came a Jehovah's Witness, called Shearer, a tall, physically awkward young man with a big nose and a very soft voice. His smile was so amiable towards everyone that it looked glaikit.

The Rev. Mr Borthwick enjoyed showing up the absurdity of his interpretation of the Bible.

So ingenuous and honest was Shearer that he did not mention that the only religious body in Germany to refuse to serve in Hitler's armies was the one to which he belonged.

The tribunal in front of Gavin paid little attention to Shearer's inquisition. Religion, they evidently believed, was without interest or use.

At last it was Gavin's turn. Rodger winked at him and whispered, "Good luck".

Gavin took up his stance in front of the high dais on which the members of the tribunal sat. Each had in front of him a copy of Gavin's statement. As they read it they kept glancing down at him.

In Sir James's glances were curiosity and pity, in Mr Cochrane's impatience and distrust, and in Mr Borthwick's suspicion and resentment.

Gavin's stand was based on Christ's teachings. This put the tribunal in a particularly difficult position. Britain called itself a Christian country. The kernel of Christianity was the Sermon on the Mount. This, unfortunately for Sir James and his colleagues, was the most eloquent expression of pacifism ever made. "Resist not evil. Love your enemies. Bless them that curse you. Pray for them that despitefully use you. If you love them which love you, what reward have you?" To dismiss all that as impracticable nonsense was to run the risk of dismissing Christianity.

"I note, Mr Hamilton," said Sir James, in his kindly manner, "that you have been a member of the Church all your life, and are at present an elder, despite your youth. I do not, however, see any letter from your parish minister."

"No, my lord."

"I take it he is not in sympathy with your views."

"That is so, my lord."

"Do you really believe that the way to overcome evil is by not resisting it?"

"That is what Christ said we must do, my lord."

"That is not what I asked. I asked if you really believed it."

"I believe Christ."

Sir James sighed and let Mr Cochrane take over.

"So if a thug attacked you in the street you would just stand smiling at him?" asked Mr Cochrane, with a sneer.

Mr Borthwick was keen to join in. "Let me put Mr Cochrane's question in another way. If you saw a thug attack an old woman or a child would you just stand smiling at him?"

"I would do my best to protect the old woman or the child, without using force."

Gavin was well aware how shamefully inadequate his answer was.

"No doubt begging the thug's pardon if you happened to step on his toes," said Mr Cochrane.

Mr Cochrane was angry. He made up his mind that no matter what Sir James advised in this case he was damned if he was going to agree to grant this pious young bugger complete exemption. The best place for a saint like him was in the Pioneer Corps, mucking out latrines. He'd get plenty of opportunity there to practise his humility.

At the end of the morning's proceedings the chairman read out the tribunal's judgements, like a headmaster announcing examination results. He did not however scowl magisterially at those who had failed badly: that was to say, who had been refused exemption of any kind. Indeed, addressing them his voice was kind and regretful. It was not, on the other hand, noticeably congratulatory towards the one applicant that morning to pass with honours, in other words who had been granted complete exemption. This was a stooped, thin, consumptive, young man, who would have failed the medical examination anyway.

Gavin himself was exempted on condition he went to work at forestry. So were the Jehovah's Witness and the history teacher. Rodger the joiner was among those transferred to the military register. He had a choice, he remarked gloomily, between Maryhill Barracks and Barlinnie. His friends were amused. Their own cases came up next week. It would be Barlinnie for them too.

Gavin went down the steps into the street with McMillan, the history teacher.

"Well, what did you think of our comrades-not-at-arms?" asked McMillan. "Rum lot, wouldn't you say? Hardly a troop of spiritual knights."

It would be more difficult for conscientious objectors than for soldiers to build up a comradeship. Consciences were too private and isolated.

"Are you satisfied or are you going to appeal?" asked McMillan.

"I haven't thought about it."

"Are you married?"

"No."

"I am. With one child, a little girl of three. Well, good luck. I may bump into you in some peaceful glade."

The expression on his fat face as he walked off was as anxious and rueful as a soldier's about to be parted from his wife and child. To be fair though, when it was all over, he stood a better chance of being reunited with them.

As he walked to the bus station it seemed to Gavin that the people he passed had become alien. They were not removed from him by any difference of language or dress or physiognomy, but by something unseen. In respect of that something they had more in common with the Germans with whom they were at war. He was set apart, like a leper in the Middle Ages. His isolation was not physical but moral. He could touch them, even shake hands with them, but he could not share their joy at victory or their sorrow at defeat.

Still, the soldier's lot was probably harder. He had to wear a uniform, he had to carry out demeaning tasks the purpose of which was to induce in him a slave-like promptness to obey orders even if he thought them wrong or foolish, he had to learn to use weapons intended to kill, and he might be sent overseas into conditions of hardship and danger. As against all that he would have the admiration of the great majority of his countrymen and all those related to him would be honoured and cherished for his sake.

Above all, the soldier, having made his decision, would never be asked to justify it, either to himself or to others. In Gavin's own case he knew he would be trying to justify it for the rest of his life.

5

I F H E H A D told the people of Auchengillan about his humorous diagnosis of moral leprosy they would have laughed, but they would have assured him cheerfully not to worry, it wasn't catching, so that if it gnawed away souls as real leprosy did fingers it would be only *his* soul that would suffer; and anyway, when the war was over, there would be an immediate and miraculous cure.

Sometimes a woman whose husband or son had been called up would sniff indignantly or shake her head sadly when he passed.

No one shouted "Creeping Jesus" or "Crapper" at him from closemouths.

Those of his school friends waiting to be called up still gave him friendly greetings. Charlie McGill, ordered to report to the barracks at Cadzow, said that he wasn't looking forward to it all that much but he thought he could put up with it. He added that he would never be able to put up with what was ahead of Gavin. He meant it too. All his life Charlie had needed to be one of the crowd, he'd hated to be left out of anything, and he had always worried about what people were saying about him behind his back.

One evening Gavin met Mrs Ferrier in Hawthorn Avenue, walking with a stick. She poked him in the stomach and glared at him with her good eye.

"They're saying it's principle," she said, "but I ken better. It's revenge. You've never forgi'en us for your faither being killed, and your mither deeing young, and you haeing to leave school, and Miss Bannatyne breaking it aff. You've said naething, for it's never been your nature to say much, but you've been holding it against us."

For the rest of that evening he kept asking himself if there was any truth in her accusation. Beneath layer upon layer of self-deceiving pride had grudge really been germinating?

He visited the Griersons to offer them the use of his house while he was away. Little Elsie climbed up on to his knee. Clasping her, he felt how thin she was.

Quietly he pointed out the advantages.

In the small scullery Elspeth was washing dishes. As she listened there was no pause in the clinking of delf or cutlery. He might have been talking about football or the weather or the war, from her apparent lack of interest.

Tommy, in bed, smoked and scowled up at the ceiling. Baby Robert lay beside him, chuckling and kicking his legs as if to make sure they were in working order.

When Gavin was finished speaking Elspeth came to the scullery door, with soap suds on her arms. Her face was grim.

"How long do you think the war's going to last?" she asked.

"They say three, four, five years."

"Don't think I'm no' grateful, Gavin—your hoose is a palace compared wi' this—but when you came back, in three, four, or five years, where would we go then?"

"You'd stay till you got a place of your own."

"We've got oor name down for a cooncil hoose," muttered Tommy, "but it's aeroplanes they're building noo."

"I hate this place," said Elspeth. "I see it ruining my weans' health. But there are men making big money in the steelwork and the pits who could pay you thirty shillings, two pounds even. We pay six shillings for this. It's a' we can afford."

"Why should you pay rent, Elspeth? You'd be looking after the house for me?"

"Hm. Whit aboot your braw furniture? The weans are at a destructive stage. I cannae be watching them a' the time."

"Children matter more than furniture."

"I think you're serious."

"Very serious."

Yet she was still not looking pleased.

"You'll hae to gie Tom and me time to talk it over."

"Of course."

"Betty McLauchlan would jump at the chance of this hoose. She's Blackie Simpson's daughter, maybe you mind. She's a widow, with five weans. She's living in a single room noo."

Gavin thought of Blackie Simpson, that big strong quiet man. Now over 60, Blackie was finding the work underground too much for him.

Drying her hands with a towel, Elspeth came into the living-room. She still looked resentful.

"Excuse me for saying this, Gavin, but I hope you're no' using us to prove onything. There's nae need. There are mony gie Christianity a bad name. You're no' one of them."

"I want you and Tommy and the children in my house. When I think of you there it'll be a help to me. I mean that, Elspeth."

"I ken you do."

The look of resentment at last faded from her face. Then she did something quite out of character. She went over, bent down, and kissed him on the brow.

6

I T   W A S   A dull August morning when he left Auchengillan on a bicycle, with his suitcase strapped to the carrier and his fiddle case slung round his neck. He passed some miners trudging home from the night-shift. He waved, but their heads were bowed with weariness and they did not notice him.

He was cycling to Lendrick where he would take a train to Glasgow Central. There another train would take him to Gourock on the Firth of Clyde. From Gourock the mail steamer *St Columba* would carry him through the famous Kyles of Bute to Port Fada on Loch Fyne. The rest of the journey would be done by bicycle.

As he passed Lendrick Cross, deserted at that early hour, he remembered, as always, Rachel Hallad. She was married to a man who had fought in the Spanish Civil War. Perhaps, like many others with high morals but no religion, she had set aside her pacifism until the evils of Fascism were expunged; or more likely, for she was always honest with herself, she had abandoned it altogether. Yet had she not come very close to a profound religious position when she had said that no person could help another? All she had needed to add was: "if the love of Christ is not between them".

As he cycled past the office where he had worked for fourteen years he recalled Mr Bannatyne's farewell words.

"You know your trouble, Gavin? Lack of ambition. You could have played football for Queen's Park or Glasgow Rangers. You could have been famous. And now, when the best opportunity in a young man's life has come, in the shape of this war, to see the world, have some fun and excitement, and meet lots of interesting people, you're sneaking off to dig ditches in some Godforsaken bog. I just don't understand."

Julia would have understood. Married to a stockbroker, she had a child now and lived in Edinburgh.

In the Gourock train a small yellow-faced sick-looking man in a cloth cap asked him jocularly if his fiddle case up on the rack contained a machine gun.

Others in the crowded, smelly, dirty, uncomfortable compartment took up the joke.

"If ony Nazis come on at Paisley mow them doon."

"They're mair likely to come on at Port Glesca."

"Juist a minute, Mrs. We're maybe bad in the Port, but no' as bad as that."

Everybody laughed. Gavin was included in the good-natured fellowship. He wondered if he was receiving it fraudulently. If they knew that he was a conscientious objector would they want to avoid him as most Germans did Jews?

Be careful, he warned himself. This isn't humility, this is aggressive self-pity. These men and women on their way to work, wearing grubby raincoats, carrying foolish gas masks, enduring the daily discomforts of crowded trains, and worrying about relatives and friends, would not readily snub or despise him. They would be more likely to show him puzzled concern. The women would be sorry for his mother or wife. One of the men, perhaps the sick-looking little man himself, might to put him at his ease mutter that it was a free country, everybody was entitled to his opinion, and anyway, God knew, maybe the only way to end wars was if everybody refused to fight in them. Instead of heaping faggots for his martyrdom they would, a bit shamefacedly, with their eyes turned away, cut him down from the stake.

Yet from his point of view their good nature, their fairness, their instinctive sympathy for outcasts, and their tolerance were all based on profound pessimism. In their hearts they did not believe that war would ever be abolished. They were sorry for Christ, not inspired by Him.

As she was getting up to go off at Greenock a stout middle-aged woman with a swollen red nose, who had been seated opposite him, touched him on the shoulder and whispered into his ear: "Cheer up, son. We're no' a' deid yet."

Her humanity was beautiful, and he acknowledged it with a grateful smile.

All the same surely it weakened his cause.

In the past Christians had been put to death for their faith. Those who had burnt or hanged or beheaded them must have been impressed by their steadfastness. In these more tolerant times, in this tolerant country, instead of the flames or the rope or the axe were words of motherly comfort and a pat on the shoulder.

If he had refused to go before the tribunal, waited for the police to come and arrest him, and in prison had eaten no food, he would have demonstrated not only the tremendous importance of his cause, but also its manliness.

Christ had shown his love for mankind by letting them crucify Him.

7

THE RAIN WAS heavy as he went up the gangway on to the steamer. All the upper deck gleamed with wetness. Gulls stood on rails and lifeboats, as if they had decided flying in such weather was no fun. Two warships were lying off Greenock further up the Clyde.

Like all the other passengers he was glad to hurry below to the saloon. Among the people seated there was a soldier in kilted uniform, fair-haired like McIntyre. Perhaps he was going home on leave, to Islay or Jura or some such remote place.

Gavin took out of his pocket the anthology of poems that Rachel Hallad had given him the day he visited her house. Comments scribbled by her were on every page. "Marvellous!" was the most frequent. He could almost hear her saying it.

The steamer was on its way when someone came and sat beside him, with a grunt that could have been a greeting or disgust at the weather. His sandy hair and raincoat were soaked. He looked aggrieved and yet, underlying it, pleased with himself.

For a few minutes he said nothing and smoked a cigarette. When it wasn't at his mouth he held it well to his right, so that the smoke drifting up from it missed his eyes and caused Gavin's to smart. Like most of the other men in the saloon, including the soldier, he kept looking at two women at the front; or rather, at the one who was so strikingly good-looking, with long fair hair flowing down from under her red woollen hat.

"You know," he said, "you're the first person I've ever seen reading poetry in public. Odd, that. We get it hammered into us at school. We're made to learn screeds of it by heart. Yet nobody's ever seen reading it in public. It's like dead birds."

He glanced at Gavin's book. " 'La Belle Dame Sans Merci.' Got that at school. 'So haggard and so woe-begone.' Is it a favourite of yours?" He bent down to see what Rachel had written. " 'Sloppy.' Well, so it is. But isn't 'sloppy' a sloppy word? Do you write poetry or just read it?"

"I just read it."

"Name's Saidler, by the way: Ian Saidler."

"Gavin Hamilton."

"I'm a conchie on my way to do my bit at Ardmore Forest, in wettest Argyll. I've a feeling you are too."

"Yes." Gavin did not like the word "conchie". It seemed contemptuous.

"I'm hoping it isn't a nest of Holy Willies. You know the sort: that never look at pretty girls' legs; that sing psalms through their noses; that think drinking and smoking are sinful; that think anything enjoyable's sinful. That sort."

He grinned as if he thought Gavin might fit the description.

"I don't trust people who say their objections to war are religious," he said. "Religion has caused a lot more wars than it's prevented. In fact, I can't think of one that it ever tried to stop. The Old Testament's steeped in gore. Are you religious, Hamilton?"

"Yes."

Saidler chuckled. "What flaw did Sir James and his henchmen find in your faith? I mean, if they had decided it was flawless they'd have given you complete exemption. But perhaps they did?"

"No. What are *your* objections?"

"Let's just say I don't fancy taking orders from ynaffs in uniform. You know, it's *you* she's interested in. The beauty with the red tammy. She keeps turning round. I thought it was me. But it's you. She must like them black-haired, soulful, and poetic. What are you going to do about it? Invite her to the bar for a drink?"

"I don't drink."

"Not even tea? She'd jump at it, Hamilton. She fancies you. I'll be big-hearted and invite her pal, who, as you can see, is small and dumpy, and probably cross-eyed. What about it?"

"I'd rather not."

"Well, I think I will. It's hellish stuffy in here. And all that fresh air outside. There's a moral of sorts to be drawn from that. Well, I'll be seeing you. Keep an eye on my case for me."

He strolled over to the girls and spoke to them. The fair-haired one glanced back at Gavin. She seemed reluctant. The two others coaxed her. She gave in. As she went out with them she gave Gavin a smile. She struck him as naïve rather than brazen.

The steamer had rounded Toward Point and was heading for Rothesay when Saidler returned with the two girls.

"Guess what, Hamilton," he said. "These two young ladies are on their way to Ardmore too. Landgirls. Would rather nurse trees than make shells. Miss Ann McTaggart and Miss Helen Lyall, of Edinburgh, erstwhile typists. Ladies, meet Gavin Hamilton, who reads poetry in public, believes in God, and neither smokes nor drinks."

They shook hands. Miss McTaggart of the fair hair gave Gavin a protective smile: he was not to mind Saidler's sarcasm. Seen close up, she was certainly pretty, with bright blue eyes, good skin, and soft red mouth. She seemed so lacking in subtleties that it almost amounted to silliness. Compared with Julia Bannatyne, she was guileless; with Rachel Hallad, dull.

They went up on deck to have a look at Rothesay in the rain.

Each of them had spent holidays there in childhood. Ann remembered the Punch and Judy at the Children's Corner, Helen the blue-bells in Skeoch Wood, Gavin the rowing boats, and Saidler the courting couples among the whins on Canada Hill.

"He's got a dirty mind," whispered Ann to Gavin, with a giggle. She seemed more amused than displeased.

She hummed a snatch of the sentimental song "Sweet Rothesay Bay". It had been one of his mother's favourites.

"You're musical, I see," said Ann.

"I play the violin a little."

"I play the piano a very little." She laughed. "I don't see why we shouldn't enjoy ourselves at Ardmore. Do you?"

In spite of the miserable weather there were holiday-makers on the pier watching the steamer come in. Among them were some soldiers in foreign-looking uniforms.

"Poles," said Saidler. "Officers, of course."

No wonder they looked so dejected, thought Gavin. They had lost perhaps forever their homes, families, and country. Would they feel recompensed if Germans were similarly to lose homes and families? They did not look as if they were raging for revenge. They were too unhappy for that.

"You wouldn't think," said Saidler, "that they used to strut about like lords."

"How do you know that?" asked Helen Lyall, a small brown-haired woman with a firm jaw and honest eyes.

One of the Poles, seeing the lovely Ann McTaggart smiling at him, clicked his heels together and gave her a gentlemanly bow. His colleagues did likewise.

"See what I mean?" said Saidler. "Every Pole not a peasant thinks he's an aristocrat."

Ann McTaggart gave the Poles a friendly wave. They all looked cheered up.

"Have you ever been to Poland?" asked Helen.

Saidler grinned. "They wouldn't be in the mess they're in if they'd let the Commie Russians in to help them."

"Maybe they'd be in an even bigger mess."

The *St Columba*, with gulls screaming about its red and black funnel, drew away from the pier.

Saidler and Helen, still arguing, went below out of the cold.

Ann asked Gavin to keep her company on deck. "I want to see the Maids of Bute."

It struck him as a childish wish.

"Those Poles," she said, with a shiver. "They looked so unhappy."

"They must miss their families."

"Are you missing yours? Ian Saidler was saying you must have a beautiful wife and three lovely children. Otherwise, he said, why were you looking 'so haggard and so woe-begone'? That's a quotation."

"Yes. I'm not married."

"I didn't think you were. Or engaged either. You have the look of a man worried about principles, not about a woman."

"Could you tell the difference?"

"Any woman could."

She gripped him by the arm. "We're going through the Kyles now. We'll soon see the Maids."

These were figures painted in red and white on a rock, in a desolate part of the island shown on the map as Buttock Point.

"There they are," she cried, squeezing his arm.

They weren't very distinct through the mist and rain.

"They look like forestry-workers sheltering," said Ann. "I've got a friend at Ardmore. She says rain's the worst part of it. It's a very wet place."

"Aren't they allowed to shelter?"

"Only after they've worked in it for some hours and are soaked through. But Sheila says that when the sun shines it's very beautiful. I'm quite looking forward to it."

She was lovely and sweet-natured and guileless, and she liked him. But he could not afford the complications of a developing friendship with her. First and foremost he must settle the problem of to what degree should he consent to be beholden.

8

ANN EXPLAINED that a bus made the journey from Culbreack to Port Fada and back every week day, passing through Ardmore. It carried not only passengers and mail but also anything that people along the road might ask to be brought. Its driver, Culbreck Charlie, was as obliging as he was imperturbable. He would take on board a bicycle with no bother.

She suggested that Gavin should travel in the bus with her and the others. The road to Ardmore was rough, narrow, twisty, and in places steep, as well as being lonely the whole way. He thanked her but said that he would cycle. He had brought an oilskin cape and a sou'wester.

Not wanting to seem too churlish he accepted her offer to look after his fiddle. The cover over the case was supposed to be waterproof but perhaps it wouldn't keep out rain as persistent as this.

As he set off from the pier he passed Saidler and the two women walking into the village. They had invited him to wait and have a snack with them, but again he had declined. All the same, as he cycled through the village and saw the brightly painted café in front of the harbour and the fishing boats, he felt that it would have been relaxing to sit in it for a while, just chatting.

Not accustomed to cycling in the rain he soon found his legs and back wet and aching, and his bottom chafed. On stony stretches of the road his feet skidded off the pedals. His long cape kept catching in the spokes. The hard work of pushing up hills made him sweat.

For some miles the road rose and fell close to the loch. In one small bay he counted nineteen stoical swans. There were other birds whose names he didn't know. In his suitcase he had brought two small books, one on birds and the other on wild flowers. He could never believe, like Rachel Hallad and her favourite poet Wordsworth, that nature in the form of beautiful scenery and with its variety of creatures and plants, made a substitute for religion, but it was all God's creation and a source of pleasure and solace.

A memory that was often with him was of Charlie McGill and Davie McLuskie poking earwigs out of rotten fence posts and transfixing them with pins. At the time, for he was only seven, he had not thought of Christ on the Cross, but years later, when the significance of the Crucifixion had became clearer to him, he had understood that cruelty even to earwigs kept the nails sharp.

The road was very lonely. The few solitary houses stood well back, behind drystone dykes and unkempt hedges, in sodden fields of rushes and ragwort. The only person he saw was a woman carrying armfuls of logs into her house. She was wearing Wellingtons. Even if her hands had not been occupied she would not have waved. She was too used to loneliness.

Leaving the lochside the road passed through a wood of low, contorted trees grey and hairy with crotal. There were boulders bright green with moss. He was reminded of the strange poem in

Rachel's book, praising the wilderness. She had commented: "Marvellous!" He had not really appreciated it until now.

At last on the hillsides on either side of the road he saw small trees in neat rows. Notices appeared warning of fire danger. Beside them were fire brooms made of birch twigs. He had reached Ardmore Forest.

Passing over a bridge under which a burn roared in splendid spate he came to the forestry houses that made up Ardmore. He had been told that the forester's office was a small hut there. Perhaps though the forester was somewhere in the forest trying to decide whether, in fairness both to his employers and to his workers, the latter should be allowed to take shelter or go home. It could well be that since he had conscientious objectors working for him now he would feel they should be kept out in the rain longer than was customary, not out of spite but out of a sense of fairness, since soldiers had to endure far worse inconveniences than rain. In that case, would the ordinary workers resent the extra hardship incidentally imposed on them, or would they gladly suffer it, knowing that its purpose was to chasten and discipline their unwelcome mates?

Near the forester's hut was a larger corrugated iron shed. At the open door some men looked out, Gavin smiled but none smiled back. They seemed not so much hostile as baffled. They were like natives into whose territory had come a stranger with human shape but alien mind.

He knocked on the hut door and was told to come in, by a Highland voice.

In khaki uniform with green collar, the forester Mr McAndrew was seated at a desk, with a pen in his hand.

He was a small stocky man with broad face and sharp suspicious eyes. He grinned at Gavin with a mixture of domination and shyness.

"My name's Hamilton," said Gavin. "I was told to report here."

"I wass expecting you, Hamilton. I was also expecting another man called Saidler."

"He's coming on the bus."

"Were there two women on the poat too?"

"Yes."

"It isn't very nice weather for a cycle run."

"No."

"Are you very wet?"

"Just my trouser legs."

"You'll be wanting to get on up to Creag and into dry clothes."

"Creag?"

"It's an old farmhouse. That's where you'll be living. Maybe a man from the city would think it is far enough. Apout a mile and a half further along the road, to the gate, and up a track apout another mile. You'll know the gate by the yellow paint that's on it."

"Can I cycle up this track?"

"I'm thinking you would need legs like a caper-tosser's. Anyway, the Creag lads keep their pikes at Granny McSporran's. Her cottage is apout 200 yards past the gate. There's a shed pehind where the pikes are kept. Anyway, you'll find Munro waiting at the gate. He's cook this week. It's part of his duties to meet the pus and carry up the groceries."

"How many are there in Creag?"

"With yourself and Saidler there will pe eleven. They will all pe there to meet you. They finished work today at three o'clock. Pecause of the rain, you see. They will be sawing logs."

"Do I report here tomorrow morning?"

"Yess. At eight o'clock. Your hands are soft, Hamilton. You have not peen accustomed to manual work?"

"No."

"But you are a pig strong fellow. I think you are a good football player, Hamilton."

Gavin was astonished. "I used to play."

"You have the palance of a footpall player. I can always tell. What is your best position, Hamilton?"

"Right-half, I think."

"Right-half would do fine. You see, Hamilton, Ardmore and district have challenged Port Fada. They think pecause they've got a pier and a picture-house they are in civilization, while we are in the packwoods. They have a team that plays fairly regularly. We have never played pefore as a team. They are saying they will pulverize us."

"The advantage would seem to be with them."

"Put I am a very good centre-forward. They are forgetting that."

He meant it seriously.

"Is the game played in Port Fada?" asked Gavin.

"Yess. You would see the field chust outside the village. It has real goalposts and nets. I would like you to play for us, Hamilton."

Gavin was about to say that he could not, for he had sworn never to play football again. But surely this game was different. It would be played in a spirit of neighbourly friendliness. As for his taking part in it it would not only help him to establish friendly relations with the local people, it could also be set against any obligations that he might not be able to avoid.

"So you can get all the plisters you like on your hands," said McAndrew, "so long as you get none on your feet."

9

AS HE CYCLED along through a tunnel of trees, looking out for the gate with yellow paint on it, he considered the inspiration, or perhaps the temptation, that had come to him in McAndrew's office: that he must, for the peace of his soul, take little and give much: for, if he allowed himself to be beholden more than was avoidable, even by the extent of a crust of bread, he would in effect be taking part in the war.

There flickered in him, once or twice, like flashes of lightning in the dark, heavy sky, angry repudiations of the right of his fellows simply because they were in millions and he was alone to order him either to prepare himself to kill or hide himself away in disgrace, like a pardoned but unforgiven criminal.

His own right to work out his salvation in this time of war was not given him by his fellow men but by God.

He passed three gates before he came to the one with yellow paint on it. Perched on the top bars was Munro the cook, playing a mouth organ. The tune was "Tipperary". He wore Wellington boots, a long dark-blue raincoat tied round the middle with rope, and a cap with its skip turned to the back. Above and all about him rain hissed on many leaves.

Gavin stopped. "Hello," he said. "Is this Creag road-end?"

Munro kept on playing but scraped his heel along the paint, as if inviting Gavin to read what it said. "This is were the yellow bellies live."

He stopped playing and shook spittle out of his mouth organ. "Are you a yellow belly?" he asked, in a gallous Glasgow voice.

He had also a Glasgow face: alert, inquisitive, humorous, and aggressive.

"Who did that?" asked Gavin.

"Some bastards from Port Fada that couldn't spell."

"When?"

"Months ago."

"Why hasn't it been scrubbed off?"

"We're waiting for those that put it on to scrub it off."

It should not, thought Gavin, be treated as a joke. For a few moments he hated those who had done it. Why should he ever act meekly towards them? More than ever it seemed necessary not to be beholden.

"Does it bother you?" asked Munro. "Better not go into Port Fada then on Saturday nights to the pictures. When you come out you're likely to find your tyres flat and the valves pinched. That means an eight-mile walk in the dark."

"Does that happen?"

"It's happened to me twice. It'll happen to you."

Every step of that walk home in the dark should be a defiance, not a penance, thought Gavin.

Then he remembered that he had not come here to defy anyone. He had come to dispel animosity if he could. Why then feel bitter at finding that it was here to be dispelled?

"My name's Munro, Bill Munro. I'm the cook this week. I'm waiting for the bus. Are you Hamilton or Saidler?"

"Hamilton. Saidler's coming on the bus. I was told I could put my bike in Mrs McSporran's shed."

"Sure. Along the road a bit. A whure of a day, isn't it? Old Charlie's late. His radiator leaks. He's to get out every couple of miles to fill it up."

"Have you been here long?"

"About an hour. I've been through my entire repertoire half a dozen times."

"I meant in Ardmore."

"Five months. But maybe not much longer."

"Are you going somewhere else?"

"I'm thinking of joining the army. It was a toss-up, heads I became a conchie, tails I joined the HLI. Heads won. But I'm thinking of tossing up again. Does that bother you too?"

"It surprises me."

"Why should it? There are as good arguments for knocking

123

fuck out of Hitler as there are for letting him trample all over you. I'm not religious, you see."

The sweat was drying on Gavin and he felt cold. The rain was still as heavy as ever. It could be heard pattering on the leaves, the road, and his cape. He felt downcast. Of all the conscientious objectors he had met so far none had struck him as, in McMillan's sarcastic words, "a spiritual knight". There was Rodger, hoping some day for a bloody revolution; McMillan himself, depending on clever arguments from history; Saidler, blaming religion for wars; and now Munro, using foul language.

As he cycled away from the gate he heard the bus coming.

Mrs McSporran's cottage stood by itself at the edge of the loch, with a brown burn roaring past it. Behind were tall trees with mist in their tops. Beyond these were sodden hills.

He put his bicycle in the shed beside the other bicycles there: the steeds of the spiritual knights, he thought.

As he walked back to the gate the bus rattled past him, with steam coming out of its radiator. The driver gave him a droll military salute, with no malice in it. There seemed to be no passengers.

Munro and Saidler had already set out for Creag. He did not see them ahead of him on the slippery muddy track until he turned a corner and came out on to a wide green space with makeshift goalposts. About 150 yards in front Munro was carrying a big box on his head, while Saidler had up on his shoulder his surprisingly small suitcase. On the boat he had said with a wink that he was just giving Ardmore a week or two's trial.

Burdened with his own heavy case, Gavin was not likely to make up on them unless they waited for him.

Once they paused while Munro exercised his neck, but Gavin had to rest too, so that he got no closer.

It might have been thought that three human beings, already isolated from the great mass of their fellows by a difference of belief, would have kept close together in this rainy solitude, to try and give one another re-assurance and encouragement.

He was too proud to shout to them to wait.

In any case if, running and panting, he managed to make up on them and asked them for that re-assurance very likely they would stare at him as if he was crazy and tell him nothing.

He was very much on his own.

10

CREAG HAD FORMERLY been a farm, keeping sheep on the rocky hills all round and a few cows in the rushy fields in front. A great deal of hard patient work must have gone into the building of the dwelling-house and steadings, all of heavy stone, in a place so far into the hills.

Even in the past when used by a family, with a woman running it, the house could hardly have been very comfortable. As a bothy for men, with not a single cushion or strip of carpet or picture or ornament it was austere enough to satisfy Gavin, though he took care not to show it. The others, he noticed, didn't grumble or look sorry for themselves but they didn't look pleased either. They accepted the roughly-made wooden chairs and table in the kitchen which was also the dining-room, the rusty wood-burning stove on which the cooking was done, the damp walls, the rotting wooden stairs that led up to the small low-ceilinged bedrooms, the dry lavatory in one of the stalls in the byre, the drinking water having to be brought from a spring 200 yards away, and the rats scraping behind the walls; but they did not regard them as evidence that they were proudly asking no favours from society.

Amidst the bustle of men in sweaters and heavy boots or Wellingtons clumping in and out of the kitchen in search of hot water to wash themselves with, Munro shouted that if they wanted to eat early somebody would have to help him peel the potatoes. Nobody paid any heed. When he then cast up, with some profanity, that they were all home two hours sooner than they should be one of them reminded him that they had earned it by working five hours in the rain at the mucky job of bottoming drains, and another that when it was his turn to be cook he hadn't noticed Munro rushing to help.

Gavin's offer to help evoked no smiles of approval. "Don't be a mug," one muttered. "He's had all day to peel them."

There seemed little spirit of community.

He soon found that Munro expected him to peel not just some of the potatoes but all of them, and there was a big heap.

In spite of his aching legs he worked at the rusty sink, in icy water, without complaint.

He was joined by McMillan, the history teacher, whom, with Shearer the Jehovah's Witness, he had found among the occupants. McMillan had greeted him with a casual nod.

"If I was you," McMillan now muttered, "I wouldn't let Bill Munro impose on me. He's lazy, and what they call in Glasgow a chancer. Into the bargain he's a rotten cook. As you'll soon find out."

"He doesn't seem very happy. He told me he's thinking of joining the army."

"He's been saying that from the day he came. He doesn't like the country. He thinks it's full of sinister presences. But one thing we don't do is pry into one another's motives. By the way, that other new man Saidler was making fun of you behind your back. Something about a girl with fair hair and a fiddle."

"How long have you been here yourself?"

"Twenty-six days. It's felt like 26 weeks. I'm thinking of bringing Mary and Sue to live in Port Fada. We could rent a couple of rooms. It would mean cycling over that road every day, but it would be better than staying here. I hope I'm not discouraging you, Hamilton. You seem to have the right temperament for this kind of life."

"Munro was saying something about tyres being let down and valves stolen in Port Fada."

"There *is* a bit of bad feeling, but Mary wouldn't be scared off by that. She's far more stout-hearted than I am. I should be just able to afford it. Glasgow Corporation has decided to treat me as if I was in the army. So they're making up my pay. I got word yesterday. It's a load off my mind."

Gavin nodded and smiled but he felt that in McMillan's place he would not have wanted that concession. It would have made him inescapably beholden.

"See you at dinner," said McMillan, and went off to write a letter home.

Munro announced that dinner was ready by banging a spoon against an enamel plate. All the plates were enamel, with black bruises. Most of the ten young men sitting round the table still wore their working clothes. Good clothes could soon be soiled or torn there.

Holding the big black sooty pot in one hand, Munro ladled out soup with the other. He looked cross. There were smudges of soot on his arms and face.

Being cook, Gavin saw, was no picnic.

The soup looked appetising enough. He took a spoonful and almost spat it out again. It was saltier than sea water.

Others were not so well-mannered. They spat it out, into their plates or on to the floor.

There were groans and sour faces.

"What the hell are you all looking so tragic for?" cried Munro. "It's a bit salty but it's not poison, for Christ's sake."

"You promised me, Bill," said Shearer meekly, "that you wouldn't take Our Lord's name in vain, in my hearing."

"Fuck Our Lord," mumbled Munro. Perhaps he meant to say it under his breath, but everybody heard it.

Gavin could have told who the Christians were from their shocked, hurt, or angry faces. They were, in addition to Shearer: Renwick, tall, with smooth pink cheeks and small tight mouth; Cunningham, prematurely bald, with small black moustache that he often fingered; and Robb, a big-mouthed ambiguous smiler with strange pale eyes.

The rest, humanists or moralists or Socialists, were more concerned about the wasted soup than the blasphemy.

Saidler, the cynic, was the only one amused.

"Well, if Your Lord was any good," muttered Munro, "there wouldn't be any war, would there? We wouldn't be here, would we? I wouldn't have salted the bloody soup twice, would I?"

"For God's sake," said McMillan, "let's be sensible. Sorry. Let's be sensible. Can anything be done to save the soup? There's a whole potful."

"It took me hours to make," muttered Munro.

"I've heard that if you boil some potatoes in it they absorb the salt," said McMaster, with his usual cheerful grin.

McMillan had told Gavin that McMaster was an atheist. Yet he seemed the most buoyant and optimistic man there. He reminded Gavin of McIntyre.

"I tried that," snarled Munro.

"What about couping out half and replacing it with boiling water?" asked red-haired McNaughton.

McNaughton's father, McMillan had said, was a Glasgow councillor. At the tribunal McNaughton had been vouched for by an ILP Member of Parliament.

"I don't know what you're all on about," muttered Morrison, who was fat. "Sure it's salty, but I like salty things. I lose a lot of sweat, so it's got to be replaced, the salt I mean."

Saidler, as one newcomer to another, winked at Gavin, as if to say: What a petty-minded lot we've landed among. He was enjoying the petty mindedness, though.

"I'm hungry," said Renwick, peevishly. "I suggest, Bill, that you serve the rest of the dinner. That's to say, if it's fit to be served."

Munro worried them all by enduring the gibe humbly.

"Pass your plates," was all he said.

The same plates were used for the second course.

Gavin because he offered, and McMillan because he was nearest to the scullery, took the plates there and emptied them into the sink.

"What we need," muttered McMillan, "is a sergeant-major."

The potatoes were soggy, the stew gristly, and the peas hard. No one complained, though some sighed or made faces.

"Did McAndrew ask you two if you played football?" asked McMaster, cheerfully. "He's daft about football. Odd, considering he was born on the island of Eigg. The wee ham from Eigg, Bill calls him."

"I told him I used to be very good at snakes-and-ladders," said Saidler.

"I said I would play on Saturday," said Gavin.

Munro blew out his breath incredulously. "No offence meant, Hamilton, but you look more like a trombone player for the Salvation Army than a football player."

"That's enough, Bill," said McMillan.

"The point about Hamilton," said Saidler, "is that he's a great obliger. Haven't you noticed? Except where women are concerned, of course."

"The Port Fada team are a tough lot," warned Munro. "Fishermen, blacksmiths, ploughmen."

"Big Dunky was saying they're not pleased with McAndrew for having conchies in his team," said McNaughton. "They're going to knock us about a bit, to test our principles."

It appeared that Munro, McNaughton and McMaster were also playing on Saturday.

"Big Dunky's a leg-puller," said McMillan.

"I intend to make it clear," said Munro, "that if I'm kicked I'm kicking back, with interest."

"Not a very good advertisement for our cause, Bill," said McMillan, with a grin.

"What cause is that, Donald? We can't even agree whether soup's salty or not."

There were groans and laughter.

"No joking," went on Munro. "We're all here for different reasons. You don't know my reasons and I don't know yours. We don't want to know. You can't call that a common cause. We're all going to stick it out till the war's over. Then we'll go back to where we left off. We just don't believe that Hitler could win and one day storm-troopers will come marching up to Creag, with sub-machine guns."

There was more laughter. Yet it seemed to Gavin that whether facetiously or not Munro was reminding them of their most terrible indebtedness, impossible to evade or cancel out. Leaving aside such considerations as that it had been the British who had declared war, and that the Germans would probably agree to a negotiated peace, the fact remained that if the Germans won they would show little mercy to pacifists, if those pacifists, as they should, refused to obey their orders. Therefore, as Munro had implied, they were depending on the protection of the armed forces which they had refused to join.

"What about the pudding, Bill?" asked Morrison, who had had two helpings of the soggy potatoes.

Munro began to dish out the singed semolina and tough prunes.

"What's of more immediate importance," said McNaughton, "is what we're going to do about walking time."

"I object to discussing such matters at table," said Renwick, angrily.

"You mean, you just object to discussing such matters?"

"That's right."

"How typical. Here's an opportunity to help your fellow workers and you don't even want to talk about it. A typical Christian attitude."

"What's this big issue?" asked Saidler, with another wink at Gavin.

McNaughton explained earnestly. "Walking time is allowed in other forests, but not here. Here you're expected to be at the job no matter where it is on the hill, at eight o'clock or in winter half-past. That means sometimes nearly an hour's walk before you start work; in the winter in the dark. In other forests you've started work as soon as you've left the nearest point on the road.

We had it out with McAndrew. So he said: 'All right, if that's what you want be at my office every day at starting-time'."

"Isn't his office the nearest point on the road?" asked Saidler.

"I suppose it is, most of the time. But, you see, it's far more convenient and sensible for us here in Creag to make straight for the job, as we're already well into the hill. So now we're faced with the hike down to the road-end and then the cycle run along to the hut; and the same in reverse at five."

"But the locals have benefited," said McMillan. "So would I if I was living in Port Fada."

"Sure, but we shouldn't let him get away with what's just a piece of spite. I propose that we all leave Creag at eight."

"I second that," said Saidler. "I'm all for another half hour in bed."

"I may as well tell you," said Renwick, "that George, David, and I have decided that we shall be at the hut at eight o'clock."

"What do you say, Donald?" asked McNaughton.

"Well, John," replied McMillan, "I think we should go a step at a time. McAndrew's given in as far as the locals are concerned. He doesn't want to lose face altogether. Let's wait a week or two and then try again."

"I don't have to ask you, Martin."

Shearer smiled benignly. "Mr McAndrew is our employer, John. He has given us an order. It is our duty to obey."

"What difference does half an hour make anyway?" muttered Morrison.

"Hamilton's said nothing," said Saidler.

"Don't heed him, Hamilton," said McMillan. "You're quite right saying nothing. You don't know what's involved."

Gavin had not intended to declare his position so soon. But, except for Sadler perhaps, he was the oldest man there. Perhaps they had a right to his opinion.

"I would rather put up with any inconvenience, hardship, or injustice than ask favours."

They stared at him in astonishment and suspicion.

"What's that supposed to mean?" asked Munro.

"I intend to be beholden as little as possible."

"Beholden?" muttered Morrison, as if he didn't know its meaning.

Were they, thought Gavin, being deliberately stupid?

"Beholden to who?" asked McNaughton. "You don't mean McAndrew, do you?"

"I mean everyone who supports the war."

They looked indignant now as well as puzzled.

"Has some old lady been telling you you shouldn't eat the food our brave sailors bring in?" asked Munro. "For Christ's sake, there's an old lady like that in every street."

"My old man's all for the war," said Morrison. "He admires Churchill."

"So does mine," said McMillan. "And I've got two brothers-in-law in the army."

"Aren't you forgetting, Hamilton," said McNaughton, "that there must be many thousands of people who support the war because they feel they have to, not because they want to?"

"Why should we regard people as our enemies just because we disagree with them?" asked Renwick. "Some of us are here, Hamilton, not because we hate our countrymen but for the very opposite reason?"

Munro pretended to be about to faint. "You mean, Dave, because you love them? You should have seen your face when you tasted the soup. You'd have cheerfully cut my throat."

"Don't talk rubbish."

"Let's be fair to Hamilton," said McMaster. "Surely we all agree that we don't want favours?"

"Wait till a rat lands on his back when he's sitting on the can," said Munro. "He'll not think anybody's doing him favours then."

"Surely as a Christian, Gavin," said Shearer, in his gentle way, "you should not be too proud to be beholden, even to your enemies?"

Saidler laughed. "Are you going to go about naked, Hamilton, eating grass and living in a cave? Surely that's the logical conclusion."

Except that, thought Gavin, I shall give some return, which will cancel out some of my indebtedness. How I face up to what's left is my business.

"Well, here's the char," said Munro, dumping a large earthenware teapot on the table. "Pour for yourselves. It's probably stewed."

11

GAVIN'S BED HAD a leg mended with wire, and musty blankets. It stood in a corner under a big damp patch on the low sloping ceiling. He had to crouch to avoid hitting his head. There were no chairs or furniture. He had to keep his clothes in his suitcase. There were nails on the wall for hanging up jackets.

McMillan was one of his roommates. The other was Shearer, who had not been invited by the three orthodox Christians, Renwick, Cunningham, and Robb, to share their room or their Bible readings. So McMillan scornfully explained. He himself was an agnostic, thank God.

There were two other rooms upstairs. One was occupied by McNaughton, McMaster, and Munro. McNaughton and McMaster were members of the ILP, Socialists with ideals but never any power. Munro was an Anarchist with impulses instead of principles. In the third room were Morrison and Saidler. Saidler would soon find, remarked McMillan with satisfaction, that he might have a steadier bed and more room than Gavin but not more restful sleep. Morrison's snores were nerve-racking. They disturbed even the rats. McMillan said he had never heard Morrison express an opinion about anything except food.

The rats were no joke. They took over the house at night. If he ever needed to relieve himself at dead of night, McMillan warned Gavin, he would have to go down the stairs and through the kitchen with great care for they were like mine-fields with baited traps and lumps of poisoned bread. Poor Shearer was terrified of rats. Fear of them added to the dampness of the house made him need to piddle frequently. To avoid perilous trips downstairs he had provided himself with two personal jam-jars. For a joke Munro one night had filled them three-quarters with water. At two in the morning Shearer had been faced with the terrible choice of contenting himself with only partial relief or going downstairs among the squealing, scurrying, dying rats. Every night afterwards he had guarded his jam-jars as zealously as he did his Bible and pamphlets.

"So you can see why I'm so keen to have Mary come to live in Port Fada," said McMillan, gloomily.

He and Gavin were lying in their beds. Shearer had gone outside for his last visit to the byre, armed with cudgel and torch.

"He keeps thumping the can with his stick. I expect he keeps praying too. Jonathan Swift said that man is never more thoughtful than when upon the stool. You'd need nerves of steel to do any thinking there. When Bill Munro spoke about a rat jumping on your back he meant it. One jumped on his."

He paused to bang on the wall with a boot to chase off rats that could be heard scraping behind it. From other rooms similar bangs could be heard now and then.

"I don't want to pry, Hamilton," he said, "but did you mean what you said about not being beholden?"

"Yes."

"I'm surprised. You look so—well, unfanatical. That's what Bill meant about that trombone player in the Salvation Army. He's a cheeky so-and-so but he's shrewd. As Tom McMaster said we're all bound to feel that we don't want favours. Not, mind you, that we're given many. There's my allowance from the corporation, true. But look at this room. Look at the whole house. Wait, too, till you've done some bottoming of muddy smelly drains in pouring rain. Consider what this place will be like in winter. No, I wouldn't say we're being favoured."

"I don't really mean favours. I mean any benefit at all that comes from those engaged in the war."

"So Saidler was justified. I thought he was being nastily sarcastic."

"He was justified."

"You *are* a fanatic, Hamilton. Is it a matter of pride?"

"A matter of peace."

"Peace?"

"Peace of mind."

"Nobody with a conscience is ever going to have that, not even in peacetime."

"I would like to be in a position where I would be able to say that whatever evil things are done in this war I am not responsible."

"We'd all like to be in that position. But it isn't possible. Perhaps it's not even desirable. Isn't it good for our souls to accept some of the blame? We're all involved whether we want to be or not. As Saidler said you'd have to eat grass and live in a cave. Even then you'd find yourself thinking of people you once knew, you'd remember books you'd read, you'd hum songs, you'd use your mind that was trained by other people. You simply can't escape involvement, Hamilton. I'm not going to pry, God help me, but you must have somebody you're fond of or who's fond of

133

you. He or she's bound to be touched by the war somehow. It can't be done, Hamilton. Don't ever try it."

They were interrupted by Shearer who came in shivering.

"My torch went out," he said. "I think the battery's done."

"Didn't you light the lamp that's there?" asked McMillan.

"It makes such eerie shadows, Donald."

He began to make preparations for bed. These included a prudish removal of his clothes and donning of striped flannel pyjamas, a surreptitious disposing of his jam-jars in a convenient but discreet place, a long read of his Bible in bed, an equally long silent prayer kneeling on the floor with his feet bare.

His goodnights were heartfelt. Then he got stiffly into bed and pulled the blankets over his face.

McMillan read for a while by candlelight. His book was a history of the Crusades. It was one of his favourites, he said. He read it often.

"Did you know, Hamilton," he whispered, after Shearer was asleep, "that once when the Christians were besieging the Moslems in Jerusalem they promised them safe-conduct if they surrendered? Well, they did surrender and were slaughtered, every man, woman, and child. Some time later it was the turn of the Christians to be besieged and given a promise of safety. The difference was that this time the Saracen leader, Saladin, made sure the promise was kept."

Evidently that was something he liked to confront present-day Christians with.

"I mentioned it to Shearer," he said. "I shouldn't have. It was like being cruel to a child. But he gave me an answer all right, just like a child. He said that Saladin, although he didn't know it, was really being a Christian when he showed mercy, and the Christians, when they were treacherous and cruel, were being heathens. Everything good is Christian, everything bad isn't. It makes him invulnerable. And insufferable."

McMillan read in silence for a few minutes.

"Human history's like an immense tidal wave of blood," he remarked, gloomily. "Pacifists are Canutes, Hamilton."

Suddenly Shearer began to mumble in his sleep. Gavin thought he could make out the name "Maggie".

"Yes, it's 'Maggie,'" whispered McMillan. "He often talks about her, in his sleep; never when he's awake. I wouldn't think a girl friend. Maybe a sister. Or a bitch he had when he was a boy."

"You shouldn't have done it, Maggie," sobbed Shearer.

"With respect, Hamilton," said McMillan, "I think he's the only genuine pacifist among us. If he saw Maggie, whoever she is, being raped he'd kneel and pray for her rapists. It wouldn't enter his head to do anything else. Speaking for myself if the alternatives were shouldering a gun or being shot out of hand I'm afraid I'd shoulder the gun. Shearer wouldn't. He'd thank the fellow that put the blindfold on. He'd assure the firing squad that Christ would forgive them. I've never heard him say an unkind word about anybody.

"The terrible thing is, nobody can stand him. Renwick and company because they think he makes Christianity look stupid. McNaughton and McMaster because he says Socialism's a sinful doctrine. Bill Munro because he's always telling him not to blaspheme. McAndrew the forester would like to get rid of him. He's so clumsy he's useless. If there's a sheugh he's sure to step right into it. The locals think he's a clown."

"Poor Shearer."

"Yes, but how can you sympathize with somebody who's so damned happy all the time? Except for the rats, of course. The only time I've seen him stuck for an answer was when Bill Munro asked him why the Lord made rats."

He shut his book and then blew out his candle.

"By the way, you didn't know Saidler before you came here, did you?" he asked.

"No."

"Why then does he dislike you so much?"

"Does he?"

"I was watching his face when he looked at you. It was full of hate."

"Surely not."

"Maybe I'm exaggerating. But he certainly doesn't like you. Good-night, Gavin. It is Gavin, isn't it?"

"Yes. Good-night, Donald."

Long after the smell of candle grease had given way to the smells of damp, sweaty socks, muddy boots, and wood smoke, and as the rats' squealing behind the walls and downstairs grew shriller, and Morrison's snores next door became louder and Saidler's grumbles grew more desperate, Gavin lay awake for some time thinking about that moral position, imaginable if not possible, where a man had cleansed himself of responsibility for all the evils of the war and so had acquired the right to pity not only those who had suffered from them but also those who had perpetrated them.

It would be like being up for smout, he thought. Smiling, he remembered McIntyre.

12

H E W A S A W A K E N E D by noises from Shearer's corner. Shearer was getting dressed by dim torchlight. Gavin peered at his watch. It was just a quarter to six. The arrangement was that Munro would wake them at half-past.

McMillan was still asleep. The rats were quiet. Outside birds were singing. The sky seemed bright.

"Aren't you a bit early?" he whispered.

Shearer crept close. "It's all right, Gavin. I've got no bike, you see. So I have to walk along the road."

Last night Morrison had offered Saidler a lift on his back-step. No one had mentioned that Shearer had no bicycle.

"I'll give you a lift," he said.

"Thank you, Gavin. But it's all right. I would just as soon walk. It's a fine dry morning."

"It seems a pity you have to walk all that way by yourself."

"I'm never by myself, Gavin. I just choose one of the prophets to accompany me. Today it will be Ezra."

"Ezra?"

"Yes. Do you remember? 'Ezra had prepared his heart to seek the law of the Lord, and to do it, and to teach in Israel statutes and judgments.' "

"I see."

"Goodbye for now, Gavin. I'll see you at the hut."

He went out and down the stairs very quietly and carefully so as not to disturb the others, or spill his jam-jars.

Why was it, Gavin wondered, that poor Shearer's consideration irritated more than Munro's lack of it? Goodwill seemed to come to him so easily that most people found it suspect. His big clammy hands too couldn't stop making gestures of benediction.

Downstairs Munro swore at the smoky stove, banged plates down on the table, and whistled "Tipperary", with the result that everyone was awake before he went to the kitchen door and bellowed, "Last down's scabby bum!"

Taking no chances, he had put just a sprinkling of salt into the porridge; also it was lumpy and half-cooked. The scrambled eggs were leathery, the tea too strong. Breakfast was eaten in bleary resignation.

It was the cook's duty to set the traps last thing at night and remove them in the morning. As they ate Munro gave them the count for the night: one corpse and one dying rat in traps, and quite a lot of poisoned bread taken. Somewhere in dark corners, he said with satisfaction, guts were being coughed up.

Nobody spoke up for rats.

"Is it necessary to poison them?" asked Gavin.

"They're fly," said McMillan. "They very quickly get suspicious of traps. We catch only the fools."

"What sort of a day is it going to be, Bill?" asked McNaughton.

"Just grand for slagging."

"Well, that'll be an improvement on bottoming," said McMaster.

"Except for the carrying of those bags. They weigh a hundredweight and a quarter each."

"He can't ask us to carry them," said Renwick, indignantly.

"Why can't a lorry or a cart take them to where it is they've to go?" asked Gavin.

"No road," said McMillan. "Just a path. Steep in places, too. And two burns to cross."

"Anybody like to change places with me?" asked Munro. "Wee Mac wouldn't mind. What about you, Donald? Look at the letters you could write home. You, Sammy? Look at the attention you could give to your moustache. You, Alistair? You could make yourself a rat stew. I'll show you where I dumped the bodies. You, Hamilton? No need to be beholden to anybody."

"He'd never admit it," whispered McMillan, "but he hates the loneliness. Creag's a very lonely place if you're here by yourself: especially if you were brought up in a crowded tenement."

Saidler, it was noticed, was very quiet. He kept yawning. He hadn't slept well. He ate very little.

He hadn't brought suitable outdoor clothing. Where the others wore a selection of thigh-length waders, Wellingtons, heavy boots, leggings, waterproof trousers, coats of oilskin, rubber, or waterproof cloth, sou'westers, balaclavas, and tweed caps, he had a hat, raincoat, and shoes suitable for a walk along a city street. If it rained, he was warned, he would be soaked to the skin inside half an hour. Even if it kept dry all day, which didn't happen all that often, and if they were sent to slag he'd find his feet painful, for the ground was rough with many tussocks and open drains. If they were sent back to the bottoming he'd be covered in peaty muck.

He just grunted.

It was pleasant walking down the track to the gate. The sun was already shining on high hills across the loch. There was blue sky. The air was fresh, silky, perfumed, and melodious. Everywhere birds were singing.

"When it's like this," said McMillan, "it's almost worth it. This is one favour you can accept, Hamilton."

Gavin smiled. "Yes."

"On a morning like this I feel that I would rather spend my life here planting trees and looking after them than teaching kids history."

"If the pay was as good, Donald," said McNaughton.

"And the hours as short," said McMaster.

"And the holidays as long," said McMillan himself, with a grin.

They went through the gate with the yellow paint.

"Shearer wanted to scrub it off," said McMillan. "We wouldn't let him."

"Why not?" asked Gavin.

They were now walking alongside the loch that was pink with morning.

"I think we're hoping that when we come down one morning we'll find that the locals have scrubbed it off. After we've proved to them that it's a stupid insult."

"And how can we do that?"

"Bit by bit. You'll contribute on Saturday. I think you'll find Bill was right. The Port Fada lot will try to put you through the mill. I hope you can look after yourself on a football field."

They got their bicycles out of Mrs McSporran's shed as quietly as if they were stealing them.

"You'll like old Granny," said McMillan, as they cycled side by side. "We pay her a bob each per week. Her grandson Neil lived with her. He was called up a few weeks ago. When we come back from week-ends home she always asks how our wives are, (if we've got any) and our mothers. I know you're not married,

Hamilton. You told me that in Glasgow. Have you got a girl friend?"

"No."

"Ever have?"

"Yes." It was not Julia he thought of, but Rachel.

They saw Shearer ahead, clumping along in his Wellingtons and swinging his arms.

"Why do I find it so hard to like him?" muttered McMillan. He rode on when Gavin stopped.

"Jump up on to my back-step," said Gavin.

There was that smile of instant goodwill. "Thank you, Gavin. I'm not very good at jumping up on to back-steps. I never mastered it as a boy. It's only another half mile. I'll be there in good time."

13

OF THE EIGHT men gathered at the hut waiting for the day's orders only one shouted a greeting "Good morning, boys" to the Creag contingent. This was Big Dunky, a tall man with a gaunt droll face and a slow raucous voice. He wore his jacket open and his cap on sideways. He had bad teeth and was smoking a clay pipe.

Gavin was reminded of the woman with the big nose in the train who had wished to cheer him up. Her humanity had seemed to him beautiful. So now did Big Dunky's.

Among the five women present were the two newcomers Ann McTaggart and Helen Lyall. Ann came running over to him, looking very handsome in khaki breeches, red shirt, and grey cardigan, with a red silken scarf over her fair hair.

"I brought your fiddle," she said. "It's in Mr McAndrew's hut. He said you could pick it up at five."

"Thanks."

"This weather's more like it."

"Yes."

The smiles she gave the other Creag men were friendly, but the one she kept giving Gavin was noticeably more eager.

She did not, though, strike him as stupid or brazen: reckless rather, in a way that indicated generosity of spirit and courageous disregard of how other people judged her and her affections.

If he were to fall in love with her Ardmore could become the most pleasant and hopeful place on earth. He might even discover a way of testifying against war as valid as and perhaps more fruitful than his intended policy of not being beholden.

"I see now what Saidler was talking about," said McMillan, when she had gone back to the other women.

"I'd let her look after my fiddle any day," remarked Morrison.

Immediately, remembering that he was among Christians, he was contrite. "I mean, she's very nice."

Angus the foreman, a healthy-looking pink-faced man with a snuffle of shyness, came out of the hut and, looking at no one, announced the day's orders.

"You, Archie, back to the fence. Jean, you and the girls back to the bracken-cutting."

Led by Archie their ganger the local men made off up a path past the big shed. Within seconds they were out of sight behind birches and scrub oaks. It would take them almost an hour, said McNaughton, to reach the fence.

The women followed. Ann McTaggart was the only one to turn and wave.

"Come on, Angus," cried McNaughton, "why don't we get a shot at an interesting job like making a fence?"

"Or an easy one like cutting bracken?" added Renwick.

Big Dunky took out his pipe and spat. "We're for the slag, boys," he said, with a grin. "It's an easy chob once you've got the slag there. My wee lassie aged nine could do it."

"Yes," said Renwick, bitterly, "once the slag's there. I suppose we've to carry it?"

Angus called to them from the shed.

The bags of slag were heaped on top of one another. Renwick quickly calculated that there were at least 60. They represented several back-breaking journeys. The place to which they had to be carried was, according to McNaughton, more than a mile away, and the path went up and down hills, across burns, through woods, and over bogs.

Still with the pipe between his teeth, Big Dunky seized a bag and heaved it up on to his shoulder. He patted it as if it was his nine-year-old daughter's bottom. "It's not like coal, you see. It lies snug."

"Apart from the weight," said Cunningham, "it's messy. We should have overalls."

"It's just dust," said Angus. "The wind will blow it off."

"Some wind," said McMillan. "Right, Dunky, let me try."

He braced himself while Dunky, helped by Angus, transferred the heavy bag on to his shoulders. He almost collapsed. He grunted and broke wind.

He didn't find it funny. "If McAndrew thinks I'm going to carry this all the way up to Glen A'Ghille he's got another think coming."

"Two men to a bag," said Angus, hastily.

McMillan let the bag fall in a cloud of grey dust.

"That's still carrying it halfway up Glen A'Ghille," he said.

"Surely any grown man worth his salt can carry half a hundredweight," said Angus.

"Your arithmetic's as bad as your logic, Angus. Half of a hundredweight and a quarter is not half a hundredweight; and it's the whole hundredweight and a quarter that we're being asked to carry."

"Why don't we carry half a bagful each?" suggested McNaughton. "It would mean the same amount being carried."

"Not enough bags," mumbled Angus. "And it would waste a lot of time."

"Aren't there any hurdles, the things you carry rolls of barbed wire on?" asked Morrison.

"That's a good idea," said McMaster. "We could carry the bags as if they were dead bodies. Hamilton could get his fiddle and play solemn music."

"Dunky will tell you," said Angus, "that the manly way to carry slag is on your back, across your shoulders."

"It depends on how strong your legs are," said McNaughton. "None of us is used to carrying heavy weights." He addressed the Creag men. "Well, what do you say? Do we go to McAndrew and tell him it's half a bag or nothing?"

"Why do you always have to turn everything into an agitation?" cried Renwick. "Come on, James, give me a hand."

He had chosen Robb as his partner in preference to Cunningham because he was stronger.

Angus had to help Robb to heave the bag up on to Renwick's shoulders.

Renwick staggered off, desperate not to waste a second. Robb, carrying his own piece-bag and Renwick's, followed behind, like a squire attending his knight, said McMillan.

Dunky too set off, carrying his bag happily, as if, murmured McMaster, it was his nine-year-old daughter.

Gavin took Angus aside. "I don't think Martin Shearer's strong enough to carry one of these bags," he said.

"It's part of the job, Hamilton."

Was there, wondered Gavin, a difference between asking a favour for yourself and asking it for someone else?

"To tell you the truth," muttered Angus, "I did mention Shearer to Mr McAndrew. That was what he said: 'It's part of the job'."

"What about you and me then, Hamilton?" asked McMillan.

"Sorry. I'm sharing with Martin."

"Oh. Suit yourself. What about you then, Andy?"

"All right," said Cunningham.

McNaughton paired with McMaster. Morrison, left with Saidler as partner, wasn't too pleased: he was afraid he'd have to do more than his share of the carrying. "It could have been worse," he muttered, staring at Shearer.

When they were all gone Angus helped to load the bag on to Gavin's back. He whispered into Gavin's ear: "If I'm about, Hamilton, I'll maybe give you a hand. Though I can't promise."

Shearer took his rôle as partner very conscientiously. He scampered on in front, breaking off twigs that he thought were in the way, lifting stones and sticks off the path, and shouting warnings about muddy or slippery patches. He was more of a hindrance than a help.

They soon passed Renwick flat on his back, panting painfully, as if he was dying. The bag of slag lay beside him like a beast he had just strangled after a fearful struggle. Robb stood with his foot on it, smiling.

As Gavin and Shearer passed Renwick sat up with grey face and bloodshot eyes.

"What do you think you're doing, Hamilton?" he yelled. "Do you want McAndrew to make us all carry a bag each? Shearer ought to do his share."

"He's right, Gavin," said Shearer, joyously. "It's my turn."

"In a few minutes," said Gavin. "Ten minutes at a stretch." He had a watch and Shearer hadn't.

"Yes, that's a fair arrangement."

Next they passed Saidler creeping along, with the bag perched not too safely on his back. In his smooth-soled shoes he kept slipping. He tried by swinging round to hit Gavin's bag with his but missed and knocked himself off balance, so that he fell with the bag on top of him.

"To hell with you, Hamilton," he shouted.

Morrison was amused. He held out his hands as if to say that though he was sharing a bag with Saidler he wasn't responsible for anything Saidler said.

"Poor Saidler," said Shearer. "He doesn't realize that the way to make any burden light as air is to pray to the Lord for strength, and to make it heavier than iron is to displease the Lord by using foul language."

Ten minutes later they came upon McMillan, Cunningham, McNaughton, and McMaster resting beside a spring.

"Carrying a weight that's too heavy is bloody degrading," said McMillan. "It makes you feel like a coolie."

"And it's dangerous," said Cunningham, who had hurt his neck.

"It's our own fault," said McNaughton. "We should have insisted on half bagfuls. I wonder if McAndrew thinks this is good training for the game on Saturday."

"You've carried that all the way from the shed by yourself, Hamilton, haven't you?" asked McMaster.

Shearer answered, cheerfully. "Yes. It was Gavin's turn the first ten minutes."

"Ten minutes! More like twenty-five."

"Is that right, Hamilton?" asked McMillan, as aggrieved as Renwick. "Have you carried it yourself to here?"

Gavin had hoped that they would understand he had done it for Shearer's sake, not McAndrew's.

His legs felt weak and his neck ached. McNaughton was right, they ought not to be asked to carry such a weight, along a rough hill path. Yet McAndrew who had given the order had not struck him as vindictive. Perhaps he felt that, as part of the process, like the tribunal, it was his duty to ensure that whether or not conscientious objection to war involved moral agonies it ought not to be physically a soft option.

McMillan had been eyeing Shearer and noticing how very thin he was. Now he got to his feet. "I'm sorry, Hamilton," he muttered. With Cunningham's help he got his bag on to his back and then, shakily, went on his way, with Cunningham following, wry-necked.

"Gavin deserves a rest," said Shearer. "Would you John and you Tom please help me to get this bag on to my shoulders?"

McNaughton and McMaster looked doubtful.

"Should we?" muttered McNaughton.

"Are you sure it'll be all right, Shearer?" asked McMaster.

"Of course. I have a source of strength, you know. Right. Up she goes." With his long legs wide apart he stooped, ready to receive the burden. His eyes were closed in prayer.

Gavin looked on.

As considerately as they could they laid the load on Shearer's back.

Immediately he sagged. His legs buckled, his face turned pale, his hands grabbed at sunlight for support. He kept smiling. With his head as low as his knees, he began to totter along the path.

"Do you think he'll be all right, Hamilton?" asked McNaughton.

"I don't know."

They watched anxiously. They knew that what Shearer was trying to do was beyond his strength. Every step he took was an act of faith, but it could well do him serious harm. He had prayed for strength, and if he were to collapse too soon he would be showing that his prayer had not been heeded. To save the Lord's face he had to keep on, for another tottering yard, and then another, more and more slowly.

"He'll kill himself," muttered McMaster.

"Look out, Shearer," shouted McNaughton, and rushed forward.

He was too late. Unable to lift his foot from the ground one single step more, but refusing to let go the bag, Shearer was dragged by its weight off the path. Down a steep bank he and the bag did not just slither but tumbled spectacularly.

Bill Munro would have laughed, thought McMaster, unable himself to stop smiling.

Then he ran forward to help McNaughton.

They found Shearer on his back, with a leg twisted under him. His nose was bleeding. His face was pale and his eyes closed. He looked dead.

"Look how skinny his neck is," muttered McNaughton.

With great care they straightened the leg.

Shearer opened his eyes and smiled. "I must have tripped."

"I don't think there's anything broken," said McMaster. "Do you feel any pain, Shearer, in your back and legs?"

"Just a bit dizzy, that's all, thank you, Tom."

"You would never have passed any army medical," said Mc-Naughton. "You should have let them call you up."

"That would have been acknowledging their right over my soul, John," he whispered.

"Well, you're not physically fit for this kind of work."

"Please don't tell Mr McAndrew. I think he wants to get rid of me."

"For your own sake, Shearer."

"He's entitled to a fair day's work," said Shearer. "I'd be all right if I didn't get heavy weights to carry. I've never been any good at carrying heavy weights."

On the path above arrived Saidler, carrying, and Morrison, squiring. The former therefore was surly and unsympathetic, and the latter interested and solicitous, when they saw below them Shearer on his back in bracken, with McNaughton and McMaster crouching over him, and Hamilton looking on.

"What happened?" asked Morrison.

"Shearer fell," replied McNaughton.

Morrison waited till Saidler had moved on a few yards. "So did Saidler," he said, hiding his mouth with his hand. "Three times. He says he's wracked his spine. He says the skin's rubbed off his neck. He says he's going to sue the Forestry Commission."

"Where are Renwick and Robb?"

"Back at the spring. They've given up. Their bag's burst and Renwick's broken his flask. He's talking about going down to McAndrew and lodging an official complaint, whatever that is."

"Why don't we all go?" asked McNaughton. "Alistair, shout on Saidler to come back."

"He'll not do that. He's been counting the inches."

"He can drop the bloody thing, can't he?"

"Dropping it can be as bad as lifting it. It was dropping it wracked his spine, he says. Saidler!" he roared. "Drop it and come back. We're having a meeting."

"What about McMillan and Cunningham?" asked McMaster. "We'd better have them too."

"Where are they?" asked Morrison.

"Ahead somewhere. Would you run on and tell them, Alistair. They can't be far."

"Right."

"We'll meet at the spring. If you happen to see Big Dunky tell him."

"Tell him what?"

"That we're having a meeting to decide what to do."

"Right." Much amused, Morrison made off.

As they helped Shearer to his feet he said: "I can't take part in a political meeting. I'm sorry. It's against my religious principles, you see."

"Yes, I see." McNaughton made his eyes go skelly.

McMaster grinned.

Together they cleeked Shearer back to the spring and sat him down carefully on the grass.

"Would you like a drink?" asked McNaughton.

"Thank you, John. Yes, I would."

Gavin looked on and said nothing. The others attributed it to exhaustion.

Seated beside their burst bag of slag, Renwick and Robb scowled at their workmates. It wasn't Shearer's plight that vexed them, but their own. They were covered in slag. A lot of it had slid down Renwick's neck. He rattled his thermos flask to show that it was broken. Robb, his face turned grey with slag and strain, forgot to smile.

"I hope you're not going to make political propaganda out of this," said Renwick. "All that's needed is for us to explain to Mr McAndrew, reasonably, that these bags are too heavy."

"Right. But suppose he doesn't agree?" said McNaughton. "Suppose he tells us that Big Dunky's nine-year-old daughter could lift one? Suppose he shows us that a wee man like him can carry one, and therefore a big man like you should be able."

"He couldn't."

"Don't you believe it. To prove us wrong he'd burst his guts."

"It's one thing lifting a bag, it's a different thing altogether carrying it for a mile and a half, over hills."

"Suppose he did that too? Not walking either, but running. Big Dunky's done it, or is doing it. We could all do it ourselves. Yes, even Shearer. It'd half kill us, it'd take hours, we'd finish on our hands and knees, we'd wrack our spines and rick our necks, but we could do it. The point is, ought we to be asked to do it?"

"You've started your council of war before the others are here," said McMaster.

"I object to that expression," said Renwick. "We're simply having a discussion. I notice Hamilton's saying nothing."

"We'd better all say nothing until everybody's here," said McNaughton.

They waited in silence.

Renwick, looking very sorry for himself, threw away his sandwiches. They were covered with slag and soaked in tea.

Shearer read the Bible that he always brought to work with him.

Gavin thought of Dunky steadfastly and without self-pity carrying his burden to the appointed place. In enduring hardship and even injustice there could be dignity; in grumbling there could be none. Their great cause was dwindled to this childish squabble about carrying something too heavy.

Soon Saidler, Morrison, McMillan, and Cunningham came along the path towards them.

There was no sign of Dunky. He was keeping out of the way. So was Angus.

McMillan put himself in a Napoleonic posture. "I ought to warn you," he said, "that councils of war seldom produce any fighting."

Renwick forestalled McNaughton by speaking first. "I propose that we go down to Mr McAndrew and tell him in a reasonable manner that we have tried and found the bags too heavy. We're willing to carry half a bag. That would mean the same amount of slag being carried."

"Didn't Angus say there weren't any bags to spare," asked Morrison, "and that a lot of slag would be wasted?"

"That was rubbish," said Renwick.

"All right," said McNaughton. "If he agrees to that, fine. But what if he doesn't? What if he decides to make an issue of it?"

"If you adopt that attitude," said Renwick," he *will* make an issue of it."

"Do you want us to go down on our knees and beg him, for God's sake?"

"You don't believe in God, so leave Him out of it. I just want us to be reasonable."

"Like Mr Chamberlain?" said McMaster, grinning.

"Look," said McMillan, "I didn't mean to say anything, but here's what I suggest. Take these bags up to where the slag's to be used. When they're empty we'll take them back down with us. McAndrew won't be able to say there aren't any bags to spare. We'll just divide a bag between two of us."

Renwick and McNaughton were united in rejecting this suggestion.

"I refuse to carry a whole bag another inch," said Renwick.

"Shearer couldn't carry one if he wanted to," said McNaughton. "He's already had one nasty fall. It's up to us to stand together for his sake at least."

Shearer looked up from his Bible. "Please. I do not want there to be any trouble on my account. I shall carry the bag. I shall be given strength."

McNaughton, the atheist, looked up at the sky and groaned.

"What you mean," said Morrison, "is that you'll let Hamilton carry it for you."

"Well, what do you think, Hamilton?" asked McMaster. "You're keeping very quiet."

So was Saidler, but nobody was interested in him.

Gavin had his answer prepared. "If carrying these bags is part of the job," he said, "then I shall carry them. I am not going to ask for favours."

"That's all very well," said McNaughton. "But what about Shearer?"

"I shall carry a bag for myself and him."

"That's the most selfish thing I've ever heard," cried Renwick.

"I don't see that," said Morrison. "I would say it's the very opposite. Hamilton was the only one of us to think about Shearer, down in the shed. He spoke to Angus about him."

"We're wasting time," said McMillan.

"McAndrew's time," said McNaughton.

"We have no right to ask Mr McAndrew to pay us for arguing among ourselves when we should be working," said Shearer.

McMillan laughed. "If I don't laugh I'll weep," he cried.

McNaughton was disgusted. "Do you wonder," he said to the gulls that had come to eat the bread Renwick had thrown away, "that the bosses have it all their own way and always will have? The workers of the world couldn't agree among themselves about the colour of shit."

He went over to his and McMaster's bag and with McMaster's grinning help hoisted it on to his back. "Don't ever ask me," he shouted, using breath he could ill spare. "Don't ever ask me." He didn't say what it was they weren't to ask him but they could guess.

"No need to be vulgar," Renwick shouted after him.

Except for Renwick and Robb who were seated beside theirs they all made for their respective bags.

Renwick and Robb had the additional problem that their bag was burst. This, as McMillan shouted back at them, had the advantage of causing it to get lighter all the time.

Still not recovered from his fall, Shearer was even less useful than before. Gavin had to elbow him gently out of the way.

Taking plenty of time to settle the bag securely on his shoulders, Gavin step by careful step climbed the bank and then set off along the path.

For some reason he remembered the girr-and-cleek forays of childhood.

14

AS DUNKY HAD said once the slag was there, on the great russet flat among the hills, the rest was easy, though after a while sore on the legs, back, and fingers. The small trees, prickly Sitka spruce, were planted in mounds that had been dug out of the ground when drains were being cut. These mounds, arranged in lines, were heavy and had to be prised up off the ground so that a handful of slag could be sprinkled beneath. After the ordeal of the bags it was to begin with exhilarating to stride unrestricted (except for tussocks of grass and deep drains) from mound to mound head up in the sunshine, with time and energy to spare for admiring the yellow tormentil and purple orchises, not to mention the butterflies, larks, curlews, and puddocks, though not the bloodsucking clegs. True, because of an oversight on somebody's part, the baskets used for holding a manageable amount of slag at a time were not available, so that piece-bags had to be used instead; but everybody, with the exception of Saidler whom no one heeded, felt cheered up by the time the lunch break came at twelve o'clock.

It was announced by Angus whistling through his fingers. He had turned up about a hour before. Anxious not be involved in the rebellion which wasn't over yet but just suspended he had not come too near them but watched from a distance, like a warder guarding dangerous prisoners, as McMillan said.

After whistling, he yelled that during the afternoon they were to go back to the bottoming of drains. Then he hurried away before they could protest that they had planned to go down to McAndrew and have it out with him about the carrying of the bags.

"Haven't you noticed," said Renwick bitterly, "how stupid people always seem to get the advantage of people smarter than themselves?"

They laughed though he had intended no joke.

They had chosen to eat in a grassy sunny hollow beside a small burn. It was an idyllic spot except that they all had the taste of slag in their mouths.

"Whatever McAndrew is," said McMillan, "he's not stupid."

As usual Morrison was first to open his piece-box.

"Good God," he yelled, "look at the ants."

They looked and couldn't help laughing. Hundreds of tiny black ants were hurrying to and fro on urgent missions over his sandwiches.

"Extra protein, Alistair," said McMaster.

"You should keep them in a tin," said Cunningham.

"What's this if it's not a tin? It's Angus's fault. If I hadn't had to use my piece-bag for the slag this wouldn't have happened. It's not funny."

If he hadn't been so horrified by the defilement of his own food he might have been amused by the faces of his companions as they discovered that their sandwiches too were infested.

Not only their sandwiches, their legs too, and their backsides. They had to jump up, banging themselves.

"Och well," said Morrison, blowing off as many ants as he could, "as my grannie used to say, hunger's a guid kitchen." He began to munch heartily without bothering to make sure that there were no ants left.

Others had more fastidious stomachs, McMillan was one.

"I've always been too damn fastidious," he muttered. "If a fly landed on my milk bottle I wouldn't drink it. Bill's pieces are bad enough without ants as well."

He threw his pieces away.

"Hold on there," said Morrison. "Anything you can't eat I will."

Renwick was especially sorry for himself. Not only had he nothing to eat he had also nothing to drink. Robb's tea was too sweet for him, Cunningham's not sweet enough. In any case, he said, he didn't like drinking out of somebody else's cup.

"Fasting is good for the soul," said Shearer, beaming. He went to the burn and scooped up handfuls of water. "Like the chosen of Gideon," he cried.

"Just as well, Shearer," said McMaster, "that you hadn't said your grace before you saw the ants. Otherwise you'd have had to eat them, wouldn't you, or the Lord would have been cross?"

"The Lord, Tom, knows how to make allowances. You mustn't think too that He has no sense of humour."

"He must be having a good laugh at you now."

"He often has a good laugh at me, Tom."

"Birds eat ants, so they must be edible," said McNaughton.

"Birds eat worms," said McMillan.

"So worms are edible too."

Morrison, his hunger assuaged, began a new conversation. He addressed Gavin. "I've been noticing, Hamilton, that you're like me. You like to work. Do you know what McAndrew said when he saw me working? He said I ought to take piece-work. So I would if I could get someone to come in with me."

"We agreed there would be no piece-work," said McNaughton.

"I didn't agree. I see nothing wrong with piece-work. I worked in a factory where it was all piece-work. We made good wages."

"Piece-work means good wages for the strong." said McNaughton.

"And the greedy," added McMaster.

"For those willing to work hard, you mean."

"If we were put compulsorily on piece-work," said McNaughton, "Shearer and Renwick would starve."

"Thank you very much," said Renwick.

"What is your attitude to piece-work, Hamilton?" asked McMillan.

"I haven't thought about it," replied Gavin.

He was though thinking about it now. There could be more independence in piece-work.

"Well, you think about it right away," said Morrison. "You and I could go into partnership. We could double our wages. We would be our own bosses. That should suit you that doesn't want to be beholden. We could do bottoming, draining, bracken-cutting, and in the spring planting. Think about it, Hamilton."

"All right," said McMillan, lying down and shutting his eyes, "think about it but don't talk about it. Let's have a litle quiet."

"Good idea."

They lay down in the sun and listened to the larks.

Only Saidler sat up, with his shoes and socks off, looking at the blisters on his heels.

When Angus whistled again there were groans. No one jumped up.

"What's he think we are?" murmured McMillan. "Sheep dogs?"

"I'll tell you what you are, the whole lot of you. Fucking slaves. That's what."

They were all startled. It was the first intelligible thing Saidler had said for hours. They had seen that he was depressed and had left him alone.

"We don't need that kind of language," said Renwick.

"You go to hell, you big phoney."

"Take it easy," said Morrison.

"You're all so damned tame that you're prepared to work your balls off for 30 bob a week. Well, I'm not."

"What are you going to do about it then?" asked McMillan.

"I'm going straight back to Glasgow."

"Isn't it a condition of your exemption that you do forestry work?" asked Cunningham.

"It's easier in Barlinnie and the food can't be worse."

"Well, you can't go straight back," pointed out McNaughton. "There's only one boat a day. You've missed it."

"Then tomorrow will have to do, won't it? Can I walk back to the house from here?"

"You could, but you'd get lost."

"Better go back down the way you came up," said McMaster.

"I've got bad blisters."

"You should have come better prepared," said Renwick.

"Too bad about the blisters," said McMillan. "But you'll still have to walk. Are you going to ask McAndrew for a half-day's pay?"

"Why shouldn't I? I've worked half a day, haven't I?"

"He'll deduct two nights' bothy rent, and you owe Creag exchequer for two days' board. You'll be lucky to have tuppence left."

"Would it not be better to wait for a day or two?" asked Shearer, sympathetically. "I assure you it's worse at the beginning."

"You shut up."

"Take it easy," said Morrison again. "He was just trying to help."

"Who's going to lend me his bike? You, Alistair?"

"And have to walk myself?" said Morrison, indignantly. "What d'you think I am? I used to get blisters too, you know."

"Somebody could give you a lift."

"No thanks."

"You can use my bicycle," said Gavin.

McMillan winked at him. Evidently he thought that returning good for evil was the best way to deal with a surly ingrate like Saidler.

Renwick didn't agree. "Is this you trying again to show us all up, Hamilton?" he said, angrily.

Saidler was having a wrestle with his pride. Of them all he disliked Gavin most. It was painful to be obliged to him.

McMillan winked at Gavin again. The tactic was succeeding.

Saidler tried to make it appear that by accepting Gavin's offer he was really showing how much he despised him.

"Sure, Hamilton," he said, "I'll use your bike. I always make a point of obliging an obliger. How would you like to lend me a couple of quid for the fare home?"

"Yes, if you need it."

McMillan's wink changed to a frown. He thought that Gavin was running the risk of being made look foolish.

"That's the other cheek turned," said Saidler. He looked round with a triumphant grin.

No one grinned back.

"I'm not sure I can find my way down to the road," he said. "How would you like to guide me, Hamilton?"

"Just follow the trail of slag," said McMillan.

"Maybe you'd like Hamilton to carry you?" said McMaster.

"We'd better get back to work," said McNaughton. "Before Angus dislocates his lips whistling."

The foreman had already whistled four times.

They picked up their piece-bags and made off across the wide sunny plain. None of them looked back at Saidler as he hirpled towards what he hoped was the path down to the road.

"Well done, Gavin," whispered Shearer.

Then, characteristically, he didn't notice a deep drain and stumbled into it.

"That was a truly Christian gesture," he panted, as he clambered out.

"Bottoming would be a good job on a piece-work basis," said Morrison. "So much per rod."

"I don't see how I can be expected to work when I haven't had anything to eat," grumbled Renwick.

"And there's Bill Munro's awful cooking to look forward to," said Cunningham.

"If Saidler does go," said McNaughton, cheerfully, "and I think he will, then he'll be the record-holder. There was a chap called McFarlane stuck it for three days. He's the present holder."

"I wonder who'll hold the opposite record," said McMaster. "I mean, who'll still be here in three, four, five years, maybe for the rest of his life?"

"Not Bill Munro anyway," said McNaughton.

"You think Bill's really going to leave us and join up?"

"I wouldn't be surprised. His girl friend keeps nagging him."

"He should tell her to go to hell," said McMillan.

As Gavin listened he was amazed by how, it seemed wilfully, they set out to be ordinary, concerned with ordinary things, and untouched by any special grace. They did not want to consider that, by refusing to help their countrymen oppose evil by evil means, they had put themselves under an inescapable obligation to oppose it, wherever it appeared, with Christian goodness. That morning they had listened to news on the wireless of air raids on London. Yet here they were beset by trivial selfish preoccupations. They thought that they had as much right as soldiers or airmen to remain their old familiar unexalted selves. They did not regard themselves as morally superior to those taking part in the war. As far as morality went, they would say, they saw little difference between refusing to kill and killing, provided that the refusers and the killers were equally sincere.

15

IT TOOK HIM only a week to decide that Munro had been right when he had accused them of having no other ambition than to keep life as bearable as possible until the war was over and then they would all go back to their respective occupations of teacher (McMillan), bank clerk (Renwick), civil servant (Robb and McNaughton), furniture salesman (Cunningham), factory-worker (Morrison), shop assistant (McMaster and Shearer), and warehouseman (Munro). None of them looked on this present experience as an opportunity to re-examine his motives, beliefs, and purposes.

They did not want anything new to be revealed to them.

They saw that he was disappointed with them and they weren't pleased. In a house like Creag it was hard not to overhear.

"What's his game then?" asked Munro once. "I think he thinks we're a shower of frauds."

"You think that yourself sometimes, Bill," said McNaughton.

"Sure. But I include myself. He thinks he's the only genuine cunt among us."

"I doubt if he puts it quite like that."

On another occasion it was Renwick talking to Cunningham and Robb. "He's worse even than Shearer. Shearer's just stupid, but Hamilton's slimy."

"Slimy, David?"

"You know what I mean. That smile of his makes me feel a snail's crawling over my face."

"I think I know what you mean, David."

McMillan too criticized him. "The history of Scotland's full of fanatics. Many were burnt to death. Through roasted lips they kept howling, 'Bugger you all, I'm right'. Or words to that effect."

Munro again, on Friday night: "Christ, I know he's a born obliger, as Half-day Saidler said; but saying he'd play in the game tomorrow was taking it a bit far. Anyway, it'll keep them from laughing at me. They'll be too busy laughing at him, not to mention kicking him."

That same night, a little later, McMillan invited him to go for a stroll as far as the spring.

"It's a fine night. Moon's shining. Mild, too."

He sounded diffident and nervous. Gavin wondered if he had been deputed by the others to convey some kind of warning.

They clattered in their heavy boots over the cobbles, past the byre. Huge clouds raced past the moon. Patches of shadow were like watching rats.

It was easy on a night like this, thought Gavin, to feel the connection between rats, stars, and human beings. That connection was God.

"I know you're not married, Hamilton," said McMillan, "and you told me you haven't got a girl friend at present. By the way, if you think I'm being too nosey just tell me to shut up. I told you we didn't pry here, so I'm really breaking a rule."

"It's all right."

"Any brothers or sisters?"

"No."

"What about your parents?"

"They're both dead."

"Oh. Long ago?"

"My mother fourteen years ago, my father 22 years ago. He was killed in 1918."

"I'm sorry. You haven't been lucky. Have you been on your own all that time?"

"I lived with my grandparents. They died three years ago."

"You certainly have been unlucky. My parents are both alive and well, thank God. I've got two sisters. And I'm happily married."

He sounded almost dismayed at how much luckier he himself had been.

They looked down on the loch, which was a blaze of moonlight.

"Maybe that explains it," he muttered.

"Explains what?"

"This obsession of yours not to be beholden. I don't think you ever have been."

Gavin remembered his mother, Rachel, and McIntyre. Yes, he had been beholden to them.

"It's a habit you could get out of," said McMillan. "Yet it's so necessary. We must depend on people. We can't live without them. We'd go mad. Anyway, I would."

He picked up a stone and threw it, as if at that madness which resulted from never being beholden. There on top of the dyke it crouched, like a rat.

"I didn't say I would never be beholden to anyone. Only to those who approve of war."

"I know that's what you meant. But some people approve of war, this war anyway, for what seem to them honourable reasons. My father's one. Yet he's given me all the support I've asked for. Am I to refuse to be beholden to him? Not to mention my sisters? And my neighbours at home who are being very fair, kind even, to my wife and little Sue? And Glasgow Corporation who are paying me the same allowance as if I was a soldier? How can I harden my heart against all those? It'd be like death. And I'd deserve it. What have we to live for if not people? Especially people we love."

The loch could have been the Sea of Galilee. Had Christ not warned His disciples that if they wanted to follow Him they must leave their families?

"Suppose you were in my place, Hamilton? Would you refuse to be beholden to my father?"

"I would have to try."

"But that's fanatical, Hamilton. You stand there as cool as moonlight, yet what you're saying is sheer fanaticism."

He picked up another stone and threw it, this time at fanaticism. They heard it rattling against a tree.

"No, wait a minute," he said. "Let's get this on to an ordinary, sensible level. Do you just mean that you shouldn't eat food brought in by sailors risking their lives? If that's all it is you're not alone. I feel that too. Every one of them up there feels it, even if they don't say it. You heard Bill Munro saying that there's always some patriotic old dear to remind you. We have to find our own justifications. Mine are simple enough. Conscientious objection's allowed by law. I think I'm sincere. I'm doing fairly useful work here, in not too comfortable conditions. Maybe too I'm doing something supremely valuable in that I'm taking a stand against war, not just this war but all war. I wouldn't want to make too much of that though, for to be honest I don't really believe war will ever be abolished. Still, I suppose that in the sixteenth century, say, sameone standing in this very place might have said that belief in witches would continue forever. Those are my justifications, Hamilton. What are yours?"

"War is evil."

"So it is. Everybody says that. I believe Hitler himself would say it."

"Everybody who takes part in it willingly, who approves of guns and bombs, is tainted by that evil."

"I'll accept that too. For what it's worth. But where's the profit to your soul in condemning and hating millions upon millions of your fellow creatures?"

"I didn't say I condemn and hate them." He remembered again

the woman in the train. All his life he would remember her with deep respect.

He spoke very carefully, for he was announcing his creed. "I do condemn the part in them that accepts war and the killing of enemies as right and natural. If I am also to pity and forgive them I must not be beholden to them."

McMillan let out his breath in a long astonished, indignant gasp. "Well, as Bill Munro would say, who the hell do you think you are, Hamilton? Sorry. But do you think they care an empty cigarette packet whether you pity and forgive them? They'd be more likely to kick your backside for impudence. Suppose though you really mean it, suppose you're a throwback to the sixteenth century or any other century of total faith, and you have a compulsion or obligation or ambition, call it what you like, to keep your soul clear of the universal infection, what then, for heaven's sake? What use are you going to make of your uniquely pure soul? It would be a terrible thing to have, Hamilton."

He picked up a third stone and threw it, this time at purity of soul.

"If you think it would enable you to convert the heathen—no, I mustn't be sarcastic—to make people kinder and happier and better, I can't agree. As you are now, Hamilton, with your soul not quite cleansed to your satisfaction—you're still pretty much beholden, you'd have to go naked and eat grass—you are the most moral—no, that sounds too pious—the most obliging, to borrow from Saidler again, man I've ever met. You lend your bike, you give away your money, to a man that did nothing but insult you. You're never surly or peevish, you never grumble. You broke your back to help Shearer. Yet what's the result? Is Saidler in Glasgow telling his pals how kind you were to him? Damned if he is. Up in the house are they saying what a good companion you are and how happy you make them feel? They are not. Well, except for Morrison maybe, who's thick in the head and sees you as a likely piece-work partner, and Shearer who's simple-minded anyway. Renwick keeps saying you're out to shame us all. Well, are you? At times it certainly looks like it. If you are you've got a damned cheek. That's all I'm going to say."

He paused, but not to let Gavin reply: he didn't want Gavin to say anything.

"When I'm in Port Fada tomorrow," he went on, "I'm going

to scout around for a place to bring Mary and Sue to. How would you like to come along and give me a hand?"

It was an offer of friendship, after the plain speaking. There was in it too a plea to Gavin to give in and be content with ordinary standards and expectations. He was sorry for Gavin, so lonely and fanatical.

What he did not understand and could never be made to understand because he did not believe in God was that any man who took upon himself the responsibilities of Christ, in however small a degree, could never be alone and was supremely sane.

"I'm sorry," Gavin said. "I promised Granny McSporran I'd play some Highland airs for her on Saturday night. So I'll have to return after the game."

"Oh. I see. One of these nights you'll have to give us a recital."

They walked back in silence to the house. Moonlight glittered on its roof.

"Tell me," said McMillan, unable to keep quiet, "if you're so set on not being beholden, why are you playing in the game tomorrow?"

"You said yourself I'm still pretty much beholden. I have to pay back my debts."

"I see. You're going to be very busy. Consider the amount of debt every one of us accumulates from the moment we're born. Maybe it's less in your case but it's still pretty enormous."

Just before they went in, McMillan, with his hand on the door handle, said, almost desperately: "You've got it all wrong, Hamilton. Believe me, you've got it all wrong."

16

ON THE FOOTBALL field in the seconds before the game began, Gavin looked round at the grinning faces of his opponents and their supporters. The latter were mainly youths still too young for war but old enough to have the required contempt for "yellow bellies", a word they chanted now and then, to the embarrassment of the orthodox members of the Ardmore and District team. Some older men reproved the contemptuous youngsters but not too wholeheartedly.

He did not think that he had got it all wrong, as McMillan had

worsted

said. He would give his life for these people but he would hide away in shame rather than be too beholden to them. They might well want to kick his backside for impudence, but they still needed to be pitied and forgiven. They would have jeered at Christ Himself.

Munro's attitude was much simpler. "Whose idea of a joke was it," he muttered, "to lend us *yellow* jerseys?"

McMillan was standing with the women from Ardmore. They all looked apprehensive. The Port Fada team contained several brawny players, eager for the onslaught.

The whistle went and the game began.

It was Port Fada's kick-off. Casual with over-confidence, their centre-forward tapped the ball to their inside-left, who with similar casualness passed it on to his outside-left; or at least that was his intention, easily anticipated and thwarted. At the right moment Gavin dashed forward and intercepted the ball. With it at his feet he had sprinted well into the Port Fada half of the field before the disconcerted defenders took steps either to rob or fell him. They were further flustered by McAndrew's imperious screams for the ball to be passed to him. In his excitement he forgot that he was then merely the centre-forward and not the boss. By this time the Port Fada left-half, left-back, and centre-half had made up their minds that collective might was needed to squash this early presumption. Together they rushed at Gavin. Their goalkeeper waved his long arms and yelled in alarm at their folly. He saw a danger that they didn't. Feinting to go one way, Gavin went the other. As a result the left-back, aiming a kick at either the ball or Gavin's leg, either would have suited his purpose, struck only air; and the centre-half, a fisherman with a chest like a herring barrel (Munro's description) trying too abruptly to change direction got his legs in a fankle. Now within range of the goal Gavin pretended that he was going to shoot with his right foot, which as a right-half he ought to have done, according to the goalkeeper's frantic calculations, but instead struck it hard and true with his left, into the net.

The referee, a butcher in civilian life, was so astonished by such an instantaneous goal that he almost forgot to blow his whistle.

It was unbelievable, yet it was not a fluke. The faces of the Port Fada players, particularly that of the goalkeeper, for he had had the best view, showed incredulity but also bitter respect.

Though themselves the crudest of acolytes they were nevertheless faithful, fervent, and knowledgable devotees of football. In the case of the Port Fada supporters, they recovered sufficiently to utter howls of defiance, disbelief, and accusation (they accused Ardmore and District of having recruited a professional), but they remained shaken. True believers, they had had a miracle perpetrated against them; and it could very well happen again at any moment for the miracle-worker, a tall black-haired conchie with the energy of an ape stuffed with bananas, was continuing to organize attacks on their goal, as well as thwarting attacks on his own.

As for his team mates, though they rejoiced at his prowess, they were as puzzled as their opponents. Munro, himself soon puffed out from too much smoking, gave him many abjectly contrite winks. McNaughton, McMaster, and Morrison, frequently under stress, kept panting expressions of gratitude as time and again he nipped in to rescue them. Representing the local men, McAndrew was pleased that they were winning but chagrined that it was owing to the efforts of one of their dubious allies.

"You didn't tell us you were such a good player," he said once, more in reproof than admiration.

Applauding as loudly as any, McMillan thought of last night's conversation in the moonlight. Surely, he thought, a man so adept at a beefy and banal game like football couldn't have meant all that preposterous high-flown stuff about pity and forgiveness.

Ann McTaggart kept pointing out to her companions, to their amusement, that he wasn't just the most skilful player on the field, he was also the most courageous and the most forbearing. Though fouled often he never once retaliated.

The game ended with a win for Ardmore and District by five goals to two. Gavin himself had scored twice. He had suffered for it. As well as a cut on the forehead he had bruises on his legs and an especially painful one on his left thigh.

Though downhearted and humiliated, the Port Fada players had to give due credit. As a conscientious objector he was more of a conundrum to them than a spear-brandishing Zulu would have been, but as a football player he was worth a hand-shake at the finish and a growl of congratulation. They again drew the line though at inviting him and the other Creag men into the pavilion.

Everybody in the Creag party, which included the girls, was excited and happy, in a mood for celebration.

"We're all going for fish and chips."

"To the Temperance for a bath first."

"To the Argyll for a drink first, you mean."

"Then to the pictures."

"You'll have to come, Hamilton," said McMillan. "We can't have a feast without the hero."

"I promised Granny."

"She'll not mind. You can play your fiddle for her tomorrow."

"Tomorrow's Sunday."

"Well, next week then. Come on, man. Be one of us. For better or worse."

"I said I would meet Martin Shearer at Creag road-end at six. He's coming with me. He's bringing my fiddle."

"Let's go then," shouted someone.

They headed in a body for the village main street. The women claimed the honour of wheeling the conquerors' bikes. Ann McTaggart took charge of Gavin's.

In the main street Port Fada folk looked on with smiles. They knew the result of the match and were amused. After all, their smiles indicated, we weren't beaten by Nazis. We were beaten by men from Ardmore and District whom we've known for years and who come in to Port Fada every Saturday to shop and have a drink and get their hair cut. Even if they were helped by conscientious objectors, what of it? Conscientious objectors were British too. They weren't the enemy. Surely for one Saturday anyway they can be made welcome. From stories we've heard they're not having it cushy while our own boys in the forces are having it hard. Besides, no bombs have ever fallen on Port Fada itself and are never likely to. It's not costing us very much then to be a bit friendly for one night.

All that their smiles conveyed.

Those who had not been at the game had Gavin pointed out to them by those who had. Even women who cared nothing for football showed interest. Their own sons were very keen on football and revered anyone who played it well. For their sakes therefore they were prepared to set prejudice aside and wish him good luck.

Ann McTaggart was hurt almost to tears when, outside the Argyll Hotel, he climbed on his bicycle and cycled off, with a quiet "Good evening".

"What's the matter with him?" asked someone, in astonishment.

"He promised Granny McSporran to play his fiddle for her," said McMillan.

"Oh, I see," said Ann.

McMillan felt annoyed that she was so ready to turn from disappointment with Hamilton to admiration for him. He knew he ought not to be annoyed. That was the way love reacted. God help her, she would do better to fall in love with Shearer. *He* might be enticed to forego Jehovah and his mysterious Maggie, but never Hamilton his quest for purity of soul.

17

O N S A T U R D A Y afternoons he did not go into Port Fada with the others but walked for miles into the heart of the hills behind Creag, far beyond Ardmore's boundaries. There in some beautiful desolate place he would sit for hours, sometimes in heavy rain, watched by hawk or deer or fox, and practise taking upon himself the guilt for all the agonies, miseries, and brutalities of the war. He took with him nothing to eat. Hunger, like cold and loneliness, was needed to induce that profundity of despair beyond which, as Christ had promised, lay absolution, hope, and joy, like a clear blue sky.

Often all he felt was a dull misery, tinged with self-derision, and he wondered if after all McMillan was right and he had got it all wrong.

"Up for smout." Yes, but as McIntyre could have explained, smout, that state of mystical grace, could often come very close but never be attained. Failure too was final.

Be one of us, for better or worse, McMillan had also said. Love Ann McTaggart. Take her to Auchengillan. Visit her parents in Edinburgh with her. Marry her. Rent a cottage somewhere in Ardmore. Through his love for her and her love for him earn the right to pity all those whose own happiness was destroyed by the war. Leave forgiveness to Christ.

Yes, but that would be to conform tamely. It would be humbly

163

begging his countrymen to look upon his conscientious objection as a pardonable aberration, caused by his too sensitive and perhaps too immature, but none the less sincere, interpretation of Christ's teachings. It would be a propitiation of the virulent hatreds that produced wars and made them atrocious. It would be not only a capitulation, it would be worse, a joining of the enemy. For the enemy was, as he had said to McMillan, that part of the human mind, the devil's part, which brought about wars, poverty, injustice, and cruelty. He had to overcome it first in himself. No other human being could help him, not even Ann McTaggart. It had to be done alone.

On Sundays he walked to the small kirk at Largiebeag, eight miles along the lochside, in the opposite direction to Port Fada. There were never more than a dozen worshippers, including the minister Mr Urquhart and his thin ailing wife.

Once, early in December, on a morning of fierce storm, with trees blown across the road and the loch raging like an ocean only the minister, his wife, and Gavin turned up. They seemed more embarrassed than flattered by his presence. If he had not come there would have been no service. This in any case was cut short. Mr Urquhart was anxious about his wife. His voice was low therefore and could not be heard for the roaring of the wind. Spume splattered the windows facing the loch.

Mrs Urquhart had a slight fever and a pain in her chest. She should have stayed in bed. She could not smell the chrysanthemums she had brought and put into the two silver vases. For years the church on Sundays had been for her as reassuring as her own home. The coming of the young black-haired man with the Papist intensity of worship had brought a disturbance. Her husband had smiled, saying that Mr Hamilton was certainly much too serious-minded for a young man, but that was all. She was not reassured. She felt unsettled, as she might have done if one of the disciples, or Christ Himself, had been present.

That morning of the storm when she caught sight of him coming across the bridge, under which the river roared, with the elm trees thrashing overhead, she felt afraid. It was as if she thought he had been sent to call her to account. When he opened the heavy creaking door, kept shut that morning because of the wind, and came into the shadowy church, she suddenly smelled an overpowering perfume of chrysanthemums and had a vision of her dead mother standing amidst thousands of the beautiful sad flowers. This was absurd and morbid, and she did not tell her husband about it when she went into the vestry to say that Mr Hamilton had come.

After the brief service she approached the young man and invited him to the manse for lunch. He declined, very graciously. He seemed, she thought, to be listening to some other voice than hers. Her husband then, having taken off his gown and put on his overcoat, offered to run him in his car to Creag road-end. This he declined too, saying that a car wouldn't be able to get through until the blown trees had been sawn up and pulled out of the way.

For the rest of the day, as her fever grew worse, Mrs Urquhart could not get out of her head the foolish notion that Mr Hamilton if he had wished could have picked up those fallen trees as if they were straws.

A few days before Christmas, on the same damp dreary day that Mrs Urquhart was being buried in Largiebeag kirkyard, McMillan at break-time, for the sake of stirring up argument, for they were all feeling cold and miserable, put forward the proposition that the reason for Gavin Hamilton's peculiarities was that he was a good man in a time of war.

The place where they were digging drains was bare and bleak, with no shelter from the chilly drizzle. Their arms and backs were weary with using rutters and hawks. Their coats were sodden and their boots thick with mud. Their hands were so cold they could scarcely hold the thermos cups full of tea. McMillan himself had chilblains.

Gavin was cook that week.

At first they responded sourly.

"Good? Who the hell isn't good?"

"That's right. There isn't one of us would put a washer in a blind man's tinny."

"But which of us would put a fortnight's wages into a tramp's hand?"

The incident had taken place a few weeks ago. Coming back from the hut on Friday evening after they had been paid, they had met a tramp seated by the side of the road stuffing his boots with grass. Some of them had stopped, wondering if there was anything they could do to help him. Angered by what he thought was their callous curiosity, he had struggled to his bare feet and groped in the ditch for stones to throw at them. Hamilton had gone up to him. They had seen him take his pay packet from his pocket and hand it to the tramp. The latter had thought he was being cruelly teased. He had yelled abuse. Then he had realized that Hamilton was in earnest. Amazed and weeping, he had taken the money.

McMillan himself hadn't been present. The others had told him about it.

"If he couldn't have afforded it he wouldn't have given it."

"Which of us, with a little sacrifice, couldn't afford it?"

"Perhaps he thought the Lord was watching."

"The Lord *was* watching and would not be deceived. He would see that it was an act of generosity and in His own time He will reward it."

"The laugh is that the tramp as soon as he got to Port Fada got blind drunk."

"You don't know that."

"He was just trying to show us up, as usual."

"Couldn't Christ's contemporaries have said that about Him?"

"Who does the lion's share of the dirty work at Creag? Who goes and empties the jakes when the rest of you are grumbling about whose turn it is?"

"We'd prefer it if he grumbled too."

"You're not really in a position to know, Donald."

For some time now McMillan had been living in Port Fada with his wife and child.

"Look at your pieces. Does anybody else ever take such care over them?"

"That's true."

"It's so bloody true that I feel I'm eating sacramental wafers."

"No need for blasphemy."

"Can an atheist be blasphemous? But maybe you're right, Donald. There is something peculiar about him. It could be goodness."

"Big Dunky says he's the only real Christian he's ever met."

"Rubbish. What does Dunky know about Christianity? He never goes to church."

"Why has he never invited Gavin to his house if he thinks so highly of him?"

"He has."

"Who told you?"

"Dunky himself."

"Why didn't he go then?"

"Maybe he was afraid the nine-year-old daughter would take him for a bag of slag and sling him across her shoulders."

"I think she's ten years old now."

"Keep your voices down. Dunky might hear."

Dunky still ate his pieces apart. It was a habit he was too shy to break. They had decided not to hurry things but let trust grow. Already buds were showing.

"I suppose it's that fanatical determination of his not to be beholden."

"Fanatical's right. What kind of Christianity is it to do good turns and then refuse to take any in return?"

"He thinks he takes too much in return. He's still too beholden for his liking."

"Did you know, Donald, that he's been working like a slave reclaiming Creag garden? He's going to plant it with potatoes and vegetables."

"We're wondering if he'll let us eat them."

"He's not humble. Far from it. He's off his head with pride, if you ask me."

"Isn't a good man supposed to be a happy man? Would you call him happy?"

"Yes, I would."

"You're pulling our legs."

"No. You should see him playing with my little girl Sue."

"I'd be more convinced if I saw him playing with the big girl Ann."

"Why must you always be suggestive?"

"Because my heart isn't pure."

"Why does he get no letters?"

"Well, he's got no family."

"Hasn't he got friends? If he's as good as you say he's bound to have lots of friends."

"I don't see how that follows. In fact, I'd be surprised if a really good man had any friends."

"Because everybody found him insufferable? You could be right."

"He's been here nearly fourteen weeks and as far as we know he's had only one letter."

"There were two other enclosed in it."

"Well, that's Dunky up again. Back to the salt mines."

"When I'm ready to drop with exhaustion I'll think of Hamilton's goodness and be miraculously revived."

"You do that, Bill."

18

THE LETTER HAD been from Elspeth Grierson. Enclosed with it were two more, one from McIntyre in Singapore and the other from Rachel Hallad in London.

He had read them lying on his bed, by candlelight. Elspeth's handwriting was as neat as the day she left school.

Dear Gavin,

How are you getting on? We hoped we would have a letter from you by this time but maybe you've been kept too busy. Tom thinks you'll be too tired to write.

If you remember before you left when I asked what to do about any letters that came for you you said burn them. Neither Tom nor me was sure whether you meant it. Well, these two came last week. They've been sitting on the brace for days. Wee Elsie kept asking when I was going to send them to Uncle Gavin. Tom said that if anybody was going to burn them it would have to be you yourself. So here they are. If we've made a mistake we're sorry.

Not much news. We're very happy and comfortable, thanks to you. The weans are looking much better already. But I've got a terrible confession to make. Do you mind the wee china bell among the ornaments in the display cabinet? Elsie loves to look at them, with her nose pressed against the glass. She craiked and craiked to be allowed to hold the bell for a minute to see if it would tinkle. Tom said no, but I was daft enough to give in and let her have it. Of course she dropped it, I think because she was trying too hard to be careful. It broke but not too badly. Tom's sorted it with glue and you'd hardly know. Elsie was terribly upset and begged me not to tell Uncle Gavin. So that's another promise broken.

Your old crony Mrs Ferrier fell last week and broke her leg, poor old soul. At her age it'll not mend easy. A touch of glue won't do the trick there.

Mr McFarqhuar the minister's very ill, it seems. There's somebody else taking his services. I hear his wife's not well either.

Coming home from the Co. the other day who should stop me and ask after you but Harold Murphy and his wife that used to be Molly Flanagan, Jim's sister. He used to be such a nasty boy up to all sorts of dirty tricks. Well, he seems sensible enough now. He was in his soldier's uniform. I except Molly's done a lot to civilize him but I've noticed it before, horrors growing up to be quiet and sensible. Anyway, he asked after you and said I'd to tell you to stick it out.

Tom and the children send their regards. Oh, by the way, what about the New Year? I know it's still some time away, but you're bound to get some holidays then, and Tom and I would be very pleased indeed if you spent them with us. Imagine the cheek of it, inviting you to your own house. Maybe you've met other friends and are planning to spend the holidays with them. Whatever you decide to do, Gavin, the best of luck from all of us here.

"News from home, Gavin?" whispered Shearer, from his corner.

"Yes."

"All well, I hope?"

"Yes, thank you."

"Praise the Lord!"

"What about yourself, Martin? Is everything all right?"

"Yes. Oh yes. Fine. Everything's fine. Thank you for asking, Gavin. Yes, everything's fine."

Always he answered questions about his people with this excessive enthusiasm, the purpose of which seemed to be to discourage further questioning.

Gavin picked up McIntyre's letter. It was short.

Dear Hamilton,

I've been wondering where you are and what you're doing. I expect you're in the army and an officer. Though I don't like to think of you in uniform. I keep remembering that day in the academy when I came to tell you I had left. It was outside the engineering drawing room where they let us eat our pieces. Walking along the streets here and through the bazaars among the faces of the Chinese and Indians I keep seeing yours, as it was that day. Did you know, Hamilton, you had tears in your eyes? How's the football? Here the only time you can play is about six o'clock when it's getting cooler, and of course that's when it gets dark.

Fortiter et recte. (You see, I still remember the old school motto.) Good luck.

As always, he gave the impression of being alone. This time, though, he seemed a little despondent. Perhaps he had not been feeling well.

In every army that had ever been there must have been men like McIntyre: obscure, brave, uncomplaining, and decent. They had done their best to kill other obscure, brave, uncomplaining, and decent men on the other side, because they had believed that it was their duty to their king, their country, and their God.

I loved you, McIntyre, he thought, I still do. I shall never forget you.

"Bad news this time, Gavin?" whispered Shearer.

"In a way, yes, I suppose so."

"I'm sorry. Is there anything I can do? If you like, I'll join you in prayer."

"No. It's all right."

"But you do pray, Gavin. I've seen you."

"Yes, I pray."

"You don't mind me talking to you?"

"Of course not."

"You know how John McNaughton and Tom McMaster like to tease me. Today on the hill they asked me if I believed that God created the germs that cause diseases like cancer and syphilis."

Gavin smiled. "And what did you say?"

"I said that it was man's unclean ways that created germs: just as it is his selfish greedy ways that cause mass starvation and wars. Don't you agree, Gavin?"

Christ had never heard of germs, just as He had never heard of high-explosive bombs. He had not known that the earth went round the sun and was a tiny speck in the universe. In many things He had been more ignorant than a child of ten today. He had not washed as often as modern standards of hygiene required. But He had known as no other human being ever had that kindness and love were good and fruitful, and cruelty and hate evil and barren. It made no difference what name was given to the source of His knowledge. That source was eternal and available to every human being: God was as good a name as any. Therefore even the most immoral and criminal of men knew in their hearts that what they were doing was wrong. Therefore too the ultimate triumph of love, kindness, and unselfishness was celebrated in every church, mosque, temple, and synagogue throughout the world.

While wars existed, and the hatred, fear, envy, and ignorance that caused them, that triumph would never be achieved.

He picked up Rachel's letter.

Dear Gavin Hamilton,

Having mislaid my own conscience in this age of brutalities I recently fell to wondering whether you have continued to guard yours as zealously and secretively as ever. I thought at first that with your religious faith you must have declared yourself a conscientious objector, but then it occurred to me that like the rest of us, in your case more soulfully perhaps, you must have decided that the stopping of German bestialities must take precedence over obedience to the precepts of the moralist of Nazareth. Like me you will wish to put our war aims no higher than that. We are not so guileless, are we, as to believe that this war, any more than the last will bring about a millenium of peace and goodwill?

I see you smiling. You want to ask me if I now believe that we human beings really can help one another; if I think that by killing a sufficient number of Germans we shall rescue the Jews, the Poles, the Czechs, and all the other victims. I do not. It is much more likely that if we ever, by some miracle, find ourselves in a position to threaten the Germans with humiliation and defeat, they will take their revenge on those victims.

It wouldn't surprise me if after this war is over, whoever wins it, the Germans and the British and the Americans, that is to say the Capitalists, gang up against the Russians, the Communists, and so another even greater war is already preparing for us.

As you may know we are bombed here almost every night. I bristle like a cat with fear and hate. Yet I know that if I were to meet one of the German pilots responsible he would most indignantly deny that he was a cowardly murderer. He would put his hand on his heart and say that he was serving the Fatherland. Patriotism is the last refuge of a scoundrel, said Dr Johnson. But who would call those blond, blue-eyed young heroes scoundrels? Not even the people I see in the mornings weeping as they try to dig out relatives and friends. That is the trap we are all in. I can't think that you have escaped.

At present I am working in a hostel for infirm old women. My colleagues are very kind people who think that Mr Churchill, that grandiloquent attitudinizer, is our saviour. I groan in the depths of my soul. Yet is it not true that he is holding firm our national resolve to fight on, and should not I therefore who want us to fight on praise him too? I do, I do. I am only too well aware that those who relish war will do more to win it than those who hate it.

I have decided never to have any children. Good luck.

"Your friends write long letters," said Shearer.
"Yes."
"You must be looking forward to answering them."
He would reply to Elspeth, but in the case of McIntyre and Rachel silence was best.

19

ON HOGMANAY there was a party in Big Dunky's house in Ardmore. All his forestry mates were invited, except the Creag men who in any case, with the exception of Hamilton, had gone home for the holiday. Accepting his invitation, McAndrew had felt obliged to make it clear that though he would be pleased to fraternize with his subordinates he hoped he would not be treated too familiarly. It was especially important in a time of war for authority wherever it appeared to be maintained at all times. Otherwise, he implied, the Nazis would be in Ardmore in a matter of weeks.

Up to midnight he was addressed very properly as Mr McAndrew. During the toasting of the New Year however and the handshakings afterwards some called him Ian. An hour or so later he found himself answering, without huff, to "Wee Mac". Far from protesting, he insisted on taking his turn to sing, and gave a lugubrious but heartfelt rendering, half in English and half in Gaelic, of "The Mist-covered Mountains of Home".

About three o'clock, when their wives had gone home and the whisky was all consumed, a mood of sadness overcame them. They remembered that the country was at war, which was the reason why the whisky was in short supply. They thought of workmates now far away, in uniform.

Somebody remarked that Hamilton was up at Creag by himself. Somebody else suggested, as a joke, that they should all go and first-foot him.

Practical objections were solemnly put forward. It was dark outside and freezing cold. None of them was fit to mount a bike far less ride one to Creag road-end. If by a miracle they did reach the house they would be sure to find it in darkness and Hamilton asleep in bed, with his blankets pulled up over his ears to keep out cold and rats. If they managed to wake him up there would be only spring water to drink with him to the New Year.

During this discussion McAndrew fell asleep in his chair. They looked with much satisfaction but little malice on the face of authority gaping so foolishly.

They continued to discuss Hamilton. They conceded that as a Christian he was probably genuine, but instead of this pleasing them it troubled them. They remembered how, though he went out of his way to be obliging he also went to lengths to avoid accepting anything in return. That too of course could be a consequence of his being a genuine Christian, but they weren't sure they approved. They exchanged stories of his courtesy. They agreed that he was a good man, probably a better man than themselves, but just the same if every man in the country had his views the German flag would have been flying from Buckingham Palace long ago.

"Why is he by himself on Hogmanay in that lonely house?"

"He would tell you that he is not alone. He would say that God is keeping him company."

"It is not every man would want God to be his first-foot."

"What is he thinking about, would you say? What is he looking forward to?"

"That is a good question, Jake. We are looking forward to winning the war and better conditions after it. What is he looking forward to, as you say?"

"Maybe he is looking forward to the time when there will be no more wars."

"That is a very long look forward, I'm thinking."

"I hear that the bonny fair-haired McTaggart woman is not coming back after the New Year. She has asked for a transfer to Strathyre Forest in Perthshire, her and her friend."

"It is because of Hamilton, I think. She had a great fancy for him."

Dunky so far had just listened. Now he wanted to speak up on Hamilton's behalf.

"McMillan was telling me that Hamilton is too sensitive. He blames himself for everything that happens in the war. Every bomb that's dropped he's to blame, he thinks."

"Well, in a way that's true, Dunky. His kind certainly make it easier for brutes like Hitler."

"I would say myself it goes deeper than that," said Dunky.

Then McAndrew woke up. He peered at them all suspiciously. He thought they had been talking about him.

"I must go home," he said.

"I shall see you to the gate, Ian," said Dunky.

"There is no need."

But there was, as he found when he had difficulty finding the handle of the door.

"Good-night, all," he said.

"Good-night, Ian," some said, and "Good-night, Mr McAndrew," said others.

Dunkey took his arm down the six steps and along the glistening path to the gate.

It was frosty. The stars were bright.

McAndrew looked up at the sky. "On Eigg, when I was a boy," he said, "we used to light a fire on top of the Sguur on Hogmanay. It could be seen all the way to Skye. Why did we not light a fire on the Fort?"

"When the war is over we surely will. That is a good idea."

They turned and looked at the Fort. This was the rocky hill behind the houses. Some stones on the top were reputed to have been part of a fort or watch-tower built hundreds of years ago by the Scots as a protection against the Norsemen. From it long-boats coming up the loch could be spotted many miles away. From it in the landward direction Creag farmhouse could be seen.

"I would like to tell you something," said Dunky. "It has nothing to do with the chob, you understand, but I would like to tell you anyway. Tomorrow, that is to say, today, this afternoon, I am to go up to Creag with a cake that Morag has baked. Calum and Catriona are to go with me."

"Who has given you these orders, Dunky?"

"Morag. She thinks it is time we treated the Creag boys as neighbours. Forby, they gave Calum and Catriona presents at Christmas."

"So I heard. I was surprised, Dunky, that you took them. All the other men with children refused, I believe. I hope they did it courteously, mind you; but I am glad they did it."

"It was their right to say no, just as it was mine, and Morag's, to say yes. I have been their ganger for months. I have worked beside them in many places, in all kinds of weather."

"You eat your lunch pieces sitting apart from them."

"That has been my fault. I have been invited to join them. In the new year I shall."

"Their principles are not our principles, Dunky."

"They are their own."

"Hamilton now, I think he would like to live by himself in a hut of stones on top of the Fort."

"Then Morag would send me up there with her cake."

"If I was you, Dunky, I would not go."

He tried to make it sound neither like an order nor a threat, but made it sound like both.

"Good-night and thank you for your hospitality."

Then he set off unsteadily along the road towards his house that stood apart and was larger.

From Dunky's house came the sound of singing. They were all joining in. It was a sad Gaelic song about leaving an ancestral island.

He was a free man in a free country. His friendship was his own to offer to whomever he pleased.

As he went up the path to his house he thought of Morag, his kind-hearted wife, and his two children, and knew that as long as he had them and their love he did not have to be afraid of Hitler himself, far less Ian McAndrew and the Forestry Commission.

20

About two o'clock Gavin was returning from the spring with a bucketful of water when he heard behind him the cries of children. Looking back, he saw coming up the track Duncan McNiven and his two children, ten-year-old Catriona and seven-year-old Calum. Their white knitted bonnets were easy to see amidst the bronze of dead bracken and the green of whins.

He had been half expecting this visit. Morag McNiven had struck him as a persistent woman who would not be content until she had returned a kindness with another. She would make it difficult for him to lighten his burden of indebtedness, which was still too heavy.

Putting the bucket under the sink, he hurried out again. The buildings prevented his visitors from seeing him as he climbed over the dyke and, crouching, went up the steep hillside. At a place where birches formed a screen he stopped and looked back.

They had almost reached the house. He could hear the children speaking to each other, the girl in a strangely authoritative way. She was used to ordering her brother about.

Gavin smiled as he remembered the good-humoured jokes on the subject of her father's boasts about her.

Duncan himself was silent. He seemed reluctant, as if unsure of his welcome. It was the little boy who knocked on the door. Catriona carried something in her hands. Perhaps it was a present for him. They would be Creag's first-foots. According to tradition it was considered unlucky to come empty-handed.

Duncan turned and scanned the hillside. He saw frosted grass, white-withered heather, bronze bracken, dark-green whins, shiny-green holly, blue-and-grey rocks, and purple birches. From the way he hunched his shoulders he seemed to suspect that Gavin was hiding. When he went to knock on the door it was without expectation.

Catriona, carefully putting down her parcel, climbed up on to the sill and looked in the kitchen window. Her brother, whistling bravely, ran down the side of the house past the gean tree to try the front door. He came running back very quickly, shaking his head.

It was Catriona who tried the door and found it unlocked. It was she who put her head in and shouted, sternly: "Mr Hamilton, are you at home?"

Two ravens, startled, flew up from among the rocks, croaking querulously.

The little boy turned in fear to gaze up at the black birds.

Duncan at last ventured in, with Calum at his heels. Catriona remained outside for a few seconds longer. Perhaps she was counting. She would have her own rules. Gavin remembered those of his own childhood.

They would see that he had been scrubbing the floors. They would smell the disinfectant.

They did not stay long in the cold house.

When they came out the little boy put his hands to his mouth and yodelled: "Mr Hamilton, Mr Hamilton".

Echoes came back from the hillside, mingled with the cries of the ravens.

Catriona's hands were empty. She had left the present in the house.

This skulking avoidance of children was hard to justify, even to himself.

Surely it could weaken no man's cause to be beholden to children. One of the worst horrors of war was that children were put in a position where they must look on other children as enemies, whose deaths might not be prayed for but did not have to be mourned.

They were not to blame, yet they were not innocent.

They were to be pitied. But who had a right to pity them? Not ministers or priests who told them that Christ's commands to love their enemies did not apply. Not politicians who promised them a guilt-free future when the slaughter was over. Not airmen who thought that the killing or maiming of children was a risk that could be honourably taken. Not soldiers who killed other soldiers who were the fathers of children. Not even their own parents who accepted as a legitimate consequence of war the deaths of other parents' children.

And who had a right to pity those ministers, politicians, airmen, soldiers, and parents?

Only someone completely uninvolved.

There was no such person, Donald McMillan had said. If there was, he had added, he would be a monster of spiritual arrogance whose contempt would be preferable to his pity.

Donald had got it wrong. The pity would not be expressed to

those being pitied. It would be felt and spoken in a place where no people were. It would be judged by God.

The visitors were about to leave. The children shouted, "Happy New Year, Happy New Year", time and again, making a defiant song of it until their father told them that that was enough.

It was growing dark when he returned to the house. He lit the oil lamp and saw on the table the present the visitors had brought. Unwrapping the brown paper, he revealed a cake with currants and raisins: the kind offered to Ne'erday callers, with a glass of whisky or sherry or ginger wine.

The rich smell of the cake evoked memories. He remembered being called into her house by Mrs Ferrier. He was six at the time and his father was away at the war. She had held out to him a plate on which were small pieces of cake like this one, and also a very small glass with the Rothesay coat-of-arms on it in gold; in this was a green liquid that smelled like medicine. Indeed, she had stood by and made sure he ate and drank the lot, as if they were meant not to be enjoyed but to do him good. Because he had been nervous crumbs had stuck in his throat. To his surprise, instead of being angry with him for choking she had bent down, with her stays creaking, and kissed him. He had been fascinated by so close a view of her bad eye.

He cut a slice of Mrs McNiven's sake and put it to his mouth.

If, like Adam, he was to take so much as a bite he would be free to go out into the world and share in its pleasures and griefs. No one would think of him as a criminal or outcast. He would be branded but not many would shun him. He could find love, with Ann McTaggart or some other woman. He could write long letters to McIntyre and Rachel. He could go home to Auchengillan and talk with friends.

After a long hesitation he went with the whole cake to the door and threw it out into the darkness. The rats would sniff at it suspiciously and decide that it was good. In the morning not a crumb would be left.

"Please understand," he murmured, thinking not only of Mrs McNiven and Duncan, but of all the people who had ever known him and wished him well.

PART FOUR

ON A COLD sunny morning in January 1946, six months after
the end of the war, McAndrew had a visit from his district officer,
Captain Pilgo-Stewart.

Before and during the war he had always greeted this young
man with involuntary servility. He had despised himself for it,
especially as it had been accepted as a natural thing, like the
fawning of dogs. The youngest son of Sir Hector Pilgo-Stewart,
Bart., of Kerrera, and educated at Eton College, the captain, now
26, had the voice and manner of an upper-class Englishman,
accustomed from birth to instant subservience from, among many
others, crofters' sons from Eigg, even if twice as able as himself.
As officer in the Argyll and Sutherland Highlanders, he had lost
an arm during the retreat from Dunkirk.

That bright morning McAndrew did not cringe. Where before
he had found the captain's unconscious haughtiness offensive and
intimidating he now found it comic. He even allowed himself the
liberty of rather liking the young man.

In the past whenever his own opinions on forestry matters,
derived mainly from experience, had differed from those of the
captain, who had a degree in the subject, he had cravenly stifled
his own. Now he listened with respect and interest and then
modestly but confidently put forward his own views, even if they
contradicted those of the captain.

He was not sure where his new self-confidence had come from
and had made no serious effort to find out. No doubt the war
had had an effect. It was scarcely possible for the country to fight
a long and bloody war for the freedom and dignity of Poles in
Warsaw without at the same time giving courage and self-respect
to a Scottish forester in Ardmore. Besides, he had a son now and
though little Ian was only nine months he had a right to have a
father he could be proud of.

McAndrew was no leveller. In the General Election at the end
of the war he had, like the captain, voted for Winston Churchill's
party and had been grieved when it was routed. He had no
sympathy with the view that all men were equal. How could he,

when he considered himself superior, in brains, resource, character, and usefulness, to every other man in Ardmore and district, not excluding the Creag men?

His wife Kirstie had once unguardedly remarked that he was being influenced by the conscientious objectors, especially Donald McMillan and John McNaughton. She had said it in her usual calm affectionate way, but he had been deeply hurt. It had mattered a great deal to him not just that she was wrong but also that she knew she was wrong. He had spent several evenings, at the fireside and in bed, explaining and persuading. She had been surprised and amused by his persistence and vehemence and had been willing enough to retract, but he had felt that she was doing it to please or rather to appease him, and not because she was really persuaded. What difference did it make, was her easy-going attitude, if they had influenced him? They were intelligent, sincere, honest, well-read men, with good intentions. In the midst of his earnest arguments he had realized that he himself could not have said why the idea of his being influenced by them was so abhorrent. He had learned to respect and like them. He would go so far as to say that they had become his friends. They had been guests in his house. But the very thought of their having in any way altered his mind was hateful.

The captain had come with two definite purposes: to discuss the question of McAndrew's transfer to a larger forest and therefore promotion to Grade I; and also to make an inspection of Creag farmhouse and outbuildings, with a view to deciding their future use when the last of the conscientious objectors had gone. A more indefinite but just as important purpose was simply to spend a few hours in a beautiful place.

The glorious winter sunshine was a stroke of luck. It lit up snow on the tops of hills, against blue sky, and it made withered grass shine like gold.

They went in the captain's car to Creag road-end.

With his stick the captain pointed to black paint obliterating the yellow on the gate.

"When was this done?" he asked, with a guffaw.

"A good while ago."

"Did you order it done?"

"I did not."

"So they finally got round to doing it themselves?"

"No. They didn't do it."

"Who did?"

McAndrew knew that some of his local workers led by Duncan McNiven had done it.

"I like to think," he said, with a smile, "that it just happened, a natural thing, like leaves appearing in spring."

The captain guffawed again.

They set off up the track. It was iron hard, with patches of bright ice.

Because he was happy in his son, and in his job, and in his country so recently victorious, and in himself, McAndrew felt that he was allowed a little sentimentality. Though above the sky was pale blue in the distance it was luminous white, like, he thought, Kirstie's breast as she fed the baby. The loch, glimpsed down at the gate and soon to be seen again as the path ascended, was the same deep blue as wee Ian's eyes. Beside the track was a great beech, hundreds of years old. In his happy fanciful mood this enormous tree, this mighty contortion of solid wood presbyterian grey in colour against the blue and white sky, put him in mind of his son's tiny hands clutching the air.

"I expect these chaps are expecting to be demobbed soon," remarked the captain.

"It appears the necessary legislation is making slow progress through the House of Lords."

"How many of them are left?"

"In Creag itself, four. There's also Hamilton, who lives by himself."

"Will they all go? Hasn't any of them taken a fancy to the outdoor life?"

"They say the pay is too low. I am not sure what Hamilton intends to do."

Donald McMillan had told him, in confidence, one night over a glass of beer in McAndrew's house, that at the end of the war Hamilton might just walk out into the hills and not come back. "Like Bonny Kilmenny. He's never said it, but I've got a suspicion something like that's in his mind. Why? I wouldn't like to try to explain. I mean, it would be mad, utterly mad, but you know there are times when it seems the only logical thing to do."

"I must say, McAndrew," said the captain, "I've never been able to understand these chaps. I mean to say, some wars in the past a fellow with an over-sensitive conscience might have thought a bit steep. The Zulu Wars, for example. And I had a master at school who used to say that in the Crimean War—the Charge of the Light Brigade and all that—we fought on the wrong side. But good Lord, this war against Hitler and the Japs, well, surely *it* was a crusade against barbarians, if ever there was one. Simply to rescue the Jews from the concentration camps would have been cause enough."

"I agree, Captain. But they would say that most of the Jews were killed during the war, perhaps as a consequence of it."

"Do they honestly think Hitler could have been reasoned with?"

"They say that perhaps the German people could have been reasoned with. In a few years' time, they say, the Germans will pe our allies against the Russians: thus showing how reasonable they can pe."

"Have you actually let them say such ridiculous things to you, McAndrew?"

"I have had to keep in mind, Captain, that one of our war aims was the preservation of free speech."

"That's all very well, but there's a limit."

They came to the spring. "Time for a rest," said the captain, laughing. He sat on a rough bench that had been put there by the occupants of Creag. There was room on it for three, but McAndrew preferred to stand.

Out of the breeze, it was warm in the sunshine.

The captain took off his deerstalker cap and exposed his delicate skull and fine brown hair. How many generations of privilege and easeful living had it taken, wondered McAndrew, to produce this refinement of bone and flesh? Extraordinary though, that the brains inside the aristocratic head should have remained so unsubtle and commonplace.

I am not being influenced by John McNaughton, the Socialist, thought McAndrew. Even as a boy on Eigg I had these doubts about the gentry.

"I expect they're all religious cranks," said the captain.

"McMillan is an agnostic, but the other three make no pones apout it and call themselves atheists. There have been religious cases here of course, but they have all gone. I understand one of them is now studying to become a minister. Hamilton is religious, though I doubt if his view of religion would be considered orthodox."

"He's the fellow who lives by himself? Didn't you say once that he's a bit off off his head?"

Suddenly McAndrew felt that though he might be breaking a confidence he must tell the captain about Hamilton. The captain's ideas of duty were honourable but too simple. He ought to be given a glimpse of how very complicated it could be.

"You may remember, Captain, the passage in the Bible where Our Lord tells a young man who wanted to follow Him that first he must sell all his goods and give the money to the poor."

The captain laughed, like a schoolboy asked some hoary old riddle.

"Is that where the bit about the eye of a needle appears?" he said. "I never knew anyone that did it, though. I mean, gave away all his goods to feed the poor. The working-class lads I met in the army held on to their pennies as tightly as any rich man to his pounds."

"Hamilton did it."

"I wouldn't have thought he ever had all that much to give away."

"He had a house and a fair amount of money in the pank. He gave it all away. He gives most of his pay away. I doubt if at this moment he has more than a shilling in his possession."

They continued on their way up to the house.

The captain was more amused than impressed. "How do you give away all your money to the poor? Do you go into the streets and look to see if a chap's down at heel and slip him a quid? Or do you go down some street in the slums and push a quid through the letter-box?"

"Hamilton did it through a lawyer in the town he came from."

"How do you know, McAndrew? Doesn't it also say in the Bible that you should do good by stealth and not let everybody know?"

"Not everypody knows in Hamilton's case. I happen to know pecause the lawyer sent a clerk here to Ardmore with some papers Hamilton had to sign. This clerk called in to see me. He wanted to make sure that Hamilton was in his right mind."

"Did you certify he was?"

"I did."

McAndrew remembered the football match against Port Fada. Hamilton that day had played with extreme intelligence. They still talked about it in the bars in Port Fada.

Since they were on a tour of inspection they went into the byre. It was very cold. On the stone floor beside the dry lavatory was a paper-back book. The captain turned it over with his foot to see its title. It was an ordinary thriller. "Thought it might be something political," he murmured.

"There used to be many rats," said McAndrew. "They got rid of them."

"How?"

"Trapping and poisoning."

"So their pacifism didn't extend to rats?"

"No. They refused once to go on a deer drive. They had to be assured that the venison would go to hospitals."

They went out into the sunshine.

"You know, McAndrew, you sound as if you admired them."

McAndrew pondered. "I respect them," he said.

"Not quite the same thing," said the captain, with a chuckle.

The back door was unlocked.

"They said it would be all right for us to go in," said McAndrew, as he led the way.

"Did that matter?"

"I think so. This house has been their home for almost six years. I would not go into any man's home without first asking his permission. Their possessions are here."

The captain loked round the living-room. "Reminds me of some field quarters I've been in."

McAndrew opened the door of the stove and put in some logs from a basket.

"It'd need a fair amount of money spent on it if we were thinking of asking anyone to take it on as a working farm," said the captain.

"It would. I hope it's done though. It would be a pity if Creag farm was to be apandoned for good."

"Why should it bother you? You'll be far away."

"Even so, it would pother me."

The captain looked at some books on a home-made shelf. *"History of the Crusades. Religion and the Rise of Capitalism. Point Counterpoint. A History of the Working Classes of Scotland. What I Believe* by Leo Tolstoy. *John Burnet of Barns.* Good Lord, I don't think John Buchan would be pleased to find himself in this company. I believe," he added, "some of them were in jail."

"Rodger was in jail. So were several others, but they've all gone. Rodger made that window weatherproof. He repaired the stairs. He's a first-class joiner."

"Did he want payment?"

"It was never mentioned. I understand he may pe staying on in Port Fada. One of the local puilders is anxious for his services. He is courting a local girl."

"So they're accepted locally?"

"Yes."

"That wasn't always the case."

"No. It took time."

"And you've no idea when they'll all have left?"

"They think it should pe within the next three or four months."

"Well, shall we go? It's not very warm in here, or very comfortable. What's the arrangement as regards a cook now that there are only four?"

"One of them comes off the hill at three. I think they prepare the soup and peel the potatoes the night before."

He lifted the lids of two pots on the stove. In one pot was soup, in the other peeled potatoes.

The captain looked at an apron hanging from a nail, a smoothing iron on the hob, and a colander in the sink.

"You know," he murmured, "I might have enjoyed a chat with them."

2

"TWENTY-SEVEN in all," cried McNaughton, his breath showing in white gusts. "I think that's it, 27."

"Counting Half-day Saidler?" shouted McMaster.

They all laughed, including Rodger, who had not met Saidler. "Who'd ever forget him?"

It was late February, several weeks after the visit of Captain Pilgo-Stewart. They were draining a flat at the head of Glen A'Ghille in preparation for planting it with Sitka spruce in the spring. Out of a heavy dark-blue sky flakes of snow were drifting more and more steadily. The piece-bags piled beside a frozen burn were already white. The air was so still that when anyone stepped on a frozen twig the sound was like a gun shot. They kept glancing up at the sky. If it began to snow in earnest they would have to decide when they could honourably stop work and make for

Creag to cut firewood, as McAndrew had instructed. They were a good hour's walk from Creag or the road, and even men familiar with the hills in ordinary weather could easily get lost in mist and thick snow.

There were five of them: Dunky McNiven, Donald McMillan, John McNaughton, Tom McMaster, and James Rodger. Dunky and John were wielding the rutters, the long-handled huge-bladed draining spades. With these they cut deep parallel lines in the ground and then sliced the earth between into mounds, which the others with hawks dragged out and arranged over the flat in straight lines. In these mounds the small trees would be planted.

It would have been heavy, weary work for novices, especially in such cold, gloomy weather, but they were all expert now and able, without any waste of time, to carry on conversations, which often had to be shouted as the work kept sending them apart.

They were amusing themselves by trying to recall all those who had been at Creag during the six years of war. There were many besides Saidler whom Rodger had not met.

Dunky took part as if he too was a Creag man.

"On a day like this," he said, "big Renwick would have brought his hot-water bag."

"That's right," cried McMaster. "First thing he'd do was light a fire."

"You mean, get Busby Bob to light it for him," cried McMillan.

"Busby could have lit a fire on an ice-flow, using icicles for sticks," said McNaughton.

"Renwick had a wee pan that he put on the fire to boil, so that he could keep his bag hot," said Dunky.

"Where'd he put the bag?" asked Rodger.

"Up his jooks," said McMaster.

"He was the coldest and the slowest man I ever saw," said Dunky.

"Except for Shearer," said McMillan.

They were all silent for half a minute.

"Talking about fire," said McMillan, "Shearer once asked me if I thought cremation was unfair to God. He was worried about the trouble God would have on Judgement Day trying to put together all the bodies that had been cremated. He was always worrying about God's difficulties."

"So he wouldn't get cremated himself?" said McNaughton.

"Maggie didn't say, if you remember."

About three years ago Shearer had gone home to Glasgow feeling ill. Within a fortnight they had got a letter from Maggie saying that he had died in the Southern General Hospital. It had been a short mis-spelled ungrammatical letter, written, it could have been, by either a girl of eight or an old woman of 80.

"Little Munro could not have been more different," said Dunky. "He was the angriest man of peace I ever saw."

"He was the one that joined up?" said Rodger.

"He didn't come back after the New Year, years ago," said McNaughton. "It was his girl's fault. She was always threatening to drop him."

"I don't believe it," said McMillan. "Bill wouldn't have let any woman talk him into doing something he didn't want to do. He used to say it had been a toss-up whether he became a CO or joined the HLI. An honest statement. Too honest."

The snow was now coming down thickly.

"I wonder how he got on in the army," said McMaster. "He said he'd write but he didn't."

"None of them did," said McMillan.

"What happened to them?" asked Rodger. "Where'd they go?"

"Most of them got jobs nearer Glasgow: in market gardens, on local farms. One or two transferred to hospital work."

"Renwick wrote once," said McMaster. "To let us know he'd started studying to enter the ministry."

"How could he do that?" asked Rodger.

"He had complete exemption."

"Why'd he come here then, especially as he hated it? Was he ashamed of being a CO?"

"Aren't we all?" said McMillan. "A bit. I'm joking. No, I'm not."

"I never was ashamed. I never will be."

"Wait till your son asks you what you did in the war."

"I'll tell him I tried to stop it."

They laughed.

"Doesn't it never bother you, Jimmy," asked McMillan, "that millions of your fellow countrymen disagreed with you?"

"Why should it? I was right, they were wrong."

They laughed again.

"Sometimes, Jimmy, you remind me a bit of Gavin Hamilton," said McNaughton.

"I hope not. He's crazy."

189

"Crazy?" shouted McMillan. "It's too easy just to say he's crazy."

"We're supposed to be his comrades, aren't we? Why then doesn't he work with us and live with us?"

"Do you want to know, Jimmy? Do you really want to know?"

McMillan stopped dragging the heavy mound. He was some distance from Rodger and peered at him through the snow.

Dunky and McNaughton, hopping along on their rutters, winked at each other. Donald was up on his high horse again.

"He's afraid," shouted McMillan, "that we'll contaminate him, morally: you Jimmy, and me, and Tom, and John; I don't know about Dunky. And let me tell you, speaking for myself, he's got a right to be afraid. Right from the beginning I've compromised and made allowances and fed my conscience anodynes. I'll soon be going home. I'll be welcomed back all right by relatives and friends that fought in the war, but they'll expect me to shut up as somebody proved wrong should. They'll not say it but it'll be plain enough that they hope I have the sense and the grace to enjoy the freedom they helped to win for me, and not whine like a loser. The difference between Gavin and me is that he's free and I'm not. He's worked hard at keeping free and today he's the freest man in the country. He's done it by wanting nothing from society. I'm not free because I want society to give me a job, a house, money to buy books and leisure to read them, and maybe the right to offer my opinion, even if humbly. Not much really, but all the same representing a surrender that'll have me lying awake at nights despising myself. I'll be aware of the stink from the foundations, but I'll keep quiet and wear the same kind of zombie smile as everybody else."

"Why do you have to keep quiet?" shouted Rodger. "Why can't you try to do something about the stink from the foundations?"

"I've told you why. Because I feel I haven't the right. But suppose I didn't feel that, suppose I thought I had a right to do something about it, what could I do? Rejoin the Peace Pledge Union? My God, didn't they desert in millions as soon as war came? Join the ILP or the Socialist Party of Great Britain? The brotherhood of true Socialists? Don't make me weep. The masses marched off to war at a snap of their masters' fingers, and they always will. Become a Quaker? Yes, but I don't believe in God. Put my trust in education? Make sure that the children I teach learn the truth about the society they live in? Hardly, for I don't know the truth, and anyway they won't want idealistic guff but the right kind of selected facts to enable them to pass examinations."

He paused for breath. His voice had become hoarse.

Dunky took the opportunity to cry: "Twelve o'clock or near enough. Time for tea."

They made their way through the falling snow to their piece-bags.

"Well, boys," said Dunky, with a chuckle, "you're still arguing as well as you did the first time I saw you on the hill. I think it was about the right way to make a steam pudding."

They laughed.

They ate their cold bread and drank their hot tea standing up.

"Suppose you're right, Donald," said McNaughton, "suppose we're all compromisers and chasers of rainbows, in what way is what Gavin's doing any better? Shut your eyes. Turn your back. What sort of freedom's that?"

"His eyes aren't shut. He's more aware than we are. But either you feel sympathy for his position or you think he's crazy. I envy him. We're supposed to be seekers of peace. Well, the only time I ever feel really at peace is in his presence."

"I'm still not quite sure what his position is," said Rodger, "or maybe I should say what you think his position is. I admit he's a very calm person to talk to. But isn't that because he's given up as a human being and left it all to God. In my book that kind of calmness is a treachery."

"I've often wondered," said McNaughton, "if it isn't a matter of pride with Gavin. On the surface he seems so meek, but beneath he's always struck me as having a terrific pride. If we give in, as Donald says, it's because we see good reason for it. We've lost. We've never been noticed. We've had no effect. Losers have to accept terms. We've accepted them. It's time somebody told Gavin he'll have to accept them too."

"He's been told," muttered McMillan, bitterly.

There was a pause. They listened to one another's breathing. Snow gathered on their eyebrows. Not another living thing was to be seen. The rest of the world seemed very far away.

Their rutters and hawks, upright, trimmed with snow, waited like dumb faithful companions.

"Well, what d'you think, Dunky?" asked McNaughton. "It's getting worse."

"I think it's time we headed for off," said Dunky, "while we can still find the way."

"Right."

"We'd better take the rutters and hawks and put them in the shed at the Barneilan burn."

"Right."

A few minutes later they were on their way, with rutter or hawk over their shoulders, like guns.

3

TO HIS SURPRISE Donald McMillan felt happy and confident, when there were so many reasons why he should have been feeling miserable and despondent. His left heel was sore, his legs were weary, the path kept going up and down, the snow was slippery, and Creag was three miles away. Also, in his war on behalf of hope, he was as usual returning not from a successful foray, but from another defeat. Above all, Mary his wife, in spite of her passionate wish to bring no more children into a world of atomic bombs, was pregnant again, and, fairly enough, blamed him. Her recent letters had been sulky with recriminations. Little Susan too, now nearly eight, influenced by her mother, had sent her curtest and least cordial note yet.

In spite of all that here he was feeling happy and uplifted. With their white blossoms of snow the whins made him think of magnolias. He felt that the sun was shining and the sky blue and clear.

His mother would have told him that he must be sickening for something: perhaps flu.

He knew the reason. It was Gavin Hamilton. Gavin was blossoms, sunshine, and hope.

He was sure that his companions, so contemptuous of religion, felt the same way. Thinking about Gavin gave them faith. They were prisoners, he was still free. Finding the burden too heavy or too shameful they had long ago put down their idealistic protest against the war. Gavin still carried his.

Like me, thought McMillan, they lie awake at night, despising themselves for adding to the world's falseness and hypocrisy. Then they remember Gavin and feel instantly absolved.

They all knew that Gavin himself was doomed. Like Cortes, he had deliberately burnt his boats, before setting forth on his long hard perilous journey that had brought him to a loneliness few people could have endured, and a spiritual fullness. Even if he wished he could never go back to the old satisfactions. He would remain here in Ardmore, carrying for the rest of his life not only his own burden of perpetual awareness but theirs too, while they back in their old lives were able mercifully to close their minds. Or he would, thought McMillan, set off one day for that last mad messianic walk into the hills.

McMillan awoke with a start. They had reached the shed. His companions were staring and listening.

Below the shed stretched the Barneilan Flat. Most of it was only slightly above the level of the burn that flowed through it. Draining it had been one of their previous assignments. After draining came the bottoming. If this was done well the water would run and the flat would be properly drained; if it was badly done the water would lie, the ground would remain boggy, and the trees planted in it would die.

The task of bottoming Barneilan Flat had been entrusted to Gavin Hamilton.

In the snowy silence they heard the sounds of a spade striking against stones. About 100 yards away, where the curtain of mist fell from sky to ground, a dark figure could be made out, working busily.

"If it's not for money," muttered Rodger, "what's it for?"

The spell broken, they went into the hut and put away their rutters and hawks.

"It's not for money," said McNaughton.

"I know it isn't. What for then? To please the Lord?"

"As good a reason as any, Chimmy," said Dunky, with a chuckle.

They came out of the shed and again stood gazing. They were reluctant to leave.

"Shouldn't we give him a shout?" asked McNaughton. "Let him know we're on our way to Creag? Ask him to come with us?"

"Why don't we go and ask him?" said Rodger.

"What d'you think, Donald?" asked McNaughton.

"Why not? But he won't come."

"Well, at least we would have asked."

"It might be the last chance we'll get," said McMaster. "I mean, we could all be away within a week or two."

"That's so."

"What d'you say, Dunky?"

"I always like having a word with Hamilton."

Over the heavy ground broken by open drains and encumbered by many mounds, they hurried with an eagerness and a lightness of foot that would have amazed a stranger. Everyone was smiling, but all their smiles were private. Each of them was taking his own wilted hopes and flourishing shames.

They would have angrily denied it. They would have said that they were smiling because they were about to speak to a man they had known for years, whom they didn't understand but had sympathy for. They might even have claimed that they wanted to give encouragement and not to receive it. But they would not have been speaking the truth.

They did not envy Gavin. They would never have changed places with him. They would have argued that by accepting the world with all its imperfections they were acting more sanely and compassionately than he. They preferred to take what society had to give them, much of it not particularly noble, like material possessions, but some of it good, like friendship and love. In return they could repay society by trying at least to make it a little less greedy, more just, and less aggressive.

Yet their eagerness to speak to him or just to stand in his presence put a beauty into their faces that had not been there before.

Or so at any rate it seemed to McMillan.

He did not expect that the actual words spoken, either by them or by Gavin, would be other than commonplace. There might even be in Rodger's voice and perhaps in John McNaughton's too a trace of antagonism, for they found it hard to concede that what flowed from Gavin, call it grace or illumination or whatever, could have its source in something as false as religion. Believers in God, they thought, were either intellectually immature, like Shearer, or intellectually shifty, like Renwick; and in both cases extinguished rather than brought light.

It was interesting too to watch Dunky, who was neutral. An irrepressible humorist, who had once called McAndrew the monkey to Captain Pilgo-Stewart's organ-grinder, he had been much amused by Gavin's more extravagant attempts at self-sufficiency: particularly the making, out of tufts of wool gleaned from thorns and barbs, of bonnets and gloves on the old spinning-wheel bequeathed him by Granny McSporran. That afternoon Gavin was wearing one of those bonnets. It looked, as Dunky said afterwards, like fistfuls of wool torn out of an old dirty ewe.

Gavin was also wearing the same long blue policeman's coat that he had had when he first came to Ardmore. It was sewn and patched in various places. His waterproof trousers had been made out of a piece of canvas picked up on the beach. Like his coat they were miry with peaty mud.

Snow sprinkled his black beard. The strain of the past five years showed on his thin face and in his blue eyes; but he had safely passed through fanaticism into serenity. Perhaps he had never been fanatical at all, only ruthlessly truthful.

"Hello, Gavin," they said.

"Hello, Dunky. Hello, John. Hello, Jimmy. Hello, Tom. Hello, Donald."

"We've packed it in for the day and are on our way back to Creag," said McNaughton.

"Before we get snowed in," added McMaster.

Years ago they would have blamed him for letting down his fellow workers by continuing to work in such conditions. They were less intransigent now. Besides, no employer or boss would ever have pointed to Gavin as an example or reproach to his other workers. Work for him was not simply what he did to earn wages or to pass the time usefully. It was a pleasing of the Lord, a kind of holy communion, a purging of the soul. If McAndrew had ever said, "Hamilton's carrying bags of slag," or "Hamilton does what he's told without grumbling," reply would have been easy. "Yes, and look what's happened to him. He talks to his spade. Would you like all your workers to be like him?"

"What about coming with us?" asked Rodger.

"How does a plate of hot soup in front of a roaring stove appeal to you?" asked McNaughton.

"Not too salty either," added McMaster.

Remembering Bill Munro's lurid blasphemy, McMillan looked up at the sky.

But if God existed, which of course He did not, He was not up there, up there extended for unimaginable millions of black empty miles. He must be here, in Gavin Hamilton's blue eyes and patched muddy coat.

I'm losing my bearings, thought McMillan. It must be the snow and the heavy sky. Or is it the effect on me of the past six years, of all the toss-ups, heads I did right, tails I made a terrible mistake? Or am I taking the flu?

"Thanks, but I made up my mind to work till three," said Gavin.

It was not the first time he had refused an invitation to Creag. He had not been in the house for over a year. They, though, had visited his cottage and helped him carry and saw wood.

They did not try to persuade him. They looked round, shivering. The snow was still falling thickly. The dull red light in the west had gone. The sky was not going to clear. It would go on snowing for hours.

"So long then," they said, and hurried away.

None of them looked back. None said anything.

It seemed to McMillan that, like him, they were secretly pleased that Gavin had not come with them. They liked to think that in this desolation he was still strengthening his resolve never to give in, as they had done. In their hearts they acknowledged that he alone of them all was entitled to say that he had no part in the enormous evils of the war or in the benefits they were said to have brought. He was one of the few in a position to pity honourably those who had suffered the cruelties of Belsen and those who had inflicted them.

Or, as McMillan himself saw it, like a medieval heretic in the flames who had earned the right to forgive and leave judgement to God.

4

IT WOULD HAVE been very pleasant going back to Creag with them.

Though they must have been over a quarter of a mile away already he heard them laughing, so still was the air. Perhaps Duncan McNiven had made some droll remark about him.

He would have laughed at it himself. He had always known that in his efforts not to be beholden there was something unavoidably comic. He had been aware of it even when praying.

More likely, though, Duncan had made one of his partly humorous and wholly serious boasts about his daughter Catriona now nearly sixteen and a brilliant scholar at the high school.

Those who laughed with Duncan liked and respected him. Laughter could be a sign of affection and goodwill.

All of them were laughable.

James Rodger, self-confessed would-be bloody revolutionary, was going to marry the daughter of a sergeant in the Port Fada Home Guard.

John McNaughton and Tom McMaster, staunchly atheistic, still had their saint-like vision of the human race come gloriously to its senses and living forevermore in peace and justice: a condition brought about by the deliberations in small stuffy rooms of handfuls of idealistic Socialists, who did not always agree among themselves. The war to them, for all its gigantic horrors, had been simply an aberration. They had even derived some confidence from it. It had shown that if mankind could be turned in the right direction then his cleverness and tremendous energies could bring about gigantic benefits. Their mission was to indicate what that direction was.

The more earnestly they pointed the more they would be ignored. That was comic. They would laugh at it themselves, and those who loved them would laugh too.

As for Donald McMillan, he was the most comic of them all. Previously plump, he was now almost gaunt. Previously eloquent on the necessity of love or at least companionship he now seemed to distrust people. He would visit Gavin and stare gloomily into the fire. Once, helping to saw wood for that fire, he had suddenly burst into one of his long semi-hysterical speeches. Consider, he had said, two men, either of whom could have been himself, at one of Hitler's mass rallies. One, hating the jubilant roars and the evilly ecstatic faces, had sat silent, consumed by shame, fear, and doubt. The other though, roaring with the rest and having the same evil ecstasy on his face, had felt great joy. Was it better to be outcast and miserable, or conformist and triumphant? "There are times," he had said, "when I can't look a sheep in the face."

Just then a sheep had bleated. They had both burst out laughing.

Here he was himself, up to the chin in a narrow ditch, trying, with holy dedication, to make the peaty bottom so smooth and so uniformly inclined that the water draining into it would flow into the burn, so that the ground, no longer waterlogged, would produce healthy trees which, in 20 or 30 years' time, might be cut down and turned into, as Bill Munro had once pointed out, ammunition boxes. Since, in his five years at Ardmore, he had with

his own hands planted over 100,000 trees he might well have sup-
plied ammunition boxes for an army.

That was funny too. Those who respected him would laugh
with him.

Funnier still was his belief that one day—why not today?—he
had a promise to keep in a place where no one waited and from
which he would not return.

But then was it not one of the supreme jokes of all time, a
carpenter's son with horny feet and dirty underwear acclaimed as
the Son of God and the Saviour of all mankind?

Suddenly he imagined that smiling down at him through the
falling snow was McIntyre, in his kilted uniform.

But McIntyre was dead. He had died in a prisoner-of-war
camp in Malaya. His mother had written to the house in Auchengillan, saying that Douglas had asked her, if anything happened
to him, to let Gavin Hamilton know. That had been four years
ago.

He often had visitations from people he had known: a consequence of his being so much alone.

Later, as he ate his icy sandwiches, McIntyre was still watching
him, with a smile.

"Still up for smout, Hamilton?" his smile said.

Yes, Gavin admitted, smiling too: still up for smout, still trying to reach smout itself, that state of grace.

It was a joke he shared with McIntyre and no one else.

He could not ask McIntyre for advice. What advice could the
dead, with their marvellous meekness, give to the living, whose
selfishness could never be sated or whose pride subdued?

He thought of his friends arriving at Creag. They would shake
their coats and caps and stamp their feet at the door. They would
stir up the fire in the stove and put on fresh wood. They would
heat the soup in the black pot. They would cut bread and dip it
in the hot soup. They would fill the kettle with spring water. They
would smile at one another, in trust and gratitude. They would
wonder if Charlie the Bus had got through from Port Fada with
the mail. They would savour the memorable sweetness of human
companionship. Perhaps they would speak of him.

He went back to work.

About two hours later, when it was quite dark, he made for the
shed. After he had put away his spade he stood outside for a
while. There was a choice of three ways. One led down to the

road at McAndrew's hut, where his bicycle waited; the second would take him across the hills to Creag; and the third, towards which he kept turning, went up to the head of Glen A'Ghille and beyond, where, if he walked far enough, into the snow and the coming night, there could be no coming back.

5

SHORTLY AFTER THREE Dunky and McMillan put on their heavy coats and came out of the warmth of Creag to walk down to the gate. Dunky was on his way home, and it was McMillan's turn to fetch the mail and bread. He took a torch. It would be dark by the time he got back.

Out of a sky the colour of stale porridge the white flakes came hurrying down, like a multitude of fragmented souls, thought McMillan. If Gavin was in earnest about vanishing into the hills, in a final gesture of renunciation or expiation, now surely was the time to do it.

Once, three winters ago, when the snow had been as heavy as this, McAndrew had lent half a dozen of his men, McMillan among them, to a neighbouring farmer whose sheep had been caught out on the hill by the sudden blizzard. They had tramped about for hours thrusting twelve-foot poles into the deepest drifts. They had learned to tell, from the feel of the pole, whether sheep lay beneath. Several had been rescued, frozen stiff. They had been carried to a big fire where they had thawed out. It had been uncanny to see them slowly become alive again. Their first bleatings had not sounded particularly thankful; but inside minutes they were eating the hay spread out for them. They had been saved from becoming mutton now to become mutton later.

Dunky was talking about his daughter Catriona. He and his wife weren't sure whether they should let her go to Glasgow University. It would be very expensive. She would have to be by herself in the city.

"You know she can come and live with us, Dunky. She knows Mary and Susan."

Catriona had met them while they were living in Port Fada.

"I mean that, Dunky. So does Mary."

"I know that, Donald. But it'll not be for another two years. You could have forgotten all about us Ardmore folk by then."

"I'll never do that. I'll be back often."

There was a warm feeling between them.

They passed McAndrew's beech. Its clutches at the air were softened by mittens of snow. But it looked more immense than ever in the murk.

"You'll be cutting your initials one of these days, Donald," said Dunky.

It was a tradition of Creag men when leaving. Even DRR, representing David Robertson Renwick, could be found there; and MS, meaning Martin Shearer.

"I don't like defacing trees," said McMillan.

"Och, it would do the tree no harm, and whenever I came by this way I would like to see your initials among the rest."

"I'll do it then."

"It could be soon."

"Any day now."

They were in sight of the gate.

"I see Charlie's got through all right," said Dunky. "Isn't that the bread on top of the gate?"

"So it is. Good for Charlie."

McMillan eagerly lifted the flap of the wooden box that Jimmy Rodger had made. Lying snug and dry in it were three letters, one white and the other two buff. The white was for him, from Mary; the buff were for him and John McNaughton. He knew what they were. He opened his. He was right. It was what he had been waiting for for weeks. Permission was given him to pack up his goods, including his conscience, and return to society, his penance done.

He did not feel like shouting for joy.

"Is that it?" asked Dunky.

"This is it."

"Well done then."

"Is it?"

"Surely. You'll get back to your wife and child."

"Children, soon. Mary's expectant."

"Well done again. Two are better."

"She doesn't think so. She thinks this is a very wicked world into which to bring children."

"It is wicked indeed, but it is not too bad."

They both laughed.

"And there's one for John McNaughton?"

"Yes."

"But not for Chimmy or Tom?"

"Maybe tomorrow, or the next day."

"So Creag could be empty by next week?"

"It could."

"When will you go yourself?"

"Tomorrow, or maybe the day after. I'd like to—well, readjust my feelings before I go home. I'd like to see Gavin too."

"If he left Barneilan at three o'clock as he said he should be along any minute."

"If he hasn't already passed."

Dunky bent down to study the road. "I see no marks of cycle wheels."

"I'll wait then. Good-night, Dunky."

McMillan watched his friend until he disappeared round a bend. He could still hear him whistling cheerfully.

Local men like Jake and Archie and Dugald would be along soon on their bicycles. They would have been taken off the hill hours ago, but McAndrew would keep them at the shed until four when he would give them permission to go home. In the old days they would have had to wait till five, the official lowsing time.

As like as not Jake would have a log like a caber balanced on his shoulder. He would be taking it home for firewood. Snow wouldn't deter him. He lived nearest to Gavin. His cottage was on the lochside, Gavin's half a mile into the hill; but that was close enough to make them next-door neighbours. "The salmon in the burn are a lot closer." Jake had once said.

At last he heard the rattling of a loose mudguard. Round the corner they came, Jake in front. He was the only one with a lamp. It cast a red light on the snow. The two others, in single file, kept close. They were cycling in one of the bus wheel marks.

They stopped when they saw McMillan.

"It's yourself, Donald," said Jake. For once he had no log on his shoulder.

"Hello, Donald," said Archie and Dugald.

"Hello. I'm waiting for Gavin. Have you seen him?"

"Not since this morning," said Jake.

"He wasn't at the shed when you left?"

"No."

"Did you notice if his bike was still there?"

None of them had noticed.

"We weren't looking for it, mind you," said Jake.

"We were too anxious to get off home," said Archie.

"He should be along soon."

"Surely," said Jake. "Dunky was telling us you and John Mc-Naughton have got your discharge."

McMillan grinned. "Yes, that's right."

Jake spoke for the three of them. "When you've gone you will have left it a better job than when you came."

"Thanks. That's as good an epitaph as any. It was easier for us. We knew we weren't going to be here all our lives."

Jake put his left foot on the pedal, about to mount. "By the way, Donald," he asked, with a grin, "did you know that Gavin took the service at Largiebeag Kirk last Sunday?"

"No, I didn't."

"The minister's ill. So Gavin was asked. It seems he did it very well."

"Calum McGregor's wife Nora was there," said Archie. "She said it was the best address she has ever heard. Mind you, she's a bit hard of hearing. She says the minister's sister, Miss Urquhart, has a great liking for him. She's 40 if she's a day, and not even her own mother would call her bonny."

McMillan was listening with amusement and disbelief. He had once met Miss Urquhart at a party in Largiebeag school. She had struck him as nearer 50 than 40. She had arthritic hands.

"Don't heed them, Donald," said Dugald. "It is chust talk."

"Good-night," cried Jake, and cycled off, laughing.

"Good-night," said his two mates, following.

Above the rattling of the loose mudguard McMillan heard Dugald, a simple solemn man who loved truth, say: "You should not have said that about the minister's sister, Archie. It is not right to mock the woman."

McMillan could not hear Archie's reply.

6

A S H E W A S getting his bicycle out of the shelter that Jimmy
Rodger had made, McMillan remembered old Granny McSporran.
All the Creag men had been at her funeral in Largiebeag kirkyard.
She had left Gavin Hamilton some furniture, as well as the
spinning wheel.

He set off towards the forestry houses. He had decided to go
and tell McAndrew that tomorrow or the next day he was going
home for good. The truth was, though, he could not bear to go
up to Creag not knowing what had happened to Gavin.

It was reassuring to see the lights in the windows.

There was no one about. He did not know where to look for
Gavin's bicycle.

He knocked on the door of McAndrew's hut.

McAndrew opened the door. He looked pleased. "It's yourself,
Tonald. Come in out of the cold. Dunky was telling me the good
news."

Suddenly McMillan's worry about Gavin was no longer vague.
He felt sure he would never see Gavin alive again.

"Have you seen Gavin Hamilton?" he asked.

"Not since this morning. Didn't you see him yourself on Parneilan Flat?"

"Yes. About one o'clock. He said he was going to leave the hill
at three. It's nearly five now. Is his bike still here?"

"I have no idea. I thought he would have gone home. He slips
past like a deer, you know."

"Where does he keep his bike?"

"Behind this hut usually."

"I'll look."

McMillan went round to the back of the hut. Gavin's bicycle
was there all right, with snow on the saddle.

He went back to the door and entered the warm hut. "It's still
there," he said. "He must still be on the hill."

"He could pe on his way down," said McAndrew, more amused
than alarmed. "We could be hearing him any minute."

"It's dark."

"There's still light enough if your eyes are used to it. Gavin
is used to walking in darkness. He would have to pe, living where
he does."

"I suppose so."

"So you're apout to leave us?"

"Yes."

"You do not look convulsed with joy."

"I'm worried about Gavin."

"Would there pe a letter for him too, do you think?"

"I don't know. Perhaps it came yesterday, or last week."

"He has said nothing to me."

"I wonder if I should get a lamp from the shed and go up the path a bit?"

"I don't think you should. You are more likely to get lost than Gavin. You're not thinking, are you, that he has gone up the glen, like ponny Kilmenny?"

McMillan smiled. McAndrew forgot nothing.

"I looked up the poem in a pook that Calum McNiven prought home from school. I'm not sure I understood it clearly. Was it heaven Kilmenny went to? 'The plackbird alang wi' the eagle flew.' There's nothing like that on Parneilan Flat."

"Hardly."

"I mind once, Tonald, when I was a wee poy my father gave me a good scolding. I did not think I had done anything to deserve it. My soul was crushed. He was ill at the time; he did not often enchoy good health. So I ran off up the hill and sat under a big rowan. I was six at the time. When it got dark I crept home. No one had noticed. My father greeted me in his usual kindly way. He had already forgotten the reprimand".

McMillan understood the parable. The small boy was Gavin, the war the unjust rebuke.

"I wonder if anything ever happened to him when he was young that he considered unfair and has never peen able to forgive?" asked McAndrew.

"His father was killed in the 14–18 war."

"It could have peen that."

"And his mother died when he was fifteen. But it's a lot more than that. In this century already, and it's not halfway through, well over 50 million people have been slaughtered in wars and revolutions: not just soldiers either, but women and children. Millions more have been dispossessed and made utterly wretched. We all know this, but we take great care not to let it bother us too much: a skelf in our fingers bothers us more. We tell ourselves we're not personally responsible, we've killed nobody, we've raped nobody, we've never looted, we've burnt down nobody's house.

In any case, most of those who have been killed or made suffer were enemies or foreigners, who brought most of it on themselves. We know all this but we push it into unfrequented corners of our minds."

He paused and smiled as if at his own exaggerations. McAndrew nodded, as if agreeing that they were ludicrous, those exaggerations.

"Suppose, though," went on McMillan, in the same quiet voice, "there was somebody so unlucky as not to be able to forget it but had it on his mind and conscience all the time, every minute of every day. Suppose he felt more and more desolated at the lack of remorse and repentance being shown. Would it be so very surprising if one day he just walked away, not wanting to see another human face again?"

"You have it all rehearsed, Tonald."

"Of course. I've thought about it dozens of times. Don't think I don't see the funny side of it. A person in a huff's always funny: all the more so if he's in a huff with most of humanity. Gavin knows himself it's funny."

"I can easily imagine him standing in the snow somewhere, in the darkness, praying; but I chust cannot imagine him walking off to his death."

"I can't either. Nobody could, today. The Bible's full of holy men so disgusted with the degenerate ways of their fellows that they hiked off into the desert. Here in Scotland, in medieval times, when faith was total, such men would have been understood. But not today. Today the leaders of all the churches are rational and realistic. They have diminished God's expectations to coincide with their own, to save Him from embarrassment."

"I thought, Tonald, you did not pelieve in God."

"I don't. If I did I think I would be on my way to Glen A'Ghille and beyond."

McAndrew rose. "Instead of which you are coming for a cup of tea. Kirstie will be pleased to see you and hear your good news."

"Thanks."

"No need to mention Gavin chust yet."

"No."

Outside the hut McMillan looked to see if Gavin's bicycle was still there. It was. Almost reverentially he swept the snow off the saddle with his hand.

Kirstie McAndrew was feeding little Ian from a bottle in front

205

of the fire. This happy task she immediately entrusted to her husband, so that she herself could get tea ready for her guest. She took cups and saucers not out of the cupboard in the kitchen where the workaday delf was kept but out of the display cabinet in the sitting-room. Any visitors to her house, whether passing tramps or officials like Captain Pilgo-Stewart, were given tea in these delicate pink-and-white china cups.

She was delighted to hear that McMillan was at last free to return home.

"Your wife will be the happy woman," she cried, "and your little girl too."

He decided not to say anything about Mary's pregnancy. Kirstie was too optimistic about motherhood. It would have been cruel to remind her that in Hiroshima many mothers had been incinerated with their babies in their arms.

Prattling away, she told him that he had had a letter a few days ago from Ann McTaggart, now back in Edinburgh.

"She always asks after you, Donald; and of course after Gavin. It's a funny thing but she's always said she's understood why he's kept so much to himself and wouldn't be beholden to anyone. The war was such a terrible hurt to him that he had to suffer it by himself."

"Yes, I know."

"I wouldn't be surprised if she still had hopes of him."

"Now, Kirstie," said her husband, "you're reading too much petween the lines."

"Maybe I am. But you wait and see. He'll come out of his shell now the war's over and done with. Whatever woman does get him will be very lucky."

McMillan thought of Miss Urquhart, the minister's 45-year-old sister with the flat chest and sunken cheeks. Would she be the lucky woman?

"Take care, Ian," cried Mrs McAndrew. "Don't let the wee soul suck on an empty bottle. That causes wind. Give him to me."

With immense care the baby was handed over.

McMillan rose. "I'm afraid I'll have to be going," he said. "Thanks for the tea, Kirstie."

"Will you be going into Port Fada tomorrow with Charlie?" she asked.

"I'm not sure. I might wait another day."

"I'll look out and give you a wave. But you'll not be away

for good. You'll come back often and bring your wife and daughter with you."

"Yes, I certainly will. Good-night, little Ian." He touched the baby's warm pink foot.

McAndrew saw him to the door.

"If there's to be a search," muttered McMillan, "I'd want to take part. Good-night."

"Good-night, Tonald. Take care."

It was still snowing. The bus wheel marks were almost filled in. Cycling would be hard work.

He was about to pass the hut when it occurred to him that he ought to take a last look to see if Gavin's bicycle was still there. He laid his own bicycle down at the side of the road and tramped up to the hut.

It was hard going in the soft snow. He felt a little apprehensive about getting safely back to Creag. Still, they would come looking for him. He would be in a known place. What would his thoughts be, he wondered, as he lay exhausted in the snow, doomed to perish if help did not come? He would have no grand thoughts about forgiveness or expiation or repentance: he would just feel regret that he would never see Mary and Susan again.

The bicycle wasn't there. Though he ought to have been expecting to find it gone, for it was surely more likely that Gavin had been belated than that he had walked off to his death, he was nevertheless taken aback. He could not believe it. He thought he must be looking in the wrong place. He went all round the hut, feeling the very air with his hands, like a blind man.

For a few seconds he felt disappointed, let down, betrayed. The intolerable burden of conscience, which he was so sick of carrying, must still be carried. Gavin Hamilton's sacrifice, he had foolishly imagined, would have lifted it off him once and for all.

Then, come to his senses, he felt great relief.

He would have to go and tell McAndrew that Gavin was safe. He would say nothing about Gavin's having weakened and given in like everybody else, he would just say that he was safe, thank God.